North American Pirates and Their Lost Treasure

by W. C. Jameson

illustrations by Kory Fluckiger

August House, Inc.
ATLANTA

Published 2018
by August House, Inc.

Atlanta, Georgia
augusthouse.com

Book and Cover art and design by Kory Fluckiger

ISBN 978-1-941460-47-4 (pbk)

Manufactured in the United States
10 9 8 7 6 5 4 3 2 1

Library of Congress Cataloging-in-Publication Data

Names: Jameson, W. C., 1942- author. | Fluckiger, Kory, illustrator.
Title: North American pirates and their lost treasure / W.C. Jameson ; illustrations by Kory Fluckiger.
Description: Atlanta, Georgia : August House, Inc., 2018. | Includes bibliographical references and index.
Identifiers: LCCN 2018011021
Subjects: LCSH: Pirates--North America--History--Juvenile literature. | Treasure troves--North America--Juvenile literature.
Classification: LCC G535 .J37 2018 | DDC 910.4/5--dc23
LC record available at https://lccn.loc.gov/2018011021

The paper used in this publication meets the minimum requirements of the American National Standards for Information Sciences—Permanence of Paper for Printed Library Materials, ansi. 48–1984.

For Laurie

CONTENTS

Introduction

Pirates – who they were and what they did – are often misunderstood and misinterpreted by the general public. Most of us hold perceptions of pirates that are largely derived from film, novels, and even comic books. The perceptions that are embraced, however, are far from the truth.

Most of us are familiar with outlaw names such as Billy the Kid, Jesse James, Butch Cassidy, and the Dalton Gang, among others. We know that they earned their reputations as banditti by stealing livestock, robbing trains, stagecoaches, and banks as well as occasionally killing people. These men practiced their criminal trade on land.

Pirates were the outlaws of the high seas. Instead of riding horses, they sailed ships. Instead of preying on trains and banks, they preyed on other ships and coastal communities, often acquiring an amazing accumulation of wealth in the form of precious metals and other valuables.

Author Colin Woodard writes, "There was . . . a democratic spirit aboard the pirates' ships, an unusual development six decades before Lexington and Yorktown." Woodard continues:

Upon seizing a vessel, the pirates turned its government upside down. Instead of using whips and beatings to enforce a rigid, top-down hierarchy, they elected and deposed their captains by popular vote. They shared their treasure almost equally, and on most ships didn't allow the captain his own cabin.

One scholar emphasizes that most pirates were "very shrewd in the way they reorganized their ships to limit the captain's power," and that there was "a real social consciousness at work there."

Among pirates' stolen goods, gold and silver coins and ingots, jewelry, and precious stones such as diamonds, rubies, emeralds, and opals were also found. In addition, valuable cargoes of rum, wine, silks, and other items were often seized. At times, the hold of a pirate ship was so full of captured cargo that the pirates were forced to offload it from time to time. Merchandise was sold at ports such as New Orleans, Louisiana, and Charleston, South Carolina, but treasures were often cached at secret locations. Pirates buried their treasures for two reasons: to lighten the ship's load so that it would move through the water with greater speed and to keep it from being seized by other pirates or pursuing authorities in the warships of America, Britain, and Spain.

According to author Woodard,

. . . unlike the aristocrats who controlled the British, French, and Spanish colonial empires, many ordinary people in Britain and British America saw pirates as heroes, as Robin Hood figures fighting a rear-guard action against a corrupt, unaccountable and increasingly tyrannical ruling class. Like the outlaws of the American West, many pirates were viewed as noble brigands, antiheroes.

Pirates, like American outlaws, have inspired plays, books, motion pictures, and television shows.

Pirates sailed a variety of ships, but those vessels associated with transporting cargoes of slaves were preferred. "Slavers" were large, very fast, and capable of being fitted with a great deal of heavy armament. According to researcher Mike Daniel, the slavers were easily converted such that they had a large, open flush deck that could accommodate many people and could maneuver with ease.

Over the years, and with the constant repetition of pirate myths in novels, film, and television, the general population has come to regard them as fact. For example, the notion of pirates forcing their condemned captives to "walk the plank" is a pure fabrication. It never happened; this style of execution first appeared in a novel and was subsequently picked up in film and repeated over and over. In truth, the pirates simply threw condemned captives overboard.

Like their counterparts on land, pirates varied in personality, behavior, and appearance. Another myth is that all pirates were male; however, piracy was an equal opportunity industry and attracted the fearless and the enterprising. Those who manifested these attributes to a high degree assumed roles of leadership, and some of them happened to be women. In the pages that follow, the reader will discover two such female pirates – Mary Anne Townsend and Ann Bonney.

Many people believe that all or most pirates were ruthless outlaws who were apt to kill anyone they confronted during a raid. While some of them were little more than craven psychopaths, a significant number of pirates approached piracy as a business and conducted their operations much as a CEO would run a company; many pirates viewed themselves as businessmen and entrepreneurs so they pursued piracy as any businessman would pursue profit. To them it was about profit and loss, efficiency, managing a payroll, and finding customers for their stolen goods.

It will be a surprise to many that one of the most notorious pirates in history, Blackbeard, was never known to kill anyone or have anyone killed, except possibly in self-defense. In fact, history records that Blackbeard had a reputation for treating his prisoners well, and many of them were eager to join him.

Another myth is that all pirates were Europeans and Americans. Surviving records reveal that Africans more often than not comprised from one-fourth to well over half of the crew on any given pirate ship. A great number of pirates came from captured slave ships. On capturing a slaver, the pirate captain normally gave the freed slaves the opportunity to join his crew.

Many pirates chose this form of livelihood over servitude. The notion of living a life of freedom and adventure, along with a promise of wealth, was a captivating one. At times the risks were high, but the rewards more than compensated.

American and British pirates primarily targeted shipping lanes and settlements along the coast of North America. The Spanish pirates preyed upon other parts of the world, notably the South American and African coasts, while the Caribbean attracted sea-going brigands of all ethnic groups.

Along the coasts of North America, pirates buried dozens of treasures of gold and silver coins and ingots, precious stones, and valuable jewelry. These caches served as the equivalent of banks for these brigands; sometimes withdrawals were made from these caches, sometimes they were added to. As the result of a variety of circumstances, a great percentage of these treasure caches were never retrieved, and they remain today where they were buried as long as two centuries ago and earlier. Hopeful treasure hunters have searched for them for decades. Once in a great while, one is found, but for the most part these treasure caches are still waiting to be discovered.

Our journey into the life and times of the pirates of North America and the treasures they left behind begins at the northern boundaries of the east coast of the United States. From there it progresses southward along the Atlantic Coast to Florida, circles around the Keys, and into the Gulf of Mexico. From there, the travels take us up the west coast where the U.S. meets the Pacific Ocean, and our journey ends in Oregon.

It is a pleasure to have your company on this voyage. May wind fill your sails, may the seas be smooth, and may each reader find treasure.

-1-

Blackbeard and the White Island Treasure

The ships' commanders were instructed to put an end to piracy, and, more importantly, capture Blackbeard or otherwise put him out of business.

Of all the pirates who sailed the seas and plundered ships and settlements, the man called Blackbeard, according to those who immerse themselves in such studies, is by far the most famous. In spite of his notoriety, very little is known about his life, and much of what has been written about him has been in error.

As pirates go, Blackbeard stood out as being somewhat odd, a bit of a departure from the perceived norm. Despite his fearsome looks and his reputation for being shrewd and calculating, along with his numerous successes, he was, in fact, as much gentleman as outlaw. In spite of the volumes written about Blackbeard portraying him as tyrannical, bloodthirsty, and bent on torturing and killing those he captured, there exists not a shred of evidence that he ever killed, or even harmed, anyone. The "gentleman bandit" image is not unknown among American outlaws, and it appears that Blackbeard could qualify for such a title.

According to writer Colin Woodard, Blackbeard's life has "long been obscured in a fog of legend, myth, and propaganda." In truth, this notorious sea-going outlaw was a "canny strategist," a natural leader, and a committed risk-taker.

So mysterious was Blackbeard that there exists confusion regarding his name as well as his origins. In spite of his "real" name's being presented in the literature as Edward Teach, he always went by the name Edward Thatch, though no one is absolutely certain of either. According to researchers, the name "Teach" resulted from a misspelling of Thatch in the Boston News-Letter. The surname, Drummond, has even been attached to this mysterious character.

Thatch was described as a "tall spare man with a very black beard which he wore very long," hence the nickname, Blackbeard. Other descriptions mention that his beard was "braided into pigtails" and sometimes decorated with colored ribbons. Captain Charles Johnson said that Blackbeard was "such a figure that imagination cannot form an idea of a fury from hell to look more frightful." The pirate had broad shoulders and was normally seen wearing knee-high boots, dark clothing, and a wide hat. Beneath his hat, Blackbeard secured lit fuses that dangled down the sides of his face such that it appeared as if he were surrounded by a halo of smoke and fire. Blackbeard was as much a showman as he was a brigand*. When Blackbeard entered into battle, he carried three pistols in a sling he wore over his shoulders like a bandolier*.

Available evidence suggests Blackbeard may well have been born into a respectable, perhaps even well-off family, most likely in the English city of Bristol. He was quite literate, could read and write, and was reputed to have a fine penmanship. Many believe that young Thatch moved with his family to Jamaica, likely for business reasons. From Jamaica, he made his way to the West Indian island of New Providence, almost 200 miles east of the southern tip of Florida.

New Providence was largely uninhabited and known to be a stronghold for pirates, thus the notion of becoming a pirate seized Thatch at a young age. At New Providence, Thatch was given a job on a ship commandeered by Captain Benjamin Hornigold who, in the early 1700s, carried the reputation of a successful pirate. In a short time, Hornigold placed Thatch in charge of an eight-gun, 90-man pirate sloop*. Hornigold and his flotilla* sailed up and down the eastern coast of North America overtaking merchant vessels and seizing the cargo, which included wine and flour. Thatch distinguished himself during these raids, and he looked forward to more of them. He had visions of capturing ships that carried gold, silver, and jewels.

Thatch soon gained a reputation as a clever and

efficient pirate. His crew was composed of former merchant and naval sailors. Although they were experienced men, they were convinced that they were involved in a social revolt against corporate ship owners and captains who had made their lives a living hell. One pirate referred to the shipping corporations as "robbers of the poor under the protection of the law" but likened the pirates to men who "plunder the rich under the cover of their own courage."

In 1717, Blackbeard attacked and captured a large French merchant vessel, renaming it Queen Anne's Revenge. Additional raids led to more captured ships, and soon Blackbeard was commanding a pirate fleet of his own, manned by hundreds of sailors and transporting crews of bold and daring raiders. He favored the waters of the Atlantic Ocean up and down the eastern coastline of North America from Maine to Florida and even into the Caribbean Sea. It was said that Thatch terrorized vessels entering the harbors of New York and Philadelphia, as well as Chesapeake Bay, never remaining more than 48 hours in one place. Most accounts have Thatch capturing at least 15 vessels.

Ships were attacked and looted, and riches including gold and silver ingots and coins, along with jewelry and precious stones, began to accumulate. Edward Thatch, the pirate, was now a rich man, and most of his wealth was carried in his ships.

One of Thatch's voyages up the eastern seaboard brought him to a picturesque location five miles off the shared coasts of New Hampshire and Maine, referred to as the Isles of Shoals, a cluster of about a dozen small islands. Composed mainly of bare rock, these islands had been a favored resting place for pirates since the early 1700s.

It is believed that Blackbeard first visited the Isles of Shoals around 1710. He spent time sailing among these remote and unpopulated rocky outcrops and exploring their shores and interiors. He noted that most of them had safe harbors, and he determined that the islands would be quite suitable as a hiding place for his fleet of ships. As Blackbeard raided and pillaged up and down the coast, he returned to the Isles of Shoals from time to time to rest his crew and repair his ships. Around 1715, Blackbeard decided that these little-known islands would be ideal for caching some of his accumulated treasure. He decided to bury a portion of it on White Island, one of the smallest of the isles, located at the southern end of this aggregation of islands. Today it is part of the state of New Hampshire.

The first treasure Blackbeard buried on White Island is believed to be a number of trunks filled with gold and silver coins, loot taken from a merchant ship off the coast of Scotland. While anchored at Glasgow Bay, Scotland, Blackbeard met with a man named Scott who told him about a fortune of gold and silver aboard another ship that had recently departed, making its way south. Scott was a small time pirate but well enough known to the authorities that he was wanted. If captured, he would have suffered the fate of all pirates at the time – he would be hanged. Following the meeting, Blackbeard introduced the newcomer to his crew as Captain Scott, who had just provided information on a grand opportunity to acquire a substantial fortune.

At dawn the following morning, Blackbeard roused

his crew and had them set sail southward out of the bay, trailing the merchant vessel. Two days later, their quarry was overtaken. Not willing to give up to the pirates, the captain and crew of the merchant ship put up a fight. For the next several hours, an intense battle ensued, with dozens of men killed on both sides. A veteran of numerous such battles, Blackbeard oversaw the action and directed his men to a victory; the merchant ship was seized, boarded, and its crew imprisoned. For the next two days, Blackbeard directed the transfer of valuable goods, including several trunks filled with treasure, from the captured ship to his own.

Blackbeard placed Scott in charge of the merchant ship, added it to his fleet, and proceeded to sail along the coasts of France and Spain, plundering ships along the way and adding to his treasure. Following these successful raids, Blackbeard and Scott returned to Glasgow Bay for rest and to replenish supplies. While anchored at Glasgow Bay, Scott went into town and returned several hours later with a woman he introduced as his mistress, who then joined the men as they set sail for the North American coast. Several weeks later, the pirate ships anchored just offshore of White Island.

On arriving at White Island, Blackbeard ordered members of his crew to offload the trunks of gold, silver, and jewels taken from the recent raids and transport them to the shore. They were all buried in a secret location.

Blackbeard decided to place his new confederate, Captain Scott, in charge of the treasure. To that end, he suggested that Scott live on White Island with his mistress and serve as an overseer with the primary responsibility of guarding the treasure. A cabin would be necessary, but because of the mostly bare rock that comprised the Isles of Shoals, Blackbeard sent his crew across the span of water to the mainland of what today is New Hampshire to acquire building materials. Weeks passed, and the crew constructed a suitable log cabin. With Scott and his mistress accommodated, Blackbeard set off down the coast in search of more ships to plunder.

Over the course of the next three years, Blackbeard returned to White Island on several occasions. Each time, he was, for the most part, occupied with caching more treasure, acquired by attacking merchant ships. Blackbeard's immense fortune now consisted not only of gold and silver coins, but gold and silver ingots along with emeralds, diamonds, and a quantity of finely crafted jewelry.

In 1718, the British government, concerned about pirate attacks on merchant vessels, ordered a fleet of warships into the Atlantic Ocean. The ships' commanders were instructed to put an end to piracy and, more importantly, capture Blackbeard or otherwise put him out of business. During its wide-ranging patrol of the North Atlantic, a portion of the British fleet was anchored off the coast of Nova Scotia when its crew learned of Blackbeard's hideaway at White Island. The fleet weighed anchor* and set sail for the Isles of Shoals.

One morning several days later, one of Blackbeard's sentries spotted the British war fleet approaching the island and sounded a warning. Blackbeard had prepared his men well. The pirate always assumed pursuit would begin at any time, and he kept his men at the ready. In less than two hours, Blackbeard and his entire crew were boarding the ships and readying the sails. From the moment of the warning, Scott was undecided as to what he should do – board his own ship and flee with Blackbeard or remain on the island and take his chances?

Realizing that if he was captured and returned to the British Isles, he would likely be hanged, Scott decided it was in his best interest to escape. He immediately ordered his crew to prepare the ship for departure. In a bizarre move, Scott ordered his mistress to remain on White Island as caretaker and to guard the treasure. He made her swear that she would never reveal its location to anyone.

One hour after Blackbeard led his fleet away from the Isles of Shoals and southward down the coast, Scott and his crewmen were readying their own ship for departure. Unfortunately, Scott waited too long. By the time the sails were hoisted, the British ship had arrived and surrounded him. Refusing to surrender, Scott fired upon the newcomers, and his gunfire was returned with more than 100 cannonballs. In a short time, Scott's ship was wounded, ablaze, and foundering in the sea. Another half hour of bombardment succeeded in sinking Scott's vessel.

Ironically, most pirates, men who made their living on the sea, did not know how to swim. Those few members of Scott's crew who could swim managed to make their way to shore but were shortly captured and placed in chains. Thankfully, Scott was not among them.

From all reports, Scott's mistress was neither harmed nor arrested by the British forces. She was, however, left to remain on White Island. Without Scott or the other pirates to provide for her, she starved to death. Along with her death went the knowledge of the secret location of Blackbeard's great treasure. The only person left alive who knew of the hidden cache was Blackbeard himself.

Blackbeard was never afforded the opportunity to return to White Island. Constantly pursued by the British, he found himself and his fleet of pirate ships often under attack, and he was often forced to fight for his very survival. His life as a freebooter* was now dramatically limited, and his dream of retrieving his treasure and retiring to some neutral country where he could live out the rest of his life in a luxurious home surrounded by wife and family was never to be realized.

Following the passage of two to three generations, some rather cryptic information relative to the huge treasure cache buried by the pirate Blackbeard on White Island filtered into the world. It was said that Blackbeard left notes including directions to the secret hiding place, but this has never been verified. Some researchers have suggested that members of his crew who were involved in hiding the treasure had also shared these tales with friends or family members who then passed along these stories of hidden treasures. In any case, it was not long before treasure hunters from far and wide arrived at White Island to search for it. Some even established temporary housing on the island while they searched. As far as we know, no one has found any of Blackbeard's treasure – yet.

Today, three centuries after Blackbeard buried his treasure on White Island, people still come in search of it. During the 1970s, a veteran hunter of Blackbeard's treasure stated that he, and others, searched the island from one end to another with metal detectors but with no success. Every now and then an artifact from the days of pirates is found on the island, and from time to time the discovery of a gold coin is reported, but the huge cache of gold, silver, jewelry, and precious stones continues to elude the searchers. Still, they keep coming, and they keep trying.

There may be an explanation for this. Part of the legend and lore of the White Island treasure is that Blackbeard had it buried, as unlikely as it seems, to a depth of 50 feet, far beyond the reach of most metal detectors. With the recent development of sophisticated technology related to locating objects underground, some suggest it may be only a matter of time before someone finds Blackbeard's White Island treasure.

-2-

Pirate Harry Thompson and the Machias Bay Treasure

Willis's search for the hidden treasure of the pirate Harry Thompson went on for weeks. It became an obsession.

175 miles northeastward along the coast from Blackbeard's White Island hangout is Maine's Machias Bay. This somewhat peaceful setting was the preferred hideout for another pirate, who built a reputation as an efficient, successful freebooter and who also attracted the attention of the British Navy. Unlike Blackbeard, Harry Thompson gradually lost his enthusiasm for piracy, preferring instead to retire to the home he built along the shores of Machias Bay, farm his land, and raise his children.

Although he was one of the least known pirates to ply his trade up and down the Atlantic Coast of America, Harry Thompson was likely one of the most successful. He was also one of the most mysterious. Thompson's origins have never been determined. Some say he was an American from a settlement located somewhere along the northeastern Atlantic seaboard. Others claim he was from England. What scant evidence is available suggests the latter is likely true. He is known to have sailed across the Atlantic Ocean from England to the colonies numerous times, preying on merchant vessels. On occasion, he ventured to Africa to capture ships carrying valuable goods as well as gold and silver.

Thompson led a flotilla of three to four ships. His raiding activities occurred during a time when British and French governments launched warships to prowl the North Atlantic Ocean, searching for brigands, arresting or dispatching them, and putting an end to piracy once and for all. In spite of concentrated effort, they never caught up with Thompson. Some authorities claimed they had never heard of him, and that others had actually committed the piracy attributed to him. Unlike many other pirates, however, Thompson tried to blend in, never behaved in a flashy manner, was never given to boastfulness, and maintained a rather low profile.

Many estimate that Thompson, along with his first mate, accomplice, and best friend, Starbird, led attacks on no fewer than 24 ships during a span of 11 years of pirating. During that time, their raids yielded a great fortune in treasure, mostly in the form of gold and silver coins. In between raids, Thompson returned to Machias Bay in the state of Maine. On the east side of this body of water, Thompson constructed a home and had plans to move his family into it. While he was sailing the Atlantic and looting ships, the family remained in England. A barn was built, livestock placed in the paddocks, and the land was tilled. Home life was good for Harry Thompson, and he looked forward to the day when he could retire permanently to this location.

In addition to never drawing attention to himself, Thompson differed from other pirates of the day in that he was frugal. After paying off his men, he spent little on personal items or pleasures. What expenses he acquired were generally related to refurbishing and maintaining his ships. The remainder of his treasure he kept for himself.

On his returns to his Machias Bay home, Thompson transported the bulk of his treasure with him, carried it to shore, and buried it in a secret location on his land. It has been estimated that his piracy activities yielded an immense fortune.

After many years of preying on merchant ships in the high seas, Thompson began to lose his passion for piracy. He longed to spend time with his family at their Machias Bay home. Finally, he decided his days of sailing and plundering were over. He sold his fleet of ships, save for the one he gave to his friend Starbird. He also presented Starbird a chest of gold and silver coins and then retired for good. Starbird set sail for South America, presumably to continue raiding. He was neither seen nor heard from again.

As Thompson set about readying his house and property, he sent for his wife and young children. They arrived from England several months later. With a staff of servants and housekeepers, as well as farm laborers, Thompson provided his family a comfortable life. His productive farm yielded abundant crops, and he raised a sizeable herd of cattle. His harvest was sold to area merchants and residents. Thompson proved to be an intelligent businessman and logged profits every year. He was a friendly sort, and got along well with everyone. None in the community were aware of his past reputation as a notorious and feared pirate.

Thompson always seemed to have enough funds to spend on necessities for the farm or his family. From time to time, when his income dwindled during the winter, when there were no crops to sell, Thompson would leave his home for as long as two or three hours. When he returned, he had a handful of gold and silver coins to spend on whatever supplies and provisions were needed. Presumably, Thompson harvested the coins from his secret cache. When asked by his wife, Thompson only replied that the vast fortune he had accumulated during his days of piracy was buried somewhere on the farm, a location he refused to reveal.

The years rolled by, and Thompson's children grew up to be teenagers. Aware that they would someday inherit the home and land he so diligently maintained, Thompson knew the time was coming when he would have to inform them of the location of his secret treasure cache. He hesitated, wary of revealing the location. He decided, instead, to devise a set of cryptic markings that would serve as signs indicating directions and distance, all related to the location of his treasure. He scratched the signs on rocks and trees on his property. Thompson believed his children would enjoy solving the mystery of the location of his secret cache.

Thompson's children were never able to decipher the markings and expressed frustration at their lack of success at locating the treasure. By this time, Thompson was an old man. He was tired much of the time and no longer derived amusement from watching his children trying to locate his treasure. He was concerned that he might die before they could find his fortune. Too infirm to walk about his farm and show them the cache site, he decided instead to sketch a map showing the location.

One evening following dinner, Thompson gathered up pen, ink, and parchment, cleared the table, and set about to sketch a detailed map showing the location of his treasure cache. With a feeble, shaking hand, he dipped the pen into the ink well, applied it to the parchment, and outlined the boundaries of his holdings. This done, he drew in the house, the barn, and several outbuildings. As he was estimating the distance from the house to the cache, the old pirate put down the pen, took a deep breath, clutched his chest, and collapsed to the floor, dead.

Thompson's widow and children applied themselves to running the house and farm, but all lacked the commitment and savvy manifested by their late husband and father. The property fell into ruin and the farm was neglected. Bill collectors came calling and were turned away empty-handed. A few years after Thompson's passing, his widow died. With no relatives nearby, the children were sent off to live with neighbors. Thompson's son, Willis, did not take well to living with his new family and ran away. He made his way to the nearest port city and found a job working on a merchant ship.

For the next 25 years, Willis crossed the Atlantic

Ocean dozens of times as he earned his living working on merchant vessels – the same kind that his father used to board and loot. By the time he was 40 years old, Willis was piloting his own vessel. He was now Captain Willis Thompson.

A few years later, Willis grew tired of sailing and longed to settle in a peaceful environment where he could comfortably live out the rest of his life. His thoughts often returned to the family farm at Machias Bay. One day, he sailed into the bay and made inquiries. The Thompson land had gone unoccupied all the years he had been gone. In a short time, he obtained a legal title to the property and moved into the house in which he grew up.

When the pirate Harry Thompson established the house and farm on the Machias Bay property, he was pleased with the fact that it was somewhat remote and far from neighbors. In the time that had passed between then and when Willis occupied the property, settlement had progressed and dozens of people were now living where there was once only field and forest. Willis now found himself surrounded by neighbors.

As Willis cleaned out the old house and made it livable again, he encountered a small and very old wooden chest that had been tucked away in a far closet. Opening it, he found a number of documents and a variety of legal papers and notes. On examining these materials closely, Willis found a note written by his father that described a great pirate treasure buried somewhere on the property. The page was yellowed and brittle, but Willis could make out descriptions and locations of marked stones and trees – markings that contained clues to the location of the trove*. He recalled his frustration with trying to decipher the clues as a youth. A generation later, he was fascinated, intrigued, and spellbound. He decided he would search for the pertinent markers at the first opportunity.

One week later, Willis found two of them, but now he was confronted with a new dilemma: the markings, little more than scratches onto rock surfaces and into the bark of trees, were difficult to interpret. To Willis, they were undecipherable. He spent weeks trying to unravel the mystery of the markings, but to no avail. Then he struck upon an idea.

For whatever reason, Willis decided that his father must have buried his treasure in one of the fields on which crops had been raised. He also assumed that the depth of the cache would be no more than two feet. Any deeper would have required a significant amount of time and energy to retrieve. Because his father had retrieved coins from the cache from time to time, it was safe to assume it would not have been buried deep in the ground.

Consequently, he reasoned that by deep-plowing the soil, he would find the cache. Willis designed and constructed a deep-plow that would cut into the ground to a depth of two feet. He rigged his invention to two stout oxen and undertook the tilling of the large field.

His work was slow and tedious, but Willis Thompson was determined to thoroughly examine every inch of the field. For weeks, he invested twelve or more hours each day to plowing the field, stopping every now and then to examine some bit of material that turned up, such as a discarded tool or a horseshoe.

Not long after he undertook the task of plowing the field, he became aware of small groups of people gathering at the edges of the property to watch him. Days passed, and the groups grew in size. Some wondered at the large and strange plow employed by their new neighbor. Others thought Willis was crazy. A few, however, had heard the rumors of pirate treasure being buried on the property by Harry Thompson, and they wanted to be nearby to witness any discovery.

Willis's search for the hidden treasure of the pirate Harry Thompson went on for weeks. It became an obsession. The weeks turned into months, the months into years, and many began to doubt that there was any treasure to be found at all.

However, the evidence suggests otherwise. Those who have studied the life and times of Harry Thompson know well that he acquired loot in the form of gold, silver, and jewels. They are also convinced that it was cached somewhere on his Machias Bay property, and that he did indeed scratch and carve signs on the rocks and trees as clues to the location. In generations past, some have claimed to see these markings but, like Willis, were unable to determine their meaning.

If the treasure is still buried, it is estimated to be worth several million dollars today. The search continues.

-3-

Edward Lowe and the Pond Island Treasure

Neither Lowe nor any of his crew involved in hiding the treasure on Pond Island lived to return to Casco Bay.

The state of Maine became a favored destination for another notorious pirate, in addition to Blackbeard and Harry Thompson: Edward Lowe. In 1690, Lowe (sometimes spelled Low and Loe) was born in London, England and grew up in poverty. What little schooling Lowe received took place in his home, his mother teaching him the fundamentals of reading and doing sums, but for the most part, he remained only semi-literate all his life.

As a youth, Edward and his brother Richard became

skilled pickpockets and thieves. As they grew older, they turned to burglary and soon attracted the notice of the police. Sure enough, Richard was arrested for burglarizing a house and hanged in Tyburn in 1707.

Soon after the death of his brother, Edward felt it was time to leave England and managed to secure passage on a ship that carried him across the Atlantic Ocean to Boston, Massachusetts. Another account has Edward migrating with his parents to New England when he was 11 years old. History records that British immigrants with the surname of Lowe were among the first wave of Massachusetts colonists.

As a young man, Lowe participated in the ongoing struggle for survival in the New World, spending much of his time working in the fields, tending livestock, and taking on jobs wherever they could be found. He eventually made his way to Boston and settled there for a time.

In 1714, Edward married Elizabeth Marble. It has been written that shortly afterward, Lowe purchased and operated a small store in the coastal town of Salem, 15 miles northeast of Boston. Elizabeth soon gave birth to a son, who died before he reached his first birthday. In 1719, following a difficult pregnancy, she went into a protracted labor that produced a daughter. The strain was too much, and Elizabeth did not survive childbirth. Lowe was devastated and did not know where to turn. In the end, though it grieved him to do so, he left his daughter to be raised by friends of the family, and he took to the seas. He booked passage on a merchant ship bound for South America.

On landing in a Brazilian seaport weeks later, Lowe

searched for work but found little that satisfied him. While there, he would stroll down to the docks and watch the great ships come and go. He also observed the comings and goings of pirates, men he had come to admire. He thought of them as bold, adventurous, and carefree. Further, they always seemed to have money, and plenty of it.

Lowe eventually settled into a job as a rigger* on a merchant vessel. In 1722, he found work on a sloop bound for Honduras, where they were to pick up a shipment of logs to be transported to Boston. Lowe's responsibilities were those of a patron, and he supervised the loading of the logs. Late one afternoon, following a day of grueling work, Lowe entered the ship's dining room, when the captain told him that he would have to wait for his meal; all they had was rum. Angered, Lowe picked up a musket and shot at the captain. Although he missed him, the ball struck a man standing behind the captain in the throat, killing him. For this act, Lowe was fired from his job and kicked off the boat. Other men on his work crew decided to follow him.

Lowe lost no time in acquiring a boat of his own, most likely by theft. He and his crew made it to Rhode Island, where they approached and boarded a sloop with the intention of overtaking it. In the process, at least one of the sloop's sailors was killed. Researchers believe it was at this point that Lowe became a pirate.

For the next several months, Lowe captured more ships, adding to his pirate fleet*. He and his band of brigands preyed on ships traveling along the Atlantic Coast between Boston and New York. He later led his growing armada to the Grand Cayman Islands, where he joined forces with an established pirate named George Lowther. During one of their raids, Lowther captured a large six-gun brigantine* named the Rebecca. He presented it, along with its crew of 44, to Lowe as a gift.

After exchanging the Rebecca, the men parted ways, and Lowe resumed pirating along the New England Coast and Canada. In Nova Scotia, Lowe attacked a fishing fleet, sank all of the boats, and commandeered an 80-ton schooner* with 10 guns. He named it the Fancy, and it became his flagship*.

For the next several months, Lowe led his men on a number of successful raids, and with each one, the chests on board the Fancy were filled with booty* including gold and silver ingots and coins, precious stones, and jewelry. Edward Lowe was becoming a very rich pirate.

Lowe's methods were simple yet effective. Flying false colors, he would approach an unsuspecting merchant vessel. On pulling alongside the vessel, Lowe's pirates would scramble aboard and take prisoners. Anyone who resisted was tortured or killed. Lowe was even known to have men burned alive. Some reports stated that he killed the entire crew of the ships he captured.

Around the time Lowe was rampaging up and down the New England coast, a Spanish pirate vessel fleeing from a fleet of three British warships arrived at Cape Hatteras on the North Carolina coast. Having just enough time to replenish supplies and water, the Don Pedro de Monclava set sail northward just as the British ships came into view. The chase continued, with the Don Pedro gradually gaining distance on the pursuers.

Days later, with the British ships finally out of sight and far behind, the Don Pedro found refuge in Casco

Bay, just northeast of Portland, Maine. After dropping anchor, the captain sent crewmembers ashore to gather fresh water and game. For a week, the Spanish ship lay at anchor in the bay, taking advantage of the time to get some hard earned rest. When all of the water barrels had been filled and the meat lockers stocked, the captain gave orders to weigh anchor and depart.

However, the Spaniards' relief from pursuit was short-lived. Just as they sailed out of Casco Bay, Edward Lowe, leading a pirate fleet of five ships, came into view from the east. Spotting the Don Pedro, Lowe took up pursuit. As swift as was the Spanish vessel, Lowe's ships were swifter. Within the hour, the Don Pedro was overtaken. Maneuvering the Fancy into position, Lowe fired his large guns at the Spaniards, and a one-sided battle commenced. Realizing he was out-numbered and out-gunned, the captain of the Don Pedro surrendered.

Lowe and a number of his pirates boarded the Don Pedro and took the captain hostage. When the Spaniard proved to be uncooperative, he was subjected to several hours of horrific torture. Before it was over, the captain admitted to transporting a large treasure of gold coins, silver ingots, and jewels in the hold of the ship.

Lowe sent crewmen below to locate the treasure and transfer it to the Fancy. It took 10 men to lift the chest of gold coins. Once the treasure was transferred, along with a shipment of rum, Lowe released the Spaniards and turned south. The pirate fleet had not covered much distance when one of Lowe's lookouts called from the crow's nest and warned him of an approaching British fleet. Not wishing to be caught with the immense treasure on board, Lowe shouted orders for his ships to sail into Casco Bay. On entering the bay, Lowe selected an island and barked instructions to anchor off its shore. He decided he would offload the treasure and bury it at this location, a rocky outcrop referred to as Pond Island.

Pond Island was less than one-half mile long and a quarter-mile wide, located just east of Bailey Island, one of the larger isles in the bay. Pond Island was named for the pond of fresh water found in the middle of this tiny outcropping.

Employing three rowboats and 20 crewmembers, the crew took the treasure from the Fancy and transported to Pond Island. Lowe urged them to be quick, and the pirates hurried to carry and drag the heavy trunks and casks filled with treasure to the pond and push them into the water. Just as the last of the gold, silver, and jewels sank beneath the calm waters, the British fleet arrived in the bay and began firing at Lowe's ships.

Piling into the rowboats, Lowe and his crew hurried back to the Fancy just in time to mount a defense against the attack. For a while the battle raged evenly, until one of Lowe's ships was sunk. It soon became apparent that the British vessels possessed superior armament*. Rather than remain and fight, Lowe decided to attempt an escape. He ordered the men to set the sails, and the pirate ships managed to maneuver around the attackers and reach the open sea. Although out-gunned, the pirate vessels proved once again to be faster than the warships, and after a week, the British gave up the chase.

The brush with the British warships was the latest of several that Lowe had encountered during the previous months. As a result, he was growing wary of remaining in these coastal waters. He decided to set sail for the Caribbean Sea, eager to try his luck plundering in a new region.

Alas, Lowe did not fare as well as he thought he would in the Caribbean. His fleet launched an attack on a merchant vessel that had more powerful armament; the heavy guns repelled Lowe's fleet with little difficulty. On another occasion, Lowe led his fleet to attack a French ship only to be surprised by steady and powerful cannon fire, which sank two of the pirate vessels. With little left of his fleet, Lowe rejoined his old friend George Lowther in July, 1723. Together, these two pirate leaders captured a single vessel off the coast of Guinea. Yet, shortly afterward, Lowther split with Lowe and sailed away with only one ship.

From that point on, what happened to Edward Lowe is a mystery, full of conflicting reports. A book released in 1742, titled *A General History of the Pyrates* and written by Captain Charles Johnson (believed to be a pseudonym for Daniel Defoe, author of Robinson Crusoe), rumored that Lowe was last seen sailing to Brazil. Another rumor published in the same book related that many believed Lowe's ship sank in a storm and all aboard drowned.

The National Maritime Museum in London maintains that Lowe was never captured and that he did indeed sail to Brazil, where he lived out the remainder of his life. Writers Charles Ellms and Rob Ossian claim that after Lowe murdered a sleeping crewman, the rest of the men mutinied. After subduing their captain, the mutineers set Lowe adrift in a rowboat. Ellms claims that a French ship picked Lowe up and promptly delivered him to the authorities on the island of Martinique. When his identity was learned, Lowe was brought to trial, found guilty, and hanged.

Neither Lowe nor any of his crew involved in hiding the treasure on Pond Island lived to return to Casco Bay. For decades, no one knew of the treasure, much less where it had been cached. Decades later, an old and long retired pirate who once sailed with Edward Lowe, and was one of the crewmembers who carried the treasure to Pond Island, confessed his role in the affair. He died a short time later.

Over the centuries, few have come to Pond Island in search of Edward Lowe's treasure, which today would be valued into the hundreds of millions of dollars. During the early part of the 1990s, a team of explorers employing a variety of remote sensing equipment arrived at Pond Island. They spent a week examining the small body of water for the treasure, but results were negative. One thing they did discover, however, was that the pond had an extremely soft bottom, composed of loosely consolidated silts and sands. The explorers suspected, given the great weight and high specific gravity of their objective, the treasure likely sank to an undetermined depth. The team made plans to return for another attempt to probe the depths of the bottom layer, but conflicting schedules and a lack of funding prevented them from doing so.

As far as anyone knows, the great treasure of pirate Edward Lowe still lies beneath the muds at the bottom of the small body of water located on Pond Island.

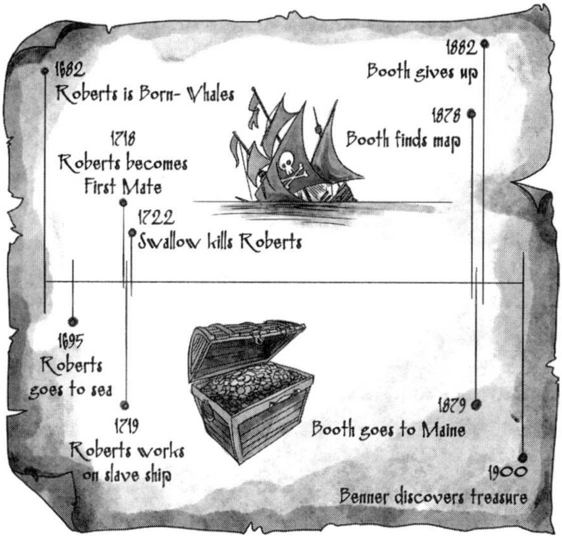

-4-

Pirates Roberts and Kennedy and the Golden Crucifix Treasure

Roberts was regarded as a competent, even vicious, fighter and completely fearless. Many claim that he and his fellow pirates were responsible for the killing of more than a thousand men.

John Roberts was born in 1682 in Wales and later became known as the pirate Bartholomew Roberts. He first went to sea in 1695 at the age of sixteen and served in a variety of capacities on several ships. In 1718, he reached the position of first mate on a sloop out of Barbados, and by 1719, Roberts was serving on a slave ship. While anchored off the Gold Coast of West Africa (present-day

Ghana), the ship was attacked and captured by pirates. Roberts, along with several crewmen, was forced to join the pirate crew.

Leading the raiders was Captain Howell Davis. Davis, a Welshman, took a liking to Roberts and soon discovered that the young man was a skilled navigator, a talent much in demand on pirate ships. Roberts took to piracy easily, and in a short time, captained his own ship. Roberts went on to pursue an illustrious career and eventually became relatively famous. In fact, based on the number of vessels he captured (about 400) historians regard him as the most successful pirate of his time.

In addition to being the most accomplished pirate, Roberts was certainly the most unusual. When he appeared in public, he was, unlike most pirates, impeccably dressed in a starched shirt with frilled cuffs and a long-tailed black coat. He remained well mannered, polite, and dignified, even when commanding a ship manned by bloodthirsty pirates. Roberts never drank liquor, smoked, gambled, or cursed. In addition, he was never known to have relationships with women. At times, he cautioned his own crewmen about the evils of drink and other excesses, though he never had much luck. Roberts even arranged to have church services conducted on his ship every Sunday. In most cases, he was the only one in attendance.

Roberts carried aboard his ship a personal barber, and prior to a raid, the pirate captain would sit for a haircut and manicure. He would then dress in clean, fresh-pressed garments and polished boots. Around his neck from a gold chain hung a large, heavy crucifix made of gold, studded with several diamonds.

In spite of his immaculate dress and bearing, Roberts was regarded as a competent, even vicious, fighter and completely fearless. It has been claimed that he, along with his fellow pirates, was responsible for the killing of more than a thousand men.

On the morning of February 10, 1722, while sailing from the West Indies, Roberts encountered a British warship named the Swallow, captained by Chaloner Ogle. Ogle, a highly decorated officer, had been given the responsibility of capturing or killing Bartholomew Roberts. Roberts was also responsible for disrupting trade between England and America, terrorizing crewmen and passengers, and sinking numerous ships.

On spotting Roberts's ship, Captain Ogle ordered the Swallow in pursuit. Swifter than the pirate vessel, it was clear that the Swallow would overtake it before long. In anticipation of a battle, Roberts, as was his custom, dressed in his finest clothes, hung the golden crucifix around his neck, and walked out onto the deck just as the Swallow fired its cannons.

For nearly two hours, the ships exchanged cannon fire, but in time, Roberts's ship suffered the most damage. One well-placed cannon shot struck a mast near where Roberts stood on deck, and a sliver of wood pierced his neck. As the fighting raged, Roberts, bleeding heavily, collapsed onto the deck. (Another account has Roberts suffering a throat wound from grapeshot*.) Moments later, he was dead.

Every week, Roberts held a meeting with his crewmen and sailors. Among other topics, he always instructed them that if he ever died in battle, they were to throw his body overboard. In response to Roberts's wishes, several of the crewmen, on noticing their fallen leader, picked him up and were about to toss him overboard when first mate Richard Kennedy stepped forward and pulled the golden crucifix from Roberts's neck. As the battle between the two ships raged, Kennedy raced below deck and hid the crucifix among his belongings.

Within the hour, it became clear that the pirate vessel could not hold out against the superior armament of Ogle's forces and would soon be defeated. The sailors and crew of the pirate ship ceased to fight and threw up their hands in surrender, all hoping they would be spared execution. A short time later, the Swallow tied onto the pirate ship, and British sailors swarmed the vessel and placed the captured brigands in chains.

On being shackled, first mate Kennedy demanded an audience with the commander of the victorious vessel, explaining that it was vitally important that he be granted one. That evening he was escorted into Ogle's chambers.

Kennedy was ready to bargain. He told Ogle that he had been present during the burial of a number of Roberts's treasure-filled chests at various locations in the Caribbean, chests that contained fortunes in gold and silver coins and ingots, jewelry, and precious stones. If the appropriate arrangements could be made, stated Kennedy, he would agree to lead Ogle to these caches. Captain Ogle was immediately interested in the prospect of growing wealthy on recovered pirate treasure. He and Kennedy discussed the matter far into the night, and an agreement was made.

One week later, the captured pirates, including Kennedy, were transported to a British garrison* on a West Indies island. They were placed in the island's prison as preparations for a trial were undertaken. Over the next 30 days, the captured pirates were tried, found guilty, and hanged. All of them save for Richard Kennedy.

Late one evening, Kennedy was taken from his cell and brought into a room to meet with several men, one of them Captain Ogle. If Kennedy could lead them to the buried caches he had earlier alluded to, offered Ogle, then the British government would grant him his freedom along with 15 percent of any recovered treasure. If he refused, he would be escorted to the gallows and hanged. Of course, Kennedy readily agreed to the proposition.

Over the next month, Kennedy led Ogle and his compatriots to several locations in the Caribbean where treasure-filled chests were dug up. By the time all of the treasures had been recovered and Kennedy paid off, the former first mate found himself in possession of a fortune that required four wooden chests to transport. During all of this time, Kennedy managed to maintain possession of the golden crucifix, which he placed into one of the chests.

With his newfound wealth, Kennedy purchased a light, maneuverable sloop, into which he loaded his four treasure chests and sailed to the Atlantic Coast in search of a place to settle. Given his recent imprisonment and related experiences, Kennedy wanted nothing more to do with piracy.

Kennedy selected Boothbay, Maine, as his destination, where he retired to a small rock house at the farthest extent of the peninsula. Over the following weeks, Kennedy explored the area around Boothbay in search of a suitable location to bury his treasure. Eventually, he sailed the short distance to the coastal town of Bath and up the nearby Kennebec River. At one point along the river, he found a location that satisfied him. After removing enough coins to last him for several years, Kennedy excavated a four-foot-deep hole on a tree-lined hill that overlooked the river. Then he placed the chests in the hole and laid two large, flat stones atop them before refilling it. After burying the treasure chests, he walked over to a nearby birch tree, peeled away some of the bark, and using a knife, carved into the trunk a simple map showing the location of his buried treasure.

A few days later, Kennedy obtained a piece of tanned calfskin. He cut an 18-by-18-inch square from it, and onto this, recreated the map showing the location of his treasure, recording distances, directions, and landmarks. At the location of his treasure cache, he sketched a star. He

referred to his cache as "the Golden Crucifix Treasure." When Kennedy had completed the map, he rolled it up and placed it into his sea chest.

Months passed, and while Kennedy was relatively content with his new life, he found himself growing bored. In spite of his capture and imprisonment, as well as his close brush with hanging, Kennedy found himself longing for the adventure of the pirate life once again. He began making plans to purchase a new vessel, arm it, and hire a crew.

As he pondered these notions, he became aware of the increasing patrols of British warships up and down the Atlantic Coast. He also learned that a number of pirates had been captured, tried, and hung. In the end, Kennedy gave up the notion of returning to piracy. Instead, he traveled to London, where he purchased a tavern.

Following several weeks of brisk business at his tavern, Kennedy decided to turn it into a brothel. Over the next year, the brothel succeeded, and it became a hangout for society's rougher elements: thieves, cutthroats, and pirates. In time, Kennedy's place grew to be an informal meeting place for gangs of criminals, where plans were made for committing a range of robberies and killings.

One evening, Kennedy became quite drunk in his own establishment. At one point during the evening, one of the prostitutes spilled a drink on him, and, in response, he beat her. Craving revenge, the prostitute went to the local authorities and reported the illegal goings-on at the tavern. For the next several days, law enforcement officials observed well-known pirates and other criminals entering and leaving the tavern. When they felt the time was right, the lawmen raided the tavern and arrested several of the patrons, as well as Kennedy.

Following an evaluation of evidence, Kennedy was charged with conspiring to kill a government official. He was tried, found guilty, and sentenced to hang. His execution was carried out a short time later.

Several days after the execution, Kennedy's possessions fell into the hands of a pirate named Booth. After opening Kennedy's sea chest, Booth removed everything of value. On coming across the rolled-up calfskin, Booth examined it but could make no sense of Kennedy's cryptic markings and notations. He decided the skin was worthless and returned it to the chest. Days later, Booth gave the chest to a relative.

The sea chest was then handed down from generation to generation in Booth's family. In 1878, Terrence Booth, a descendant, spotted the chest in a storeroom. Curious, he opened it and examined the contents. When he unrolled the calfskin, he recognized it for what it was – a treasure map. On the spot, Terrence Booth decided that as soon as he could obtain the funds, he would travel to Maine and look for Richard Kennedy's buried treasure cache.

In 1879, Terrence Booth set sail for Maine. His only luggage was the sea chest, which contained his clothes and the treasure map. By the time the ship reached the coast of Maine, Booth's meager funds were exhausted, and he was forced to find employment. For a year, he served as a hatter's apprentice in Portland, Maine. He worked at the job long enough to save sufficient money so that he could continue his search.

Due to his unfamiliarity with the region, as well as poor directions and confusing information he received from residents, Booth had a difficult time determining which of the many streams was the Kennebec River identified by Kennedy's treasure map. After several weeks of hiking and sailing along the coast, Booth ran short of money once again and went in search of work. By the end of 1882, he had made no progress in his search for the Golden Crucifix Treasure and decided to forego his quest.

In search of a job, Booth learned that a timber company in Vermont was hiring workers. Desperately short of money, he undertook the long journey to the site two states away. Weary of transporting the sea chest, Booth looked for a place to store it. He spotted a fine house a short distance from the road and decided to take a look.

Booth discovered that a woman by the name of Emmeline Benner Lewis owned the house. Booth knocked on the door, introduced himself, and asked if he could leave his chest until he returned. Mrs. Lewis agreed to store the chest for a small sum and instructed Booth to place it in the attic. However, Terrence Booth was never to be heard from again.

George Benner, Mrs. Lewis's nephew, frequently visited his aunt. With the typical curiosity of a young boy, he inquired about the strange trunk in the attic from time to time. He longed to see what lay within, but Lewis forbade him, telling him it was someone else's property, which would someday be reclaimed.

By 1900, it was clear to Mrs. Lewis that the young man who left the trunk was not going to return for it. Benner, who was now in his twenties, had maintained his curiosity about the trunk. One day, Lewis finally granted him permission to open the old chest, and inside he found several letters, one of which was dated 1830. He also found a quadrant*, a number of sea shells, and a rolled-up calfskin. After unrolling the skin, Benner realized it was a map, and even better, a treasure map. He was fascinated. Every day for a week, he pored over the map, trying to make sense of the symbols and notations.

Benner was familiar with much of Maine's coastline. On the map he recognized Casco Bay, Boothbay Harbor, and the mouth of the Kennebec River where it emptied into the sea. At one point on the map, a star had been placed at a location along the river. In one corner of the map was the inscription

STAND ABREST QURTSBOLDER
BRING TOP IN LINE WITH HILL 1/2M
IT LISE 12 FATHOM N. E.
NEAR BIG TREES UNDER STONE

Two months after parsing out the meanings of the map's notations, Benner, along with a companion, rented a boat at Boothbay one morning and sailed up the Kennebec River. Slowly making their way upstream, Benner and his friend spotted a large granite boulder glistening with quartz crystals. Believing this was the "QURTSBOLDER" indicated on the map, Benner beached the boat and explored around the area.

Approximately one-half mile north of the boulder, Benner and his friend approached a low hill with only a single tree growing near the top. After climbing to the summit, both men spotted the trunks of other trees that had died back years earlier. Benner and his friend decided that this must be the hill indicated on the map.

By this time, it was close to sunset, so Benner decided to return to Boothbay, purchase some supplies, and return the next day.

Getting an early start, the two men arrived back at the hill a few minutes after dawn the following day. They brought with them two shovels, a number of canvas sacks, and a long iron bar. With the bar, Benner probed the ground, driving the instrument deep into the soft earth of the hill every few feet, in hope of striking a treasure chest. At one point in their search, the tip of the bar struck a rock-like substance two feet beneath the surface, near a very old tree stump. Encouraged, the two men commence to dig.

Following twenty minutes of excited and hurried labor, Benner and his friend came to a large, flat rock lying horizontally in the ground. With considerable effort, the two men tilted the rock onto its side, only to discover a second one beneath. After removing the second stone, the diggers' hearts raced as they gazed down onto the collapsed lid of a wooden chest. After pulling away the rotted wood, the two men were speechless as they sifted through the hundreds of gold coins that lay within the chest. As fast as they could, they filled the canvas sacks with the coins.

When they had retrieved the entire contents of the chest, they undertook the digging of a second hole. Once again, at two feet, they encountered another chest. On opening it, Benner and his friend also found it filled with gold coins, and atop the coins lay a large crucifix made of gold and studded with several diamonds, which had belonged to none other than the legendary pirate Bartholomew Roberts. After removing the coins and placing them in the remainder of the canvas sacks, the friends resumed digging. They excavated two more holes but found nothing.

Exhausted by their labors and the excitement of their discovery, the two men decided they had found all of the treasure and made plans to return to Boothbay. After resting for nearly an hour, they gathered up their tools, the canvas sacks filled with treasure, and the calfskin map and departed. They had no way of knowing that within inches of one of their excavations were two more wooden chests, each one containing a king's ransom in gold coins.

In the years following Benner's discovery, the topography of the lower valley of the Kennebec River changed dramatically, as a result of numerous floods and expanding human settlement. The granite boulder described by Kennedy on the map is no longer there.

Beyond the banks of the river lie a number of low hills. Atop one of them, as far as anyone knows, remain two of Richard Kennedy's treasure chests, each filled with gold coins that could be worth a small fortune.

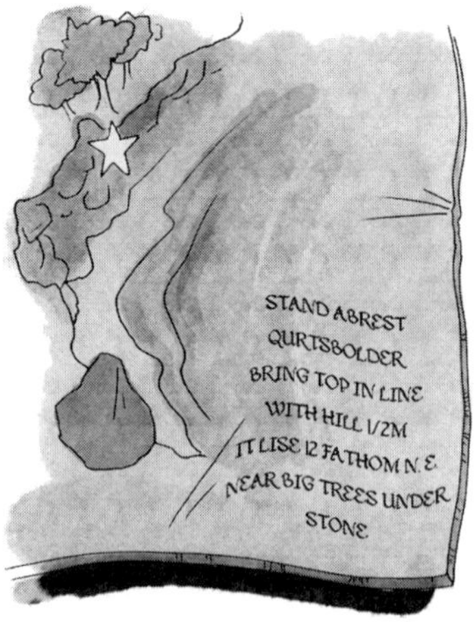

-5-

Pirate John Quelch and His Lust for Gold

> *"I am not afraid of death, I am not afraid of the gallows, but I am afraid of what follows. I am afraid of a Great God and a judgment to come."*

The Isles of Shoals, located near the borders of New Hampshire and Maine, were not only an attractive treasure burial site for Blackbeard, but they also appealed to the pirate John Quelch, who, many believe, buried millions of dollars' worth of gold on one of the rocky islands.

Quelch was born in England in 1666. He got his start in piracy in a rather ironic way. He served as a crewmember on a private ship commissioned by the British government. Many of these vessels employed a number of privateers to track down and eliminate the pirate menace along the east coast of America. By all accounts, Quelch, who served at his job for years, was a quiet and dependable crewman who went about his tasks without complaint, but that soon began to change.

One day, the privateer on which Quelch served caught sight of a Spanish pirate ship off the coast of Florida and gave pursuit. The swifter privateer caught up with the Spanish vessel after several hours and, when in range, began firing its cannons. The bombardment caused heavy damage, and following several devastating hits, the Spanish ship sank in shallow water 200 yards from the shore.

The captain of the privateer was convinced that the Spanish ship carried treasure, so he ordered several of his crewmen to dive to the wreck, explore it, and if treasure was found, to bring it to the surface. Quelch was one of the divers.

Following several attempts, the divers penetrated the hull of the sunken ship and located the treasure – hundreds of gold ingots. One by one, the ingots were brought to the surface and loaded into the privateer. John Quelch handled dozens of the gold ingots, and each time he did, he experienced a sensation unlike any he ever thought possible. For weeks following the retrieval of the gold ingots, Quelch thought of little else.

As time went on, Quelch grew obsessed with gold and the thought of possessing as much of it as possible. He thought often of the wealth it would bring him, but he was also infatuated with the touch, texture, taste, and smell of the precious metal. Gold had a narcotic-like effect on the young man. It was a preoccupation that was to remain with him for the rest of this life.

It gradually dawned on Quelch that piracy appeared to offer far more rewards than working as a crewmember on a privateer, assuming one could escape pursuit from British authorities. Quelch began to discuss this concept with other crewmembers, and before long, several men aligned themselves with his way of thinking. In order to pursue the life of a pirate, one needed a ship, and subsequent meetings were devoted to planning ways they could take over the privateer.

One morning, as the captain exited his cabin, he was jumped by several crewmembers, tied up with sail cord, lowered into a rowboat, and shoved toward the nearest shore. With the captain gone, the privateer was now under the command of John Quelch. Within a year, Quelch had attacked and plundered ships and coastal towns and amassed uncountable wealth.

Weeks later, the Quelch-led privateer set sail for the coast of Spain. It was the Spanish ships that Quelch was after, for he knew that these ships transported fortunes in gold, silver, gems, and jewelry. Of all the riches carried by these vessels, it was the gold he was after, the treasure he coveted the most. For months, the privateer plied the waters off the coasts of Western Europe and Africa, attacking and taking over Spanish and Portuguese vessels. Each of them yielded treasures in a variety of forms and quantities, and before long, the privateer labored under the weight of thousands of pounds of such wealth. When he was convinced the privateer could hold no more treasure, Quelch returned to the New England coast in search of a suitable place to cache his fortune.

After sailing up and down the east coast for several weeks, Quelch finally decided to hide his treasure on the Isles of Shoals. He identified Star Island as a favored destination. The island is the second largest landform of this complex of rocky outcrops perched above sea level, located on the New Hampshire side of the boundary.

Quelch anchored off Star Island and, in the company of several crewmen, rowed to shore. Once on the island, Quelch spent a full day exploring every inch of it in search of the ideal location to hide his treasure. At a location known only to him and the crewmen who accompanied him, Quelch ordered several deep holes excavated to accommodate his treasure.

On returning to the ship, Quelch had his accumulated treasures brought up from the hold and placed on deck. Here, he separated the gold ingots, coins, nuggets, dust, and jewelry from the rest. After spending considerable time with his fortune, touching, caressing, and admiring the gold, he pointed to the remainder – the fortune in silver and gems – and informed the crew that they could divide it among themselves.

The next morning, Quelch supervised as men loaded his gold into several rowboats that would transport his wealth to the nearest shore of Star Island. After unloading the fortune from the rowboats, Quelch's men carried it to the several holes that had been excavated the previous day. Each hole was filled nearly to the top with the precious treasure and covered over. Over the years, it's been estimated that Quelch's gold cache is worth several million dollars.

The privateer lay at anchor off Star Island for a week while the crew rested up. Men were sent to the nearby New Hampshire coast to procure fresh water and to hunt for game, all of which was plentiful. Quelch considered that when his piracy days were over, he might return to this area and live out the rest of his life.

During the ensuing years, Quelch led his fellow pirates on raids across the Atlantic Ocean and back, each time acquiring more booty and more gold. When the privateer became full of treasure, Quelch would sail back to Star Island, have fresh holes excavated, and his treasures placed within. Quelch once confided in one of this crewmen that he was so concerned someone would come to the island to take his gold away from him that he wanted it hidden so that no one could ever find it.

Weeks later, Quelch set sail down the New England coast with the intention of raiding several small towns, port cities that dotted the coastal landscape. Before he was able to launch a single raid, however, American warships chased him away. It was a close call, and Quelch grew concerned that with the growing numbers of British and American patrols consisting of large, well-armed ships, his piracy days were numbered. After giving the matter considerable thought, he turned his privateer over to his crew and returned to Star Island, where he intended to live out his days.

John Quelch looked forward to endless peaceful days living on Star Island. When the mood struck him, he would dig up a portion of his gold, spend time with it, and rebury it. Life was simple and satisfying for Quelch. Unbeknownst to the former pirate, however, his time in paradise was about to end.

Though Quelch was no longer an active pirate, he was still wanted by American authorities. He had long been classified as a dangerous criminal involved in piracy, an identification that was still on the books. It wasn't long before officials discovered Quelch's Star Island refuge. One morning, a small fleet of warships, commanded by Major Sewell and Captain John Turner, traveled from the Boston harbor to the Isles of Shoals with a mission to capture Quelch.

Quelch, who lived on Star Island with two former crewmembers, was surprised to find American warships anchoring off the Star Island shore. A short time later, a force of two dozen armed sailors, led by Turner, approached Quelch and placed him under arrest. Knowing that pirate Quelch had stolen gold and other riches from merchant vessels over the years, Turner interrogated him about the whereabouts of the treasure. Quelch remained silent; he was not about to relinquish his life's passion. He would die first.

Quelch's cabin was searched, but all that was found was a small leather sack containing a few gold coins. Believing the bulk of the pirate's treasure to be buried somewhere on the island, Turner organized a search for a likely cache. Though the American sailors scoured the entire island from its shoreline to the interior, nothing was found.

John Quelch's ultimate fate is shrouded in mystery. One version has the pirate taken to Boston where he was tried, found guilty of piracy, and sentenced to life in prison. For years, John Quelch reportedly lived in a tiny cell less than 100 miles from Star Island and his fortune in gold. Never again would the ex-pirate touch, smell, or taste the incredible wealth he had accumulated. After a few years in prison, it was reported that Quelch died from consumption, or the infectious disease now known as tuberculosis.

Another version has Quelch found guilty of murder and sentenced to death, a version that is supported by a number of written reports from eyewitnesses. On June 30, 1704, he and six of his crewmen, who were also found guilty, were marched to Scarlett's Wharf by the sea. The condemned were escorted by a platoon of musketeers, a number of governmental officials, and two clergymen.

On reaching the gallows, which had been constructed on the wharf, the condemned men were subjected to a lengthy sermon delivered by one of the clergy. All of the men manifested various levels of regret and repentance for their piratical deeds as the nooses were tightened around their necks – all but John Quelch.

It was reported that after ascending the stairs and reaching the platform of the gallows, he addressed one of the ministers, saying, "I am not afraid of death, I am not afraid of the gallows, but I am afraid of what follows. I am afraid of a Great God and a judgment to come." Taking off his hat and turning to face the spectators, Quelch said, "I am condemned only by circumstances. I forgive all the world, so the Lord be merciful to my soul." A moment later he was hanged. The bodies of the executed were buried between the high and low tide markers.

Sixty years after the death of John Quelch, a man was rummaging through an old vacant house in Gloucester, Massachusetts, when he came across an old wooden trunk in the attic. Inside the trunk, he found a journal, one that had been used nearly to the point of tatters. Inside the journal was an account of a great fortune in gold ingots buried at some secret location on Star Island. Researchers believe that the journal belonged to John Quelch. Unfortunately, while the description of the treasure in gold was vivid, there were no specific directions leading to the cache. When the contents of the journal were revealed, hordes of treasure hunters descended on Star Island in search of Quelch's treasure, but it was never found.

During the 1790s, a seawall was constructed around a portion of Star Island. The materials used for the seawall were the native rocks harvested on the isle. While selecting some suitable stones near the western end of the island, one of the workers uncovered several gold ingots. This discovery set off another round of searches by treasure hunters; still, nothing more was found.

John Quelch never enjoyed the fame and notoriety of other pirates such as Blackbeard, Jean Lafitte, and Captain Kidd, but this suited Quelch just fine. He was a man who preferred to maintain a low profile, remain anonymous, and allow the scrutiny of the authorities to fall upon others. Outside of Captain Turner and Major Sewell and a handful of other commanders who pursued him, few were aware of John Quelch's existence. Likewise, Quelch wanted his treasure to remain just as isolated. He once related to a crewman that he wanted his treasure so thoroughly hidden that no one could ever find it. In that aspect, the pirate succeeded. Explorers still search for Quelch's treasure to this day but to no avail.

-6-

Pirate Sandy Gordon and the White Island Treasure

Gordon, determined never to be taken alive, seized a torch and headed for the ship's magazine. There, he ignited the store of powder.

Historians and writers describe pirate Sandy Gordon as ruthless, fearless, and evil. He was, indeed, all of that, as the record of his raids and plunders reveal. Gordon may have also been insane. In addition, evidence indicates that Gordon buried millions of dollars' worth of treasure in gold and silver coins on New Hampshire's White Island. Unfortunately, within a year of establishing this fabulous cache, Gordon blew himself up, along with his ship and crewmen.

As a youth growing up in Glasgow, Scotland, Sandy Gordon was constantly in trouble. So dedicated was he to mischief and thievery that his parents threw him out of their house and left him to fend for himself, wandering the streets of town and pilfering whatever he could along the docks. Young Gordon spent countless weeks in jail while still in his teens, mostly for stealing from shops and dockside warehouses.

One afternoon in 1704, Gordon was roaming the docks waiting for an opportunity to steal something when he was offered a job as a crewman on a merchant vessel, the Porpoise. Excited by the prospect of going to sea, Gordon accepted the offer and signed on.

The Porpoise had been several days out in the ocean when Gordon realized that his "opportunity" amounted to little more than scrubbing decks, painting wooden fixtures, and polishing brass fittings. In a short time, he grew disappointed and bored, so he resorted to entertaining himself by stealing from his fellow crewmen.

On this voyage, the captain of the Porpoise, John Herring, brought along his 18-year-old daughter, Martha. During those days, it was considered bad luck to have a woman on board a sailing vessel. This, too, turned out to be true for young Gordon.

While engaged in his daily chores of scrubbing, painting, and polishing, Gordon often positioned himself such that he would encounter Martha during her daily walks around the deck. In time, the two grew to be very friendly, and Martha agreed to meet Gordon late one night in her cabin. Just past midnight, when he thought everyone would be asleep, Gordon crept from his bunk and made his way to Martha's room. He knocked softly on her door, and a moment later, she opened it and invited him in.

Captain Herring had long suspected that Gordon had designs on his daughter. Herring also learned from some of the crewmen and sailors that they suspected him of stealing from their sea chests when they were away from their rooms. On this evening, Herring made the rounds of the ship and noticed that Gordon was not in his bed. He raced to his daughter's cabin, burst through the door, and found the two locked in an intimate embrace. Herring summoned a pair of crewmen to place Gordon in chains.

The next morning, Gordon was tied to the mainmast and his shirt ripped away. Deftly wielding a short whip, Herring administered 100 lashes. Before Herring was finished, Gordon had fallen unconscious and was held upright only by his bonds. His back had been flayed so severely that short lengths of skin hung from his back, and a pool of blood had gathered at his feet. After being cut down and having his wounds treated, Gordon was once again locked in chains and placed in the ship's brig for 30 days.

When Gordon was released from confinement, he returned to work. Herring informed him that he would be removed from the ship as soon as it docked on the Atlantic Coast. Gordon couldn't wait to get off the ship. He was fed up with the drudgery of his menial assignments as a deckhand, but his passion for being at sea still burned. Gordon decided he wanted to command his own ship. When he wasn't looking forward to reaching some American port, his mind was occupied with thoughts of revenge against the hated Captain Herring.

As the days wore on, Gordon encountered other sailors and crewmen who had also felt the sting of Herring's lash. He discovered that the majority of the crew despised Herring and, like Gordon, thought often of revenge. Days passed, and as the men talked, they planned how to take over the Porpoise.

One week later, the mutineers took control of the ship. Herring and the first mate were taken prisoner, and with Gordon giving the orders, the captain was tied to the same mast where the young crewman had suffered a severe lashing weeks earlier, but this time, Gordon held the whip. As he ripped Herring's shirt from his back, Gordon began laughing and gleefully applied himself to the punishment. He doled out exactly 100 lashes to Herring, each strike fiercer and more violent than the previous one. By the time Gordon finished, Herring was nearly dead.

Grabbing a knife from a nearby sailor, Gordon cut the captain down. Walking over to the forge*, he withdrew a red-hot poker and burned the captain's eyes out, all the while cackling with laughter. Gordon, now raving, then ordered the men to throw Captain Herring overboard.

Gordon was recognized as the leader of the mutineers, and the men now regarded him as the new captain of the ship. He announced to one and all that he was dedicating himself and this vessel to piracy, and any who were not with him could jump overboard. Gordon set sail for the British Isles and the European coast. Over the next three years, he attacked and plundered dozens of merchant vessels and raided a number of coastal communities.

During the raids, Gordon accumulated a significant amount of treasure in the form of gold and silver coins and jewelry. In spite of the great riches taken from the ships, Gordon paid his crew only meager wages, keeping the vast bulk of the treasure for himself. In the evenings, Gordon would lock himself in his cabin, open his chests, and gaze upon his riches. He counted coins for hours at a time. According to his crewmen, Gordon grew noticeably more insane.

With time, Gordon's crewmen and sailors grew resentful at not being awarded a greater percentage of the spoils, but Gordon refused to listen to their complaints. It wasn't long before his crew mutinied. They seized his chests filled with treasure, placed him in a rowboat, and set him adrift on the ocean off the coast of Scotland.

With difficulty, Gordon managed to reach the shore along a sparsely settled portion of the Scottish coast. He took refuge in an old abandoned farmhouse with a freshwater spring nearby, where he gathered shellfish for food. With his mind and body depleted, Gordon decided to remain there and somehow survived by living a subsistence life.

Years later, Gordon, with long, matted hair and a disheveled beard, was walking along the shore near the farmhouse when he spotted a sailing vessel on the horizon. The ship appeared to be headed in his direction and, two hours later, glided into the bay, lowered the sails, and dropped anchor. Gordon watched as several men climbed down a ladder, entered a longboat, and rowed toward the shore where he stood. On beaching the craft, several crewmen climbed out, each one hoisting a water barrel. They approached Gordon and asked where they might find fresh water. Gordon led them to the spring.

As Gordon visited with the newcomers, he learned that they were pirates serving under Edwin Thatch, also known as the infamous Blackbeard. Interested in meeting the famous pirate, Gordon begged the crewmen to take him back to the ship with them. Though they thought him mad, they agreed to do so. Once on board the vessel, Gordon repeated his request to meet with Blackbeard, and he was eventually ushered into the captain's cabin. Gordon described his years of successful piracy and asked to join the noted brigand and return to the sea. Blackbeard listened and, though skeptical, agreed to give his strange visitor a chance. Blackbeard also informed Gordon that if he failed, he would be killed.

Gordon, true to his claims, turned out to be an experienced seaman and a fearless fighter. Gordon's skill with the sword impressed Blackbeard, and the captain later attributed a number of successes to the efforts of his new recruit. In spite of Gordon's accomplishments, Blackbeard regarded him as deranged and dangerous. Yet, he rewarded Gordon with his own ship, a recently acquired Spanish merchant vessel, which Gordon renamed the The Flying Scot.

With his own ship and a newly recruited and competent crew, Gordon set about raiding along the European coast once again. In time, the hold of The Flying Scot was filled with treasure estimated to be worth many millions of dollars. Gordon decided to sail to America, search for a suitable location in which to settle, and conduct raids on the trading vessels he knew to frequent the area.

Gordon eventually arrived at White Island, one of the smallest in the complex called the Isles of Shoals, located just off the coast of New Hampshire. Gordon liked the island for its solitude and the fact that, in his mind, it could be easily defended. In no time at all, Gordon oversaw the construction of a sturdy cabin. Once the structure was completed, Gordon cast about for a suitable location in which to bury his treasure. Once he selected a site, one not far from his cabin, he worked under the cover of darkness and away from his crew's prying eyes. He carried handfuls of his fortune in gold and silver coins and jewelry from the ship to the island and buried them at the selected location. In all, it took weeks to move the entirety of his treasure.

Gordon enjoyed his newfound life on White Island. Whenever he felt a craving for adventure, he summoned his crew and sailed The Flying Scot along the Atlantic Coast, conducting raids on villages and trading ships. As Gordon's treasure grew, it was carried to his secret location and buried with the rest.

Gordon had been residing on White Island for a year when he learned that a fleet of British warships was sailing in that direction from the east. Their assignment was to search out and destroy pirates. Early one morning as Gordon was enjoying a walk around his island, he spotted the British fleet approaching. They appeared to be headed to the very harbor in which his pirate ship was anchored.

Knowing that the British hanged captured pirates, Gordon knew he had to escape quickly. He ran to the barracks where his crew stayed and alerted them to prepare The Flying Scot for a hasty departure. As the crewmen hoisted the sails and raised the anchor, Gordon prepared to give the order to sail out of the bay and into the open sea. Looking around, however, he saw that the British fleet was almost upon him and that flight was now impossible. The only alternative was to engage the invaders in battle.

Gordon, never one to negotiate, fired first. His volley was promptly returned from all of the British ships, and it soon became clear that the pirates, out-manned and out-gunned, would not survive this encounter; they would either be captured and sent to trial or they would be killed. Gordon, determined that he would never be taken alive, seized a torch and headed for the ship's magazine*. There, he ignited the store of powder. The Flying Scot exploded, the blast hurling burning timbers and men dozens of yards in every direction. Everyone aboard the sinking ship died. The insane Sandy Gordon took not only his own life, but also that of his entire crew.

As a result, not a single soul remained alive who knew the location of Gordon's secret treasure cache. Although the remains of his cabin have been located and identified, the site of the treasure cache remains unknown.

-7-

Arthur Doane's Discovery of Pirate Treasure in Massachusetts

His heart pounding with the exertion and excitement, Doane looked into the chest and saw nearly two dozen canvas bags, each packed tightly with Spanish coins.

Today, Chatham, Massachusetts is a popular tourist destination on Cape Cod. Located on the seaward side of an elbow-shaped peninsula, this small town boasts picture postcard streets, shopping, fine food, and other attractions. However, unknown to many, this location also harbors a mystery of buried pirate treasure.

During the 1830s, John Eldridge, a long time Chatham resident, owned a successful tailor shop in town. Eldridge was a well-respected member of the community and provided well for his family. Another Chatham resident, Arthur Doane, was a fisherman and occasional day laborer. Doane and Eldridge were good friends, and from time to time, Doane would drop by the tailor shop to visit.

One afternoon, Doane arrived at the shop while Eldridge was putting the finishing touches on a suit coat, and the two men chatted amiably. However, during the conversation, Doane appeared to be preoccupied. Finally, Doane asked Eldridge if it were possible to exchange foreign coins for American currency. Eldridge replied that it was possible and explained that some banks and coin collectors in Philadelphia, Boston, and elsewhere could handle such transactions.

As Eldridge finished the coat he was working on, Doane sat pondering this information. Then, Doane asked Eldridge if he could exchange some foreign coins for him during his next visit to Philadelphia. The tailor agreed. Standing, Doane pulled six gold pieces from his coat pocket and handed them to Eldridge. The coins were Spanish in origin and bore mint dates of 1810.

After examining the coins, Eldridge told Doane that exchanging them for American money would be no problem and that he would do so the next time he traveled to Philadelphia to purchase cloth. Curious about the coins, Eldridge asked Doane how he happened to be in possession of them. However, while he came by them honestly, Doane preferred not to reveal the source. He thanked Eldridge and departed.

Two weeks later, Eldridge made the journey to Philadelphia to conduct business. While he was in Philadelphia, he carried the coins to a noted collector. After examining them, the collector said the coins had a very high gold content. Eldridge was given American money for the lot.

When he returned to Chatham, Eldridge handed the money over to Doane who, in turn, paid the tailor for his trouble. Still curious, Eldridge asked once again how Doane had come into possession of the coins, but his friend responded by saying that it was best for Eldridge not to be concerned.

For the next several months, Doane would stop by the tailor shop at least once a week. Each time, he brought six more Spanish coins and asked Eldridge to exchange them for American money. This odd arrangement continued for the next 46 years. During that time, Eldridge estimated he returned close to $60,000 to Doane, an impressive fortune at the time.

About one year after Eldridge began exchanging Doane's gold coins for American money, Doane got married, eventually fathered a son, and settled into a stable family life. The fisherman continued to harvest cod and other fish from the sea and used his money to purchase new and better equipment. His fishing enterprise thrived. Doane had managed to save quite a bit of money, and after the passage of several years, his neighbors regarded him as a wealthy man. Most Chatham residents assumed he had made his money from fishing.

Then, disaster struck. Doane's wife passed away, and a short time later, his only child died from an illness. Doane also became very ill and was almost completely bedridden. His only visitors were his physician, his housekeeper, and his old friend John Eldridge. One day, realizing he did not have long to live, Doane summoned Eldridge to his bedside so that he could tell him the history of the coins.

Doane explained that 50 years earlier, he had been fishing off the coast of Chatham Beach when he decided to pull into port to visit a young girl. Doane had become enamored with the girl, but her father did not care for the fisherman. So he and the girl arranged to meet secretly on the beach. That night, as they were sitting among the dunes, the two lovers watched as a rowboat landed on the beach some distance away. Several men climbed out of the boat, and Doane noted that they were dressed like pirates. They removed several shovels from the boat and then lifted a large, heavy, wooden chest out if it. They carried the chest to a spot on the beach not far from where Doane and his sweetheart were watching. As it was dark and the two lovers were behind some low-growing brush, the pirates did not see them.

Twenty minutes later, the pirates had excavated a hole sufficient to accommodate the chest. They lowered it into the hole, refilled it, returned to the rowboat, and rowed out to sea, presumably to an awaiting ship that lay beyond sight in the darkness.

The next morning, Doane borrowed a spade from a neighbor and returned to the site of the buried chest. After looking around to make certain no one was watching, he dug into the sand. An hour later, his shovel struck the wooden chest. After several more minutes of effort, he managed to open it. His heart pounding with the exertion and excitement, Doane looked into the chest and saw nearly two dozen canvas bags, each packed tightly with Spanish coins.

Doane's first thought was that he needed to find a new hiding place for the treasure before the pirates returned for it. He closed the chest, refilled the hole, and started exploring the surrounding area for a suitable site. Four hundred yards away, he spotted a relatively high, somewhat prominent sand dune. The dune began approximately 30 yards from the shoreline and extended another 70 yards toward a dirt road that led to Chatham. Doane decided he would rebury the chest next to the dune.

Doane returned to the area an hour past sundown. When he was certain no one was around, he excavated a large hole near the dune. He then walked over to where the pirates had buried the treasure chest, removed the sacks filled with coins, and carried them over to the new excavation near the dune. It took several trips until finally, he returned for the chest, pulled it from the excavation, and dragged it to the new location. He lowered it into the hole and refilled it with the bags of coins, keeping one sack out for himself. He then refilled the hole, smoothed over the sand, and erased his tracks and the drag marks of the chest.

For years, Doane kept the secret of the buried treasure to himself in fear that the men who originally buried it would return, find him out, and kill him. Having never had much money in his life, Doane was uncomfortable about handling the incredible wealth he had come into. After the passage of several years, and feeling certain he would not be detected, Doane approached Eldridge about exchanging the coins. The arrangement worked out well for both men, and when Doane ran low on funds, he would return to the south side of the large dune at night and retrieve another sack full of gold.

As Doane lay dying on his bed, he pointed to a cherry wood dresser on the opposite side of the room and told Eldridge to look in the top drawer. On opening the drawer, the tailor found 18 gold coins lying in the bottom; it was all that remained of Doane's most recent acquisition. Doane presented the coins to Eldridge as a gift and told him that when he needed more to go to the dune and dig them up. Growing weaker, Doane, in a halting and raspy voice, provided directions to the treasure cache.

The next morning, Eldridge made the short journey out to the beach and located the dune described by Doane. Carrying a spade and the fisherman's directions, he paced off the necessary steps and proceeded to dig into the sand. Not used to such heavy work, the tailor was forced to pause often to catch his breath and rest. After an hour of digging, he was relieved to hear the sound of his spade striking the top of the wooden chest. After opening the lid, Eldridge found seven sacks of coins lying within. He removed one of them, closed the chest, and refilled the hole. The next day, he closed his shop, traveled to Philadelphia, and sold the coins for a total of $4,500.

On returning to Chatham, Eldridge deposited the money in his bank account and rushed over to Doane's house to inform him. On arriving, however, the housekeeper told him that Arthur Doane had passed away the previous evening. Saddened by the loss of his friend, Eldridge descended into a pit of depression and remained there for several days as he worked quietly in his tailor shop.

One evening, two weeks after Doane's passing, Eldridge decided to take a walk out to the dune the following morning and remove the remaining six sacks of coins. As he was preparing for bed, Eldridge closed his windows against an approaching storm. The horizon grew quite dark with the rising squall, and the tailor said a prayer that all of the local fishermen would be safe. That night, one of the most violent storms in Chatham's history blew in from the Atlantic Ocean and struck the area, causing tremendous damage to boats, piers, and homes for many miles along the northern shore.

Late the next morning as the sky was clearing, Eldridge, carrying his spade, set out for the beach. When he arrived at the approximate location of the sand dune, he was horrified to discover that it had been completely washed away by the storm of the previous night. His heart sank as he walked about the beach seeking any sign of the buried treasure chest. He found none.

At various spots, the tailor would pause to excavate a hole with the hope that he would encounter the chest, but after a full day of searching, digging, and finding nothing, he returned home exhausted and discouraged. On dozens of other occasions, Eldridge returned to the beach to search for the treasure chest. Time and again, he made excavations in places where he was certain he would locate the cache, but each time he encountered only failure.

The remaining sacks of gold coins have been estimated to be worth around $25,000 in 1880 values. Today, such a treasure would be worth considerably more, perhaps into the millions of dollars.

Many people are aware of the tale of lost treasure, and occasionally come to the beach to search for it. In 1994, one such searcher was rewarded with the discovery of a single coin, which he found lying three inches deep in the sand. It was Spanish in origin, almost pure gold, and bore an 1810 date. Many people believe that either Doane or Eldridge accidentally dropped the single coin during one of their recoveries. The chances are great that the wooden chest containing the rest of the gold coins is still buried somewhere deep in the sands of Chatham Beach.

-8-

The Mystery of the Byfield Treasure

It is estimated that from the time it was originally buried, hundreds have searched for the so-called Byfield treasure, a fortune in gold coins once possessed by the pirate Roger Hayman.

Captain Roger Hayman was a native of Great Britain and had been given command of a merchant vessel that carried trade goods from the Caribbean Islands to England. From time to time, Hayman was forced to deal with pirates during his voyages. More often than not, his ship was swift enough to outrun them, but on occasion, he was attacked and his ship was plundered.

During his contacts with pirates, it occurred to Hayman that the brigands often came into a significant amount of wealth in the form of stolen gold and silver coinage and ingots, as well as jewelry and precious stones. The average pirate, it seemed to Hayman, made a considerably better living than he did. Further, Hayman was envious of the adventurous life he presumed was led by these outlaws of the sea. In 1800, Hayman made a major decision: He decided to become a pirate.

Familiar with the Caribbean Sea and most of the islands located therein, Hayman launched his raiding expeditions throughout the area and established his headquarters on the island of Haiti. In time, he commanded a large fleet of pirate ships – sometimes as many as 15. He attacked ships throughout the Caribbean and then expanded his territory to include the Atlantic Ocean along the eastern seaboard of the United States.

Hayman proved to be a capable pirate leader. He feared no one and never retreated. In addition to attacking merchant vessels, he even chased and captured warships belonging to both Great Britain and the United States.

One winter, a fleet consisting of three American warships and one British warship arrived in the Caribbean in search of Hayman. By this time, he had earned a fearsome reputation and was wanted, dead or alive, by both countries for piracy. The two governments had grown weary of losing cargo to the notorious brigand and intended to put him out of business once and for all.

When he learned of the approaching warships, Hayman formed an armada of his 10 best and most well-armed vessels to meet his pursuers head-on. On encountering the warships, Hayman let loose with a volley, the initial barrage sinking one of the American ships. Moments later, he came alongside the British ship and tied onto it. Once the vessels were secured, Hayman's pirates swarmed the British ship, killing the officers and crew. In the hold of the ship, Hayman found two wooden chests, each containing gold coins minted between 1794 and 1799. The shipment was part of a payroll for the British Navy.

Hayman had the chests loaded onto his ship, but soon after, the American warship attacked him. During the ensuing battle, Hayman suffered a dozen wounds. Because Hayman was now unable to command effectively, his forces fell into disarray, and the tide of the battle shifted. A short time later, the American warships sank three of the pirate vessels. Struggling to remain upright, Hayman ordered his fleet to set sail for the open sea in an attempt to outrun the Americans. As the pirate leader tried to organize the escape, the American warships sank five more of the pirate ships and captured another, leaving only Hayman's vessel, which managed to to escape. However, the battle marked the end of Captain Roger Hayman and his band of cutthroats' domination of the Atlantic Ocean and Caribbean Sea.

Once safely out in the Atlantic, Hayman sailed to England, where he anchored off a remote part of the coast, north of Liverpool. Hayman had his two treasure-filled chests hauled to shore and buried. The pirate then paid off his crew and sent them on their way, and then he had the ship scuttled*. A few weeks later, Hayman dug up the two treasure chests, moved them to a new location near downtown Liverpool, and reburied them.

In Liverpool, Hayman intended to reunite with

his wife and children, but on arriving, discovered they had moved to New York. Fortunately, they left a message for him to join them. However, he decided to remain in Liverpool to recover from his wounds. When he was feeling stronger, Hayman made plans to join his family and booked passage to America. Before departing for New York, Hayman unearthed his treasure chests and had them loaded onto the brigantine that would take him to New York.

At this point, the story of Hayman's two treasure chests begins to take on a bizarre life of its own with a truly remarkable tale filled with treachery, betrayal, and deceit.

As stewards struggled with carrying the heavy chests across the gangplank*, they were observed closely by two men lurking in the dockside shadows, a physician named Griffin and a businessman named Stearns Compton. Days earlier, the two men recognized the pirate Hayman and correctly assumed the two chests contained treasure. Silently, they watched as the trunks were dragged into the purser's* cabin. The door was secured as Hayman stood by. Convinced that his treasure was safe, the pirate, in severe pain and growing weak from his wounds, was assisted to his private cabin. Shortly thereafter, Griffin and Compton boarded the vessel.

Several days later, as the ship was sailing across the Atlantic Ocean, the purser summoned Dr. Griffin to Hayman's cabin. The purser informed the doctor that Hayman was very sick and appeared to be dying. After examining Hayman, Griffin told the purser there was little he could do and that the man was likely to die from his wounds before reaching New York.

A few more days passed, and Dr. Griffin was disturbed by a knock at his cabin door. On opening it, he found the purser standing before him. The purser asked to speak to Griffin in private, and the doctor invited him inside. The purser informed Griffin that Hayman had died. Before passing away, Hayman had related tales of his career as a pirate and told the purser of the two treasure chests filled with gold and silver coins.

The purser told the doctor that Hayman's family planned to meet Hayman at the dock in New York and that they were to take him and the treasure to some remote location in the interior of the state. When he was certain that he had Griffin's attention, the purser proposed that the two of them arrange to have the treasure chests secretly removed from the ship and later divided between them.

Playing along with the purser's suggestion, Griffin agreed. Later that same evening, however, he told his friend Compton about the visit and the offer. Griffin and Compton then concocted their own scheme to make off with the treasure. Faced with the difficulty of unloading the heavy treasure chests at the busy port of New York, Griffin and Compton decided to remove them during the first scheduled stop, at Newburyport in northeastern Massachusetts.

When the ship pulled in at Newburyport, Griffin went into town on the pretense of sightseeing. Once there, however, he arranged for the rental of a stout wagon and a pair of sturdy horses. While Griffin was in town, Compton waited aboard the ship for the purser to disembark on some errand. When the purser was safely away from the vessel, Compton broke into his cabin, hacked open the treasure chests, and removed all of the coins. He placed then in canvas sacks that, in turn, he stowed in steamer trunks belonging to himself and Griffin. Not long afterward, Griffin arrived at the dock with the wagon and, while no one was looking, the two men dragged their trunks from the ship and onto the platform. With the aid of four nearby dockworkers, Griffin and Compton loaded the trunks onto the wagon and drove away.

The two robbers intended to transport the gold coins to a location near the town of Byfield, a few miles inland, and bury it. Then after waiting for five years, long enough for others to forget the incident, they planned to return to the area to retrieve it.

Griffin and Compton drove the wagon down the old Andover Road until they reached the Parker River, which flowed near Byfield. They stopped near the bank of the river and, with difficulty, pulled the chests from the wagon. From this point, they dragged the chests to a nearby granite boulder. As Compton began excavating a deep hole, Griffin chiseled the letter "A" onto the boulder to mark the site. With the hole four feet deep, the two men lowered the chests into it, one on top of the other, refilled the hole, and covered the spot with forest debris.

Unbeknownst to Griffin and Compton, they were being observed the entire time they were caching the treasure. After the two men drove away in the wagon, young Howard Noyes climbed down from the tree where he had watched them bury the two chests. Noyes ran home, where he informed his parents of what he had seen. Noyes's father thought the boy was making up the tale and administered a beating and sent him to bed. The following morning, as Howard Noyes woke up, Griffin and Compton returned the rented wagon and horses and then boarded a ship bound for New York.

In spite of the punishment he received, Noyes continued to try to convince his mother and father about the truth of the buried chests. Finally, tiring of the boy's insistence, the father agreed to go to the site with his son. They arrived at the granite boulder and saw the "A" scratched on its surface, but young Noyes was unable to determine the exact spot where the trunks were buried.

Between Howard Noyes and his father, the story of the buried treasure made the rounds in Byfield and the surrounding area over the next few weeks. People arrived at the site of the boulder and a few holes were dug, but the chests were never found.

Five years after burying the chests, Griffin and Compton met to discuss their future. For whatever reason, they agreed to postpone their return to Byfield. They were aware that the residents of the area were familiar with the story of the buried treasure, and the two men must have feared their presence might arouse undue scrutiny. More time passed, and a variety of circumstances kept Griffin and Compton from returning to Byfield to retrieve the buried treasure chests. By 1850, both men had passed away, and the two chests filled with Hayman's gold coins remained undisturbed.

Several decades later, in 1923, Compton's great-granddaughter discovered his journal, which contained a detailed description of the theft of the gold coins and their burial near Byfield. The great-granddaughter was so fascinated with the possibility of locating and recovering the treasure that she began making plans to travel to the small New England town.

When she arrived at Byfield, the great-granddaughter learned that a number of the residents still recalled the story of the buried treasure, a tale that had been handed down over many generations. In time, she located the granite boulder near the junction of the Parker River and the old Andover Road and organized the excavation of several holes nearby. After several days, she found nothing and departed, never to return.

The great-granddaughter's visit to Byfield stimulated renewed interest in the lost treasure of gold coins. Soon afterward, other hopeful seekers arrived from the New England area to try their luck at finding buried chests. The efforts proved fruitless until 1932, when a significant discovery was made – one that was purely accidental.

During the spring of that year, a laborer named Chauncey Braden was employed to dig a well for a Byfield resident. Braden earned his living doing odd jobs and, though quite poor, possessed a reputation for honesty and dependability. He was told that the buried treasure was located by the Parker River, near a granite boulder with the letter "A" scratched onto its surface.

The long, slow, and arduous work of hand-digging the well took a toll on the aged Braden, and he was forced to stop often to rest. One afternoon, as Braden was sitting in the shade of a nearby tree, Orlin A. Arlin, a Byfield resident, stopped to chat with Braden while on a walk. Every day thereafter, Arlin would make it a practice to pause and visit with Braden.

One afternoon, a week later, Arlin paused by the unfinished well, but there was no sign of Braden. Arlin approached the excavation and peered within. He was surprised to spot a number of fragments of old and rotted oak panels, along with some metal hinges and leather straps, the remains of what Arlin thought might have been a wooden chest. He searched all around the area for his friend but could find no sign of Braden. In fact, Chauncey Braden would never be seen again.

Several months later, Arlin was visiting the town of Salisbury, just a few miles north of Byfield, when he heard a remarkable story. A storekeeper told Arlin that another Byfield resident had stopped by a few months earlier, selected a variety of goods, and paid with gold coins. The storekeeper still possessed several of the coins and showed them to Arlin. They had all been minted in Britain and were dated 1794 through 1799.

When Arlin asked the storekeeper to describe the man who paid with the gold coins, it was clear that it had been Braden. Arlin searched all through Salisbury and the surrounding area for his friend Braden, but could never find him.

It is estimated that, from the time it was originally buried, there have been hundreds of searches for the Byfield treasure, a fortune in gold coins once possessed by the pirate Roger Hayman. Dozens of holes were excavated and nothing was found until Chauncey Braden accidentally encountered the treasure while digging a well, but there is one more twist to this bizarre story.

Orlin Arlin recalled years later, after hearing the tale of the two buried treasure chests, that when he initially peered into the excavation, he saw the remains of only one chest. Therefore, it is very possible that the second treasure chest still lies only a few feet below the surface near the granite boulder, next to a hand-dug well.

-9-

The Lost Gold of Bloody Tew

Tew would have the dead men hung upside down from the ship's railings as trophies.

Generations of writers have referred to a number of different pirates as "notorious," "bloodthirsty," and "brutal." In truth, many deserved these labels but no one more so than Joseph Thomas Tew. Historians have yet to determine the year that Tew was born, but most of them agree that he was originally from Maidford, Northamptonshire, England. As a child, Tew migrated to the American colonies with his family and settled in Rhode Island, though clear evidence for such claims is lacking. It has been affirmed, however, that at some point, Tew resided in Newport, Rhode Island as a husband with two daughters.

According to reports, Tew was engaged as a privateer around 1690, primarily chasing after French and Spanish ships. It was also around this time that he turned to piracy, and in 1691, Tew moved to Bermuda, where he associated with the noted pirate Captain Want. Then, in 1692, Tew obtained a commission from the governor of Bermuda, which provided him with a ship, the 70-ton Amity.

The sloop carried eight cannons and boasted a crew of 46 men. Tew was sent to destroy a French factory located on the coast of West Africa. On the way, Tew made the decision to turn to piracy. He was convinced that the rewards were far greater, and he would have the opportunity to organize his own raids. Tew gave his crew the option of remaining with him, and every man decided to align with him. Tew had a flag designed and produced, which flew boldly from a mast. The flag consisted of black cloth upon which was portrayed a white arm wielding a scimitar*.

Tew sailed to the Red Sea in order to determine the prospects for piracy. In time, he encountered a large Indian dhow*. Despite having a well-armed crew of dozens of soldiers, the captain of the vessel surrendered. Tew took possession of a large amount of gold and silver, along with ivory, silk, precious stones, and spices. His first raid was a huge success, and Tew paid his men well for their efforts.

Legend grants Captain Thomas Tew a certain colorful flair. He reputedly dressed in a black, heavy, long-tailed woolen coat topped by a long, flowing cape. Tew cultivated a well-trimmed goatee and wore a long silk scarf around his neck. Wide leather belts encircled his waist and crisscrossed his torso. His belts carried pistols, swords, and knives.

According to legend, the daring Tew would also line up as many as 10 captives on his deck and engage them in a sword fight, one by one. Reportedly, Tew laughed and smiled throughout the competition as he dispatched his victims, one after the other. When he was finished, Tew would have the dead men hung upside down from the ship's railings as trophies. It was around this time that he earned the distinction "Bloody Tew."

Following months of successful raiding, Tew accumulated an impressive fortune in gold, silver, jewelry, and precious stones. Though it was never verified, it was rumored that Tew kept an extra ship in his fleet for the sole purpose of transporting his large and ever-growing treasure.

The business of piracy was good to Thomas Tew, but time and again, he was subjected to pursuit by British, French, and American warships. On occasion, Tew was forced to retreat. During one skirmish, Tew nearly lost the ship transporting his treasure, and he grew concerned. Later, during a battle off the coast of Virginia, Tew's treasure ship was sunk in deep water, his immense treasure lost to him forever.

Growing weary of the constant pursuit, Tew finally decided to retire from pirating. He changed his name to Carter, purchased and settled onto a plot of land outside of Newport, Rhode Island in 1694. Even though he had lost most of his fabulous treasure, he still possessed an estimated $200,000 in gold coins. Once he moved onto his property, he located a suitable site and buried his treasure.

On occasion, Tew would have Tolliver, his servant, drive him into town in a horse-drawn carriage. While Tolliver purchased provisions, Tew would stroll to the nearest pub and guzzle pints of ale. When in town, Tew would be seen wearing his long coat, cape, and a red sash. He rarely had interactions with the citizens of the town. It was said that Tolliver was very fearful of his employer, the ex-pirate.

Tew's time in Newport was peaceful, but after a while, he began to miss the sea, the adventures, the raiding, the thrill of combat, and the acquisition of booty. Early one morning, three of Tew's former crewmen appeared at his residence and begged him to consider returning to piracy. Apparently, Tew was impressed, and he lost no time in making plans to return to his lucrative career. The pirate informed Tolliver that he would be away for a few months. That same afternoon, after packing a bag, Tew departed with his companions.

In spite of his profession, Tew became good friends with the "royal governor" of New York, Benjamin Fletcher. In November 1694, Tew was granted a letter of marque* from Fletcher and set off on a new raid. Tew returned to the Red Sea, where he believed he would be able to duplicate his earlier success. By the time he arrived, however, he found other pirates had already discovered the opportunities he had experienced. However, Tew recognized a new opportunity, so he met with the rival pirate captains and, together, they decided to sail as a combined fleet.

In September 1695, a Persian convoy* consisting of 25 ships sailed through the Red Sea's Mandeb Strait, somehow managing to elude the pirates who were patrolling the region. When Tew learned of this, he and his pirate comrades set out in pursuit.

Tew's Amity was the first vessel to overtake the convoy and closed in on one of the ships. As the Amity neared the Fateh Muhammad, Tew fired his cannons. Rather than surrender, the Fateh Muhammad returned fire, and the battle was on. During the conflict, Tew died, reportedly disemboweled by a cannon shot. As a result, his crew surrendered immediately.

Within weeks of Bloody Tew's passing, the news reached Newport. Shortly afterward, the citizens learned that Bloody Tew had been none other than their quiet neighbor, who had gone by the name of Carter. Three months after this news reached Rhode Island, a young man arrived in Newport. He was dressed in an expensive and fancy manner and drove a brand new carriage pulled by two fine horses. He identified himself as Richard Tew and drove directly to the property of the late pirate. Tolliver, who was in the process of packing his own belongings and closing up the house, greeted the young Tew at the door. Richard Tew informed Tolliver of his identity, along with his intention to occupy the house, and asked Tolliver to remain.

After Tolliver carried young Tew's belongings from the carriage into the house, he unhitched the horses and led them into the barn for grooming. While the servant was thus occupied, young Tew approached and asked Tolliver if he knew where his father had buried his treasure. Tolliver told Tew that he never knew, but that on occasion, his father would disappear into the woods behind the house for a time and would return with a sack filled with coins.

Over the next several days, Richard Tew searched the woods behind the house for trails but found none. His father, he determined, was always careful and wary, so he most likely took a different route to his treasure cache each time he needed some funds. Having no luck finding a path, young Tew enlisted Tolliver's help. Together, the two men searched throughout the woods for signs of excavation. Again, their efforts were met with failure.

As Tew and Tolliver explored the woods during their searches for the treasure cache, they often passed a large tree that possessed an extremely thick trunk. About eight feet from the ground, a large hole in the tree could be seen. When Tew asked Tolliver about it, the servant replied that he sometimes hunted squirrels that came out of the hole.

For the next three years, Richard Tew resided in his late father's house. A week never passed when he did not venture into the woods, searching again and again for some sign of the pirate's cache. Finally, convinced that he would never find the gold, Richard Tew sold the house and property, paid Tolliver a handsome severance, packed his belongings into the carriage, and drove away. Richard Tew was never seen or heard from again.

The story of Bloody Tew's buried treasure circulated throughout the colonies, and men sometimes arrived to search the property behind the house. Though dozens of holes were excavated, nothing was ever found. The location of the treasure of Bloody Tew became a perplexing mystery, one in which the solution escaped all who sought it. After years of fruitless searching, many people came to believe that the treasure cache of Bloody Tew was simply a tale and nothing more, that it probably never existed. Though the legend of Bloody Tew and his lost treasure persisted, few bothered to continue searching for it.

However, in 1880, an event occurred that revived interest in the legend of Bloody Tew's treasure. During the spring of that year, a fire raged throughout the region and destroyed much of the forest along the northeastern edge of Newport. When the fire finally burned out, investigators who entered the remains of the forest determined the blaze was caused by a lightning strike to a particularly large tree not far from the old house of pirate Bloody Tew.

Years passed, and the burned out forest was well on its way to recovery. By 1886, young saplings were springing up from the ash and debris of the burn, and wildlife was returning to the region.

One day, in the fall of 1886, a man named Peter McCallister was hunting in the rejuvenating forest when the toe of his boot stubbed a heavy object buried in a soft pile of leaves. On investigation, McCallister found a heavy, oddly shaped mass. When he cleaned the dirt away from it, he was startled to discover that it was comprised of dozens of coins that had been fused together, presumably from the fire. The coins appeared to be gold.

McCallister carried the mass of consolidated coins into Newport and took it to a blacksmith shop owned by Charles Smith. Smith, after examining the lump, determined that it consisted of about two dozen coins that had been melted together by intense heat. When word of McCallister's discovery spread through Newport, residents flocked into the old Tew woods with the hope of finding more treasure, but none were successful. For months, the mass of gold coins was placed on display at a local bank, but in the summer of 1887, it was removed and its subsequent whereabouts never determined.

Years later, in 1910, a Newport librarian was filing a collection of decades-old local newspapers donated by a resident, who found them in an attic trunk. Occasionally the librarian stopped to read articles from more than two decades earlier. The librarian was aware of the story of Bloody Tew and his lost treasure, as well as the discovery of the lump of coins by Peter McCallister. She suspected there was a connection between these two events, so she undertook extended research into the matter and arrived at an amazing conclusion.

The librarian suggested that the pirate Bloody Tew had hidden his treasure in the large and presumably hollow tree in the woods behind his house, retrieving a few gold coins at a time when needed. When lightning struck the tree and the resulting fire raged throughout the area, the cache of gold inside the burning tree was subjected to extremely high temperatures, and melted and fused into irregularly shaped clumps. Given estimates of the large size of Bloody Tew's treasure, the librarian deduced that a great deal more of the gold was yet to be found around the remains of the old tree.

The librarian called a meeting of four close friends and presented the results of her research. Together, they went into the woods to try and find some of the treasure. Once there, however, they discovered that the ravages of the 1880 fire, along with 30 years of decomposition and new forest growth, had eliminated all evidence of the old tree.

Then, during the 1950s, workers cleared a wooded

region on Newport's northwestern edge to prepare it for a subdivision. Throughout the area, new roadways had been created, and a few houses were under construction. Following behind a bulldozer that was cutting through a group of trees in one section of the subdivision, the foreman of the crew spotted a curiously shaped object the size of a shoe sticking out of the freshly turned earth. The foreman picked it up and was surprised at its great weight. On brushing the dirt away and examining it closely, he discovered the heavy mass was composed of dozens of gold coins melted together. On one of the coins, the foreman could see enough to determine it was of Spanish origin and bore the date of 1690.

Several days later, newspapers carried the story of the discovery, and once again, treasure hunters descended on the area. This time, however, they arrived too late, for the subdivision's roads were already paved and new concrete foundations for homes were poured. Today, the remains of Bloody Tew's pirate treasure lie buried under this suburban expansion. It is very probable that more clumps of valuable gold coins are hidden mere inches beneath the streets and lawns of this Newport neighborhood, unknown to the residents living above it.

Addendum: It is not known where the body of Thomas "Bloody" Tew was buried or if he was simply thrown into the sea. Years after his death, rumors circulated that he was the father of Ratsimilaho, a mysterious man who established a kingdom on the east coast of Madagascar.

-10-

Joseph Bradish's Block Island Treasure Cache

When Bradish's crew arrived at Newport, they were immediately identified as pirates, seized, and thrown in the town's jail.

Joseph Bradish came into the world on November 28, 1672. Most researchers believe he was born in Cambridge, Massachusetts. According to legend, Bradish served with the famous pirate Captain Kidd for a short time in 1698. Unlike many of the famous pirates who sailed near the Atlantic coast, very little is known about Joseph Bradish.

Joseph Bradish sailed his three-masted vessel, the Adventure Galley, toward the shores of New England following a succession of successful raids of Spanish merchant ships in the Caribbean Sea. The hold of the Adventure Galley was filled in part with gold and jewelry, as well as other goods and provisions taken from the Spaniards. Documents listing the information that Bradish had seized four bags containing 2,805 pieces of eight* and another bag of jewels.

After bringing this treasure on board the Adventure Galley, Bradish had the loot placed in a wooden trunk and arranged alongside other trunks that were also filled with treasure. Flush with the exhilaration of his victories, Bradish planned to launch a series of invasions on the numerous small settlements located along the Atlantic shore from Massachusetts to South Carolina. On reaching the port of Charleston, South Carolina, Bradish intended to unload the treasure, pay off his crew, dismiss them, and then sell his ship. Bradish had grown fond of this port city, and he planned to retire from his life of piracy to live a comfortable life as a wealthy man; but first, there were other matters that needed his attention.

During one of the raids on a Spanish ship, the Adventure Galley suffered severe damage to one side of the hull, the result of a well-placed cannonball. By the time the ship reached the Atlantic coast, Bradish determined that repairs would need to be made before any further travel. He ordered his crew to steer the ship to Block Island, a location used by Bradish in the past as a retreat and sanctuary. There, the repairs could be made on the ship.

Block Island is a prominent isle some 12 miles south of the Rhode Island shore and separated from the mainland by Block Island Sound. The island suited

Bradish's needs well, for it could be easily defended, and it was close enough to the mainland such that hunting parties could be sent out to acquire game. Barrels were filled from fresh-water springs and returned to the campsite on the small island.

After inspecting the damage to the Adventure Galley, Bradish determined his ship required some new planking and metal fittings. He selected six of his crewmen to row to Newport, Rhode Island, 18 miles to the northeast, to purchase the necessary equipment and have it delivered to Block Island. This seemed like a simple enough undertaking, and Bradish anticipated no difficulty, but he was in for a surprise.

During Bradish's absence from the area, communities up and down the Atlantic coast had been subjected to a number of pirate raids and as a result were on the defensive. In many of the settlements along the coast, preparations had been made to defend themselves from pirate raids. When Bradish's crew arrived at Newport, they were immediately identified as pirates, seized, and thrown in the town's jail. During the intense interrogation that followed, which was accompanied by a bit of torture, one of the crewmen broke down. He admitted that they were part of Joseph Bradish's crew and that the notorious pirate and his crewmen were encamped on Block Island.

Bradish was growing increasingly concerned. Three days had passed, and there was no sign of the men he had sent to Newport. When dawn broke on the fourth day and there was still no sign of his men, Bradish decided that they must have been identified as pirates and been detained. He further determined that it was only a matter of time before authorities were alerted to his presence on Block Island and that a raid would soon follow.

Worried that the crippled and unseaworthy Adventure Galley was not up to fleeing a potential attack, Bradish ordered his crew to unload several of his wooden chests of gold and jewelry from the ship. Then he had the chests carried to a location on the island's southern beach and buried. A number of holes were excavated, the chests lowered into them, and the holes filled. Near the location of the buried treasure, Bradish noted a stunted oak growing out of the crevice of exposed granite bedrock. Bradish decided to use this tree to mark the location of his treasure cache.

The next day, Bradish sent three men to Newport to determine the fate of his comrades. The crewmen were to land their rowboat some distance down the coast from the town, sneak into the heart of the community, and acquire the necessary information. It didn't take long. The town of Newport was abuzz with news of the capture of the pirates, the notion that Bradish and the remainder of his crew were camped a few miles away on Block Island, and that a raid was imminent. Word had been sent to nearby communities, and dozens of armed men arrived in Newport, eager to participate in the assault. After learning this information, the crewmen raced to the rowboat and hurried back to the island to inform their captain.

On hearing the news, Bradish decided on a plan he felt certain would thwart an attack. He had the Adventure Galley scuttled and sunk. Further, he had the temporary shelters torn down so that the island appeared as though it had been abandoned. Should the ruse fail, Bradish made certain his men were well-armed and in a position to defend the island. For two days while remaining in hiding, Bradish and his pirates kept their eyes on the surrounding waters, awaiting the attack.

Around sundown of the second day, one of Bradish's scouts arrived with the news that a force of close to 400 men, all armed and eager, were gathering at Port Judith, just 12 miles north of the island. The mob, according to the scout, was planning to row out to Block Island at dawn of the following day and attack.

Realizing he and his men were out-numbered and out-armed by a wide margin, Bradish knew well they could not withstand an attack. The pirate captain ordered the hasty construction of several makeshift rafts from some of the materials that were to be used to repair the Adventure Galley. Under the cover of night, the pirates loaded what they could carry onto the rafts and rowed away toward the northwest, hoping to make it to the Rhode Island shore near the settlement of Weekapaug before dawn. There, Bradish planned to stay out of sight until the pursuit had died down. Once he considered it safe, he planned to steal a ship, return to Block Island, retrieve the treasure, and escape southward along the coast.

For nearly a week the pirates remained hidden, but they had exhausted their supply of food and fresh water. They were growing desperate, so Bradish, along with five of his crewmen, decided to hike into the nearby Weekapaug settlement and barter for provisions. The moment the residents of the village spotted Bradish and his men, a cry went up. Arming themselves, several of the townsmen apprehended the pirates. After determining that they had the fearsome Joseph Bradish and some of his men in custody, the Weekapaug townsmen had them bound, placed in a boat, and transported to Newport, where they were jailed.

While Bradish and his men were locked up, Newport officials learned that the British government was offering a large reward for the brigand. The British were notified of Bradish's capture, and weeks later, a British naval ship arrived at Newport for the express purpose of transporting Bradish to England to stand trial for his crimes on the high seas. The pirate was manacled and chained, carried onto the ship, and returned to England. Another account reports that Bradish was taken captive when he sailed with Captain Kidd off the coast of New York. In London, Bradish was tried, found guilty of a number of charges of piracy, and hanged in 1700. He was only 28 years old.

Twenty-one years after Joseph Bradish was executed, one of the pirates who [had] assisted him in burying his treasure was released from prison in Newport, Rhode Island, after serving over 20 years of hard labor. Having heard what became of his former captain and the rest of the sailors, the newly freed man was certain that the great treasure in gold and jewelry was still buried on Block Island. He decided to return to the island, dig up the fortune, and purchase passage to South America.

The former pirate rented a skiff* and, passing a number of fishing boats in the sound, rowed out to a beach located at the southern end of Block Island, where he believed the treasure had been buried. He recalled the stunted oak that had been pointed out by Bradish years earlier and searched for it, but to no avail – he could not locate the tree. He searched the area from the waterline to the exposed bedrock above the beach but found nothing familiar about the landscape. Finally convinced that he had landed on the wrong beach, he decided to search all of the beaches on the southern end of the island but had no better luck. After four days of fruitless searching, he returned to Newport and was never seen again.

Throughout the generations that have passed since pirate Joseph Bradish buried his great treasure on Block Island, the story has been told and retold. Over time, these stories have led a number of treasure hunters to search for the buried treasure.

In 1872, a man named Winston Lockhart arrived in Providence, Rhode Island from Virginia. In his possession was a parchment map he claimed was given to him by a descendant of one of Joseph Bradish's crewmen. On the map was a clear and precise representation of the coastline of Rhode Island and an accurate rendering of southern Block Island across the sound. At a point on the southern shore of the island, the map manifested an "X" along with the notation, "Treasure buried here." Not far from the location of the X was an illustration of a stunted tree. Lockhart made arrangements to rent a boat with a small crew to take him to Block Island.

On arriving at the precise beach marked on the map, Lockhart undertook a search for the stunted tree. To his utter dismay, Lockhart encountered dozens of trees, all of them undersized as a result of clinging to life in the cracks of the granite bedrock and coping with the strong winds from the Atlantic. Lockhart, with help from the crew, excavated hundreds of holes near many of the trees but found nothing. Discouraged after several days of searching, Lockhart returned to Virginia. What became of the map is unknown.

However, many decades later, in 1964, two men camped on the southern shore of Block Island. By day, they fished the water around the island, and by night they retired to their simple campsite. While preparing breakfast one morning, one of the fishermen spotted three gold coins in the sand near where he knelt. He placed them in his pocket and returned to his chores.

Several days later, back at his home on the mainland, the fisherman showed the gold coins to a friend. The friend grew excited and related the tale of pirate Joseph Bradish and his lost treasure on Block Island. He suggested that the coins might be part of the treasure. The fisherman had never heard the tale of Joseph Bradish's lost treasure before, but he was so excited about the prospect of becoming wealthy, he made arrangements to return to Block Island and search for the treasure cache. One week later, the fisherman, accompanied by three boatloads of friends, made his way back to the island.

On arriving at the south shore of Block Island, however, the fisherman was uncertain of the exact location of his earlier campsite. Though he and his companions searched up and down the beach, no sign of the treasure was ever found.

It wasn't found, that is, until 1978, when a Providence automotive mechanic named Mark Kennedy came upon a wooden chest, partially buried in the sand, while exploring the southern shore of Block Island during a weekend visit. From time to time, Kennedy would motor out to the island to spend a relaxing day hiking along the beach and enjoying the silence. Assuming the chest belonged to someone nearby, he simply walked on and left the chest alone in the sand.

Days later, Kennedy related his discovery of the chest to a friend, and like the fisherman in 1964, listened to the story of Joseph Bradish's fabulous pirate cache. Kennedy wasted no time in returning to the island. On arriving, however, he was unable to relocate the chest. Since pirate Bradish had buried his treasure over two centuries ago, storm winds and strong tidal surges had deposited heavy loads of sea-borne sediment across the southern shore of Block Island. At other times, the fickle winds and waves served to remove some of the sands, carrying them away or depositing them farther down the shore. In this manner, items were sometimes uncovered and at other times covered up again. It is likely that Mark Kennedy spotted the exposed wooden chest at a time when the winds and waves were removing sand.

Someday, someone exploring the southern shore of Block Island may find one of the lost chests uncovered by the of the actions of the wind and waves. If one of the wooden treasure chests is ever discovered, most assuredly several more will likely be found nearby.

-11-

Pirate David Marteen and the Treasure of Gold Coins

On a moonless night, Marteen, along with several crewmen, moved the heavy treasure chests from the ship to the cache site and buried them three feet into the ground.

David Marteen was born in the Netherlands and, at an early age, took to the sea. After working his way up from cabin boy to first mate, he eventually secured a position commanding a Dutch privateer based out of Tortuga in the Caribbean Sea. Marteen conducted raids on Spanish strongholds in Mexico and Nicaragua between the years 1663 and1665. Marteen was known in some circles as a pirate hunter but later turned to piracy himself and conducted raids on Spanish merchant vessels and Mexican shoreline communities. In 1655, Marteen attacked and captured the Spanish galleon Neptune. In the ship's hold, Marteen found several wooden chests filled with gold coins. Their value was estimated to be around $20 million. After transferring the treasure to his vessel, Marteen killed the Neptune's crew and scuttled the ship. Then he retreated to Tortuga, a small island off the coast of Venezuela that was easy to defend and where he could refurbish his ships and rest.

While at Tortuga, Marteen had sentries posted along the shoreline around the island, keeping a lookout for any ships. Fearing that other pirates, as well as British authorities, were in pursuit of his treasure, Marteen had the chests offloaded and buried at a secret location above the beach. Two weeks later, Marteen again set out in search of more ships and communities to pillage, and this time, he set his sights on the Atlantic Coast shoreline of America. His great treasure was left buried on Tortuga, its location known only to Marteen.

For eight months, Marteen attacked and plundered trading vessels and conducted raids on defenseless coastal towns. Unlike his previous expeditions, this one proved to be somewhat less profitable, and Marteen was thinking of returning to Tortuga. He was also concerned about his treasure cache and wanted to check on it. During his entire time at sea, Marteen fretted about his cache, fearful that someone might discover it and steal it. Finally, he decided to hasten back to Tortuga, unearth his treasure, and rebury it where no one would ever find it.

For nearly a year, Marteen carried his treasure chests in the hold of his ship as he sailed about the Atlantic

Ocean. In 1657, while preparing for a series of raids on Atlantic Coast settlements, Marteen discovered the quiet waters of the bay where the Connecticut River flowed. Intrigued and impressed with the width and depth of the river, Marteen sailed upstream as far as he could, exploring the countryside on both sides, searching for a suitable location to hide his treasure.

With favorable winds, Marteen sailed his ship a considerable distance upriver, finally anchoring at a point east of the present-day town of Windsor, nearly 40 miles from the ocean. Today, Windsor is a city with a population of over 12,000 souls, but during the mid-seventeenth century, it consisted of only a few scattered farms, a church, and a tavern. After landing near the west bank of the river, Marteen spent several days searching the area for an ideal site to cache his treasure.

During the time the pirate ship lay anchored in the Connecticut River, Windsor townsfolk sometimes gathered atop the low hills overlooking the river and observed the newcomers. Though the citizens never approached any closer, Marteen noted their presence. He also saw that they were well-armed and appeared to be hostile.

One afternoon, Marteen was searching the woods, far from the scrutiny of the Windsor citizens, for an ideal cache site. He found one. That same moonless night, he and several crewmen moved the heavy treasure chests from the ship to the cache site and buried them three feet underground. After covering the cache with forest debris to make it look like any other part of the woods, Marteen ordered his crew to prepare to sail away in the morning. An hour after sunrise the following day, the pirate ship was making its way down the river to the ocean. From there, Marteen intended to continue his raiding and pillaging.

After two more years of active piracy, Marteen began worrying again that someone might find his treasure and steal it from him. He decided to return to the site and check. As before, he steered his vessel up the Connecticut River and anchored at the same location. It wasn't long before the Windsor residents became aware of the pirates' return and took up another watch from the hills.

Two days after the pirates arrived, a group of watchers approached the ship and sought an audience with the leader. During the subsequent discussion, the villagers informed Marteen that they were uncomfortable with the presence of the brigands so close to the town. They told Marteen the pirates were not welcome and demanded that they leave immediately.

Marteen was enraged. At first, he was inclined to fight the citizens, but a quick appraisal of the group indicated that he and his crew were out-numbered by a wide margin. Instead, Marteen exuded charm when he informed the visitors that he intended no harm, and he requested permission to remain anchored at the location for another two weeks. After that, he promised, he and his crew would sail away and never return. The villagers agreed to this proposition and returned to the town.

Marteen considered retrieving his chests filled with gold coins and replacing them in the hold of his ship. Instead, he decided to search the area for a new and better hiding place, perhaps even farther inland. Assembling a team of several stout crewmen, Marteen had the chests unearthed and carried northwestward from the river. After circling around Windsor, this odd caravan continued deep into the Connecticut woods. Eventually, the pirates arrived at the bank of another river. From the description, researchers have determined it was the east fork of Salmon Brook and less than a mile from where the stream converges with the west fork. At this point, Marteen ordered the chests be reburied. The site was marked with cryptic signs scratched onto some nearby rocks ranging in size from a milk carton to a basketball.

After returning to the ocean, Marteen once again set out for more plundering. One year later, Marteen directed his ship to attack a British merchant vessel. But to Marteen's surprise, the merchantman unleashed a barrage of cannon fire at the pirate ship. Marteen was killed during the battle, so he never returned to Connecticut to retrieve his treasure.

During the 1920s, a Hartford County, Connecticut resident by the name of Nelson encountered a reference to Marteen's buried treasure chests while researching some old documents in a Boston library. Subsequent research, along with a number of interviews, led Nelson to believe that the treasure was buried near the town of East Granby on the banks of the east fork of Salmon Brook. For months, Nelson searched throughout the area for some indication of the cache.

One day, while hiking along the east fork of Salmon Brook, Nelson encountered a large, exposed rock that bore a number of strange symbols and odd lettering. Over the next several weeks, he found similar markings on other stones in the general area. Nelson was certain that the inscriptions represented information pertaining to Marteen's buried gold cache. Unfortunately, he was never able to interpret any of the markings.

Three years later, Nelson invited a friend, Anthony Ruches, to help him try to interpret the signs and locate the buried pirate treasure. Together, the two men explored up and down the east bank of Salmon Brook for miles. During their searches, Nelson and Ruches gathered up all of the stones they found and carried them back to East Granby, where they could be studied at leisure.

Years passed and Nelson, now elderly, grew too infirm to continue his quest to find the buried treasure of David Marteen. In 1970, Nelson passed away. A few weeks after Nelson's funeral, Ruches sent drawing of the markings to an archeologist at a university in New York. Several months later, Ruches received a report that confirmed what he and Nelson had believed all along – the symbols indicated that there was a buried treasure at some location along the bank of the east fork of Salmon Brook. The markings also provided an estimated value of the cache in mid-seventeenth century values, as well as the name of the pirate who buried it. Some of the inscriptions, according to the archeologist, bore the name of either "Robert Campbell" or "Robert Caldwell." Additional research by Ruches revealed that a pirate named Robert Caldwell had served with Captain David Marteen during his voyages up the Connecticut River.

In addition to what Ruches regarded as good news, the archeologist also included a disturbing comment. He wrote that the information found on the rocks in terms of distance and direction was only valid if it was interpreted exactly where the rocks were originally located. Unfortunately, it had been years since the two men had moved the rocks, and Ruches had no recollection of the original positions or locations.

Ruches returned to Salmon Brook many times over the next few years, always hoping to find additional rocks with markings, but it was not to be. As he aged, he grew crippled from arthritis and had to abandon the search.

Today, it is estimated that David Marteen's treasure cache would be worth well over $250 million. Buried near the bank of Salmon Brook over 300 years ago, it is likely still there waiting to be discovered.

-12-

Pirate Charles Gibbs and the Barron's Island Treasure Cache

The pirates had been in the water for only a few minutes when the sky darkened, the wind picked up, and a violent squall struck the area.

For a decade, Charles Gibbs raided, looted, and pillaged up and down the eastern shores of America as well as throughout the Caribbean Sea. Lacking glamor or charm, Gibbs was little more than a ruthless outlaw, a petty criminal whose domain was the sea. He has been characterized as cruel, brutal, and cowardly, and his successes depended largely on the work of others he enlisted.

Gibbs was born James D. Jeffers on November 5, 1798, in Newport, Rhode Island, the son of a sea captain who had served as a privateer during the Revolutionary War. At age 17, Jeffers found work aboard a Newport-based brigantine and went to sea. Jeffers told one of his early biographers that he got his start in privateering in 1816 aboard a schooner called the Maria. He was one of the ringleaders of a mutiny, and once in control of the ship, turned toward piracy. Jeffers started out as navigator and within weeks became captain.

Jeffers soon gained a reputation for his cruel treatment of prisoners. On capturing a merchant vessel, Jeffers would hack off the captain's arms and legs. On another occasion, it was reported, Jeffers set fire to a captured merchant vessel, burning the entire crew alive.

On October 21, 1821, Jeffers, in command of a fleet of four ships, attacked three merchant vessels off the coast of Cuba. As Jeffers was firing upon his prey, the USS Enterprise, under the command of Lieutenant Commander Lawrence Kearny, arrived. Jeffer's fleet was no match for the heavy armament carried by the Enterprise, and following a brief battle, all of the pirate's ships were destroyed. Jeffers, along with his surviving crew, swam to shore and fled into the dense jungle on the island.

Little is known of Jeffers's whereabouts during the nine years following his escape. He claimed to have returned to the United States, where he allegedly lived for several years. He also claimed that he served in the Argentine War as a naval officer and later joined the Barbary Corsairs, pirates who operated out of North Africa. Time passed, and Jeffers returned to America following a succession of profitable raids. He decided it was time to retire from piracy before he was captured and hanged. He steered his ship into Boston Harbor and sold it to the first person who made an offer. After paying off his crew, Jeffers loaded all of his belongings, along with his treasures, into wooden trunks and booked passage to England where he lived under another alias for two years.

During his time in England, Jeffers lived well and soon exhausted his wealth. Needing money, as well as longing for the adventure of the high seas, he signed on as a sailor on the brig Vineyard using the alias, Charles Gibbs. The Vineyard was transporting a shipment of cotton, molasses, and a rich cargo of gold and silver coins that had been minted in Mexico. In a short time, Gibbs, along with a cohort named Thomas J. Wansley and several other crewmembers, led a mutiny on November 23, 1830. During the process of taking over the ship, they killed the captain, William Thornby, by crushing his skull with an iron bar. His body was thrown overboard. The first mate was apprehended and the psychopath Gibbs took cruel pleasure in chopping his hands off. As the first mate bled heavily from his amputations, he was tossed into the sea.

Now in charge of the Vineyard, Gibbs set a course for New York. Once there, he intended to remove the treasure from the vessel, bury it on Long Island, scuttle the ship, and go into hiding for a time. When he was convinced no one was looking for him, Gibbs planned to return to Long Island and retrieve the treasure.

On arriving off the coast of New York, Gibbs had the Vineyard run aground on a sandbar, causing serious damage to the hull. He divided the treasure among his crew, keeping a significant amount for himself. After placing the coins into empty nail kegs, Gibbs and his crew loaded their belongings into longboats and rowed toward Long Island.

The pirates had been in the water only a few minutes when the sky darkened, the wind picked up, and a violent squall struck the area. The waters grew choppy and difficult to navigate in the light rowboats. Dense rain fell, obscuring the coastline from the sight of the pirates. Following more than an hour struggling against the elements, the pirates finally landed on a sandy beach. Ignoring the storm, they unloaded the kegs filled with gold and silver coins, carried them to a location on the beach several yards above the waterline, and buried them in a number of separate holes. Then the pirates hiked a short distance inland in search of shelter from the storm.

By dawn of the following day, the storm was still raging, though somewhat weaker. An American gunboat patrolling the waters off the New York coast spotted the grounded Vineyard. A short time later, the abandoned rowboats were discovered on a nearby shore. The commander of the gunboat selected a dozen sailors, loaded them into a longboat, and rowed ashore to investigate. An hour later, they encountered pirate Gibbs and a number of his crewmen huddled under a makeshift shelter against the heavy rain.

Under questioning, Gibbs told the commander that the captain and first mate of the Vineyard had fallen into the sea and drowned during the onset of the storm. A moment later, he said, the ship had hit the sandbar. Fearful that they would perish if they remained on the vessel, Gibbs explained, they had loaded into the rowboats and come ashore to Long Island. The commander informed Gibbs that he must have become disoriented in the storm, for he was not on Long Island but on Barron's Island.

The commander, unaware of Gibb's identity, told him of a Barron's Island resident named Johnson who lived a short distance inland and who could provide fresh water and food. Johnson would also assist them in getting to the mainland. The bedraggled pirates made their way to Johnson's place where they were welcomed and accommodated. During the next several days, while the pirates were camped at Johnson's farm, one of the crewmen, a man named Jack Brownrigg, revealed to Johnson the circumstances under which the pirates had come to the island, as well as the killing of the captain and first mate of the Vineyard. Brownrigg also told Johnson about burying the several kegs of gold and silver coins on the beach. Johnson wasted no time in alerting the local constable who, accompanied by a posse of several men, arrested the pirates.

With the constable in tow, Johnson went to the beach to look for the treasure caches. During the storm, however, the surging waves had washed across the beach, obliterating all evidence of excavation. Nothing could be found.

Charles Gibbs and Thomas J. Wansley, along with their crew, were taken to New York City to stand trial for mutiny and murder. The two men were found guilty and sentenced to hang. The crewmen were given life sentences. While waiting for their sentences to be carried out, Gibbs and Wansley were incarcerated at Bellevue Prison. On April 22, 1831, the two pirates were taken to Ellis Island where they were hanged. Gibbs was 33 years old.

Among treasure hunters, some controversy has existed over whether or not it was actually Barron's Island where the pirates landed and buried their treasure. One writer insists that the loot was cached on nearby Pelican Island but provides little in the way of evidence for such a claim. A handful of researchers believe the treasure is to be found on yet another island – Great Barron's Island. However, a careful reading and analysis of the pertinent documents points to Barron's Island as the probable location.

Over the years, treasure hunters arrived at Barron's Island hopeful of locating and recovering Charles Gibbs's buried treasure. Then, in 1986, a treasure hunter found a gold coin on the beach along the southern shore of the island. After the coin was cleaned and examined by a collector, it was positively identified as being Mexican in origin and likely part of the cargo transported by the Vineyard. Currently, a team of salvage recovery experts plans to grid off the beach and employ sophisticated electronic metal detection equipment in an effort to locate and recover the lost coin caches of Charles Gibbs and his pirates. The treasure could easily be worth several million dollars in today's values.

-13-

Joseph Bradish's Long Island Treasure Cache

The existence of this fabulous cache would never have been known had it not been for one of the captured pirates, who revealed the location to his jailer.

A few days before Joseph Bradish pulled his pirate vessel, the Adventure Galley, into his sanctuary at Block Island off the coast of Rhode Island, he stopped at Montauk Point, the easternmost tip of Long Island, to bury an estimated one-third of a million dollars' worth of gold and silver coins and jewels. As a result of Bradish's earlier unfortunate experience at Block Island and the subsequent attention given the treasure he buried there, the cache at Montauk Point has faded into near obscurity. Neither Bradish nor any of his crewmen were able to return to the Long Island site to retrieve the treasure. In addition, the severe storms and offshore winds that have ravaged this area over the decades have obliterated or altered all of the pertinent landmarks noted by the pirate. The treasure, consisting of loot taken from a series of raids on merchant vessels, is still hidden somewhere on the island.

As Bradish and crew made their way toward the favored rendezvous location at Block Island, the first mate of the Adventure Galley reported a problem with the tiller*. Even though they were only 25 miles from Block Island, Bradish did not wish to risk further navigation with a faulty tiller and ordered the ship to be anchored just off Montauk Point. While several crewmen worked at repairing the tiller, Bradish and five sailors rowed to the shore.

Walking about the beach, Bradish identified several sites that he felt were suitable for caching some of his treasure. Bradish was adamant about not caching his booty all in one place, and as he planned on burying some of it on his arrival at Block Island, he decided Montauk Point was an ideal location to hide more of it.

Bradish and his sailors went into the hold of the Adventure Galley, opened the trunks containing the treasure, and removed approximately $300,000 worth of gold and silver coins along with some gems and jewelry. The treasure was tied into pieces of canvas sailcloth, carried topside, and placed into longboats. Several trips from the interior of the hull to the deck were required.

The pirates, directed by Bradish, rowed to a pre-selected location on Montauk Point, believed to be on the northeastern shore. On landing, Bradish's men hoisted bags of treasure onto their shoulders, and he led them to what he considered to be the ideal site to bury it – a location midway between the shore and a small inland pond. Here, the men excavated a deep hole and deposited the bundles of treasure within. After filling the hole and obliterating all signs of excavation, Bradish paced off the distance from the cache to the shoreline, made a note of direction and distance, and returned to the longboat. Thirty minutes later, the pirates were back aboard the Adventure. By the afternoon of the following day, the tiller had been repaired, and the ship sailed on to Block Island.

It wasn't long before authorities captured Bradish, who was eventually executed in England for his piratical activities. The pirate would never return to Montauk Island to retrieve his treasure. The existence of this fabulous cache would never have been known had it not been for one of the captured pirates, who revealed the location to his jailer.

While Bradish was jailed in Newport, Rhode Island, following his capture at Weekapaug, his jailer came into possession of what he believed was valuable information regarding the pirate's buried treasure – information that could make him a very wealthy man. He began to make plans to travel to Montauk Point and retrieve the treasure. For reasons unknown, he instead revealed the information to his superiors. Time passed, and the matter was forgotten, but not before the jailer recorded the event and all of the pertinent information in his diary.

Decades later, the jailer's diary was found in a

storeroom. Several hand-written pages detailed the caching of the treasure by pirate Bradish and his crewmen. Specific directions and distances were recorded in the diary relating to the cache site at Montauk Point on Long Island. The diary was turned over to a local storekeeper who, after reading the text, grew intrigued with the possibility of traveling to Montauk point and retrieving the buried cache of gold and jewels.

After acquiring a small but sturdy sailboat, the storekeeper enlisted the help of two companions and sailed from Newport to Montauk Point. According to the diary, the treasure was buried somewhere on the northwestern shore. On landing at the prescribed site, the storekeeper constantly consulted the diary and examined his surroundings, searching for the indicated landmarks. After three hours of exploring the region, the three searchers came to the inland pond, which was located approximately one-half mile from the shoreline.

Excited about the potential discovery, the storekeeper returned to the shoreline and, following the directions of the diary, paced off 177 steps back in the direction of the pond. At the 177th step, he placed a marker and told his companions that this was the location of the treasure cache. The three men excavated a hole six feet deep and eight feet wide, but found nothing. The storekeeper returned to the diary and read it over and over. Based on the information contained in the diary, he kept returning to the same location. Unfortunately, there was no treasure to be found. Disheartened and discouraged, the three men returned to Rhode Island.

News of the storekeeper's failed expedition for the buried treasure spread throughout his hometown, and friends dropped by to offer condolences. One of these visitors, however, was a man he had never seen before. He was an old man, who had clearly experienced several decades as a seaman. He informed the storekeeper that he possessed information about the Bradish treasure at Montauk Point. After listening to his visitor for nearly an hour, the storekeeper was instilled with renewed hope.

Several years earlier, the visitor explained, a severe storm had struck the easternmost end of Montauk Point and caused a great deal of damage. Huge waves surged across the tip of the island, eroding beaches and carrying away tons of sand. The entire configuration of Montauk Point's northeastern shoreline was significantly rearranged, according to the old man, and a large portion of land completely eroded away. The visitor explained that the present shoreline was actually several dozen paces farther inland than it had been during the time that Bradish buried his booty.

The storekeeper was so excited with this news that he immediately began making plans to undertake a new search for the treasure. He secured the boat and enlisted the assistance of his two friends. By the time he arrived back at the island, however, he determined he was no better off than before; it was impossible for him to determine the location of the shoreline during Joseph Bradish's time. The storekeeper wandered about the immediate area of the island interviewing longtime residents, but none of them were any help. After spending three days on the island, the storekeeper finally gave up and, along with his friends, returned to Rhode Island. Whatever became of the jailer's diary is unknown.

Joseph Bradish's Montauk Point treasure cache is

not widely known except among a handful of professional treasure hunters. Without the diary and any specific information on which to base a search, they have devoted their energy to other more potentially productive searches. As a result, the Joseph Bradish Montauk Island treasure cache has never received much attention. Since so few people have undertaken this quest there is a great chance that it is still there waiting to be found.

-14-

The Stone Harbor Treasure

As Barnett looked over the ship, he felt a shiver of fear: The ship was flying a flag with the skull and crossbones.

During the age of piracy, many seagoing outlaws made names for themselves, and their reputations spread far and wide. Many more, however, operated under a cloak of anonymity and carried out their nefarious deeds without anyone ever knowing exactly who they were or where they were from. Researchers believe that one such group of pirates buried a large wooden chest filled with treasure somewhere on Seven Mile Beach near Stone Harbor, New Jersey.

The year was 1710, and it was a popular time for

pirate activity throughout much of the North Atlantic Ocean, particularly along the eastern coast of America. Pirate raids on small coastal communities were common, sometimes resulting in numerous deaths. As word spread up and down the coast of this ongoing threat, some towns were abandoned, and the citizens moved farther inland, where they believed they would be safe from predators. In other instances, the community members armed themselves in preparation for a pirate attack.

On the Atlantic Ocean side of the southern peninsula of New Jersey is a location known as Stone Harbor. Today it is a quiet community with a population of just over 800 residents, but in 1710, the area could claim only one resident: a former sea captain named Eli Barnett. Barnett boasted of a half-century of seafaring. Retiring to Stone Harbor in his sixties, he manned a rescue station near the southwestern end of Seven Mile Beach. With little else to occupy his time, Barnett often scanned the Atlantic Ocean on the lookout for ships. If one experienced troubles and appeared to be sinking, Barnett would launch a longboat and row to the scene to pick up survivors. More often than not, however, Barnett was on the lookout for pirates.

For hours each day, weather permitting, Barnett would search the ocean with a telescope he had used for years on his own ship. Early one morning during late spring of 1710, when Barnett walked out onto the beach to scan the ocean, he spotted a three-masted schooner approaching directly from the east. As Barnett watched, the ship anchored one half-mile offshore. Within the hour, a rowboat dropped into the sea, and moments later, the ship's crewmen lowered a heavy wooden chest into it using ropes and pulleys. As Barnett looked over the ship, he felt a shiver of fear: The ship was flying a flag with the skull and crossbones. His worst fear had been realized – a pirate vessel had arrived at Stone Harbor.

Moments later, five men descended a ladder, entered the rowboat, and began rowing toward the shore. Barnett sought shelter, dashing to a hiding place among a grove of trees located above the beach.

When the prow of the rowboat hit the beach, one of the occupants, apparently the one in command, climbed out and walked up and down the beach, making note of landmarks. After an hour of examining the landscape, the pirate walked back to the rowboat and ordered the other four men to unload the chest. Leading the way, the first pirate directed the others to follow him. The weight of the chest was so great that they could barely keep up, and Barnett assumed, from years of experience, that it contained gold, silver, or jewels, or a combination of all three. As he watched, the party disappeared from Barnett's view behind a large sand dune. Fifteen minutes later, one of the pirates reappeared, running back toward the rowboat, where he obtained two shovels and then ran back to the far side of the dune. An hour passed, and the five men were spotted walking back to the rowboat without the wooden chest. They climbed into the boat and returned to the ship.

From his hiding place, Barnett burned with curiosity to know what was in the chest. He wanted desperately to go in search of it, but he feared that the men on the ship might spot him walking along the beach. He decided to wait until the vessel departed.

Early the next morning, Barnett ate breakfast,

dressed, and with his telescope in hand, stepped out of his modest cabin and walked back toward Seven Mile Beach. All night long he had thought about the treasure chest and the wealth he would soon come into when he recovered it. However, as he neared the beach, he was greeted with yet another surprise. The pirates had returned, their rowboat landing once again on the beach at the water's edge. Barnett retreated to his hiding place and watched.

The same five pirates climbed out of the rowboat, two of them carrying shovels. After leaving the boat, they proceeded once again down the beach and around the large dune, presumably to the spot where they had buried the chest the previous day. As Barnett watched in hiding, he noted that the wind was picking up and the sky was darkening, indicating an oncoming storm.

Nearly two hours passed before the pirates came into sight again. On reaching the rowboat, they engaged in a brief conversation, climbed in, and returned to the ship. By this time, the rain had begun to fall and the winds were generating whitecaps on the open sea. During the onset of the storm, the pirate vessel hoisted up its anchor, raised its sails, and moved eastward out of sight.

Though wishing to follow the pirates' tracks to the treasure cache site, Barnett opted instead to return to his cabin in order to get out of the pounding rain. For three days, the old sea captain waited out the tempest, unable to leave the shelter of his home. Finally, on the fourth day, the clouds parted, and the sun shone through. Barnett buttoned up his coat, pulled his hat low against the brisk winds, and walked onto the beach.

As a result of the severe storm, it was impossible to locate any sign of the pirates' tracks. Barnett went to the dune where he had last seen them carrying the chest but could not determine the destination. For two hours, Barnett searched for some sign of excavation but could find none. For several weeks, the old seaman retraced the path to some point behind the dune, trying to determine where someone might bury a treasure chest. Now and then he dug holes in what he considered to be some likely spots, all to no avail.

Barnett continued to live in his little cabin near Seven Mile Beach for the next 10 years. During that time, he continued to search for the buried treasure chest, but the exact location eluded him. As time passed, he told others of what he had seen and welcomed them to the area to assist in his search for the treasure, but nothing was ever found. More time passed, and Eli Barnett eventually passed away, never succeeding in locating the pirate treasure.

The story of the buried treasure made the rounds over the years, but most who heard it chalked it up to colorful folklore and were convinced that Barnett had only imagined the caching of a large treasure. But that attitude changed in 1944, when an amazing discovery focused people's attention on Seven Mile Beach.

One Sunday afternoon in 1944, a New Jersey family by the name of Young was visiting relatives in the town of Swainton, located six miles north of Stone Harbor. The family packed a picnic lunch and traveled the short distance to Seven Mile Beach. There, the parents spread out blankets on the sand, and following the meal, watched as their children played in the water. Growing tired, the kids retreated to the beach, where they frolicked among the dunes and built sand castles.

After spending much of the afternoon on the beach, the Young family returned to their home in Atlantic City. The following morning, after Mr. Young departed for his job, Mrs. Young gathered her children's dirty clothes and readied them for the wash. As she was going through the pockets of her youngest son's shorts, she retrieved five odd-looking coins. When she asked him where they came from, he told her he had taken them out of a "wooden box" that he had found in the sand near where they were playing the previous day. It was a large wooden box, he explained, and it was filled with similar coins.

That evening, Mrs. Young showed the coins to her husband when he arrived home and related what her son told her about the discovery. Intrigued, Young took the coins to a noted Atlantic City collector for an examination. After cleaning a thick residue from the objects, the collector examined them and declared them to be Spanish in origin, minted in 1706, and nearly pure gold.

One week later, Mr. Young, accompanied by his youngest son, returned to Seven Mile Beach. Although they spent over two hours searching the dunes for the wooden box, they found nothing. It was presumed that recent strong offshore winds had shifted the beach sand and covered the chest.

When asked by local residents what he was doing, Mr. Young told the story of the gold coins. In no time at all, dozens of area residents began searching the beach, hoping that they would find the long-buried pirate treasure. Over the next several weeks, treasure hunters (both professional and amateur) arrived at Seven Mile Beach to pursue the quest. A few had some luck. In all, about two dozen coins were found, and it was presumed that the Young children must have dropped them while they were playing. The chest, however, was never found.

To this day, there has been no more information accounting for the chest filled with coins: where they came from, where they were bound, whether or not they had been stolen. Likewise, no one has ever identified the pirates responsible for burying the treasure, or why they never returned to retrieve the chest.

-15-

Captain Kidd and the Millsboro Treasure

In time, a Royal Navy officer officially declared Kidd a pirate. The officer attempted to arrest Kidd, but the pirate ignored him and sailed away.

The pirate Captain William Kidd was known to have buried treasure in a number of locations up and down much of the east coast of the United States. Over the years, Kidd returned to many of these locations and retrieved his booty, but according to historians and pirate enthusiasts who have studied the man, much of it remains buried and lost. One such cache that was never recovered was buried not far from Indian River Bay near the Sussex County town of Millsboro in Delaware. The cache reportedly consists of several chests filled with gold, jewels, precious stones, and uncut diamonds.

Although many debate his origins, most researchers believe that William Kidd was born on January 22, 1645 in Greenock, Scotland. Documents reveal that the family name was spelled "Kyd." His father was a sailor who was presumably lost at sea when Kidd was just a boy. As a young man, Kidd somehow made his way to New York City. Researchers believe that he worked as a seaman apprentice aboard a pirate ship and served in that capacity when he arrived in New York.

By 1689, Kidd was a full-fledged member of a pirate crew plundering ships in the Caribbean Sea. During this time, the crewmen mutinied, took over the ship, and sailed to the British colony of Nevis in the Caribbean's Leeward Island chain. The ship was renamed the Blessed William, and Kidd was subsequently elected captain. A second account has Kidd named captain of the vessel by Nevis governor Christopher Codington. With Kidd's agreement, the Blessed William became part of Codington's fleet of ships, employed to defend the colony from the French. Codington could not afford to pay Kidd and his crew but encouraged them to take plunder from any French ships they captured. Around this time, Kidd and his men attacked the nearby French island of Marie-Galante. They looted the town of its gold and then burned it to the ground.

Kidd went on to greater successes serving as a privateer. On May 6, 1691, he married Sarah Bradley Cox Oort, a twice-widowed woman only in her twenties. Oort was regarded as one of the wealthiest women in New York as a result of inheritances from her former husbands.

On December 11, 1695, Richard Coote approached Kidd to request that he go in search of and attack any pirates preying on British ships along the Atlantic Coast. Coote was the First Earl of Bellomont and had been appointed governor of New York, Massachusetts, and New Hampshire by England's William III. The sought-after pirates included Thomas "Bloody" Tew, John Ireland, Thomas Wake, William Mays, and others. Kidd was to pay 10 percent of any plunder to the crown.

As time passed, Kidd fell into disfavor with British royalty, as well as the military. He had gained a reputation as "bloodthirsty" and was reputed to kill his own crewmen when they did not immediately respond to his orders. Kidd was also known for torturing and killing crewmen and sailors of captured ships as well as attacking and plundering any ships that were friendly to the British crown. He was transitioning from being a privateer to an outright pirate. In time, a Royal Navy officer officially declared Kidd a pirate. The officer attempted to arrest Kidd, but the pirate ignored him and sailed away.

Over the next few years, Kidd preyed upon merchant vessels in the Atlantic [and] the Caribbean and even ventured into the Indian Ocean. During this time, the British Navy mercilessly hunted for him.

Captain Kidd allegedly buried treasures in several locations along the Atlantic Coast. Sometime during 1699, Captain Kidd guided his vessel into the quiet waters of Indian River Bay in southern Delaware. Two streams flowed from the mainland into the bay: Indian River and Pepper Creek. Kidd arrived there following several successful raids on merchant ships along the Atlantic Coast.

Typically, while at anchor, Kidd would have his men replenish the fresh water supply and hunt for game. But this time, Kidd had another objective: He had grown concerned that the great weight of stolen cargo was causing the ship to ride dangerously low in the water, and he feared running aground on a shallow reef or sandbar. Kidd decided it was necessary to unload some of the cargo and bury it at this location. A significant amount of the heavy load consisted of several chests of stolen gold and other valuables.

As Kidd pondered the situation, a lookout shouted from the bow that the ship was only clearing the bottom of the bay by a couple of feet. At that point, Kidd ordered the anchor to be dropped. This done, he assigned several crewmembers to bring the treasure chests from the hold to the deck. After opening each of the chests and admiring his treasure, Kidd instructed his men to lower them into the longboats. After the chests were placed into three longboats, Kidd retrieved a cannonball from one of the gun placements, lowered it into one of the boats, and placed it between two of the chests.

Kidd climbed into one of the boats and directed his oarsmen to head for the nearby southern shore. The crewmen struggled to unload the heavy chests from the boats, and following Kidd's orders, carried and dragged them up the beach to a location near a single oak tree. Kidd assigned one of the crewmen the task of carrying the cannonball, and he ordered another two men to excavate a hole six feet deep. As the men dug, Kidd opened each trunk to re-examine their contents. One contained gold coins taken from a recent raid on a British merchant vessel. Another contained gold ingots from China.

A third was filled with jewelry and precious stones, including emeralds, sapphires, and rubies. The last trunk was filled nearly to the top with uncut diamonds.

After each trunk was closed and locked, Kidd watched as they were lowered into the hole. Once the hole was covered, Kidd carved a diamond-shaped figure into the trunk of the oak tree. The cannonball was placed directly over the buried cache. The job completed, Kidd and his men returned to the ship.

Kidd continued to attack and plunder ships. Knowing he was a wanted man and that the penalty for piracy was death by hanging, he kept a wary eye out for pursuit. Soon, the pressure of the pursuit became too much for Kidd, and he looked for ways to retire from piracy. As he considered bargaining for his freedom by offering officials a share of his treasure, he received a message from Governor Coote. With the promise of forgiveness, Coote invited Kidd to meet with him in Boston, Massachusetts, but when Kidd arrived, Coote had him placed under arrest. It was July 6, 1699. Kidd was installed in solitary confinement in Stone Prison. His wife, Sarah, was also arrested and placed in prison. While in prison, Kidd was subjected to beatings and other forms of cruelty. There is evidence that the conditions and treatment drove him insane.

After a year in Stone Prison, Kidd was shipped to England for questioning. The Tories* were in power, and they wanted to use Kidd to discredit the Whigs*, who had backed the pirate in the past. Kidd refused to cooperate, which angered officials, who subsequently ordered him to stand trial for piracy and murder in England's Admiralty Court. While awaiting trial, Kidd was confined to Newgate Prison.

Kidd entered court with two lawyers who were not much help. He was found guilty on five counts of piracy and one of murder. His punishment was to be death by hanging. On May 3, 1701, Kidd was brought to the gallows at Execution Dock on the River Thames at Wapping in London. The noose was fitted around his neck and the trap sprung. As Kidd reached the end of the rope, it broke and he landed beneath the gallows, stunned but alive. He was promptly marched back to the platform, forced to undergo the process once again, and this time the rope held.

Kidd's body was left at the gibbet* on the dock to hang over the river for three years as a warning to other pirates. Kidd's six associates – officers on his ship – were also found guilty but were pardoned minutes prior to Kidd's hanging.

Over the generations, the legend of the pirate Captain Kidd grew, in large part based on the belief that he had buried a great deal of treasure in a number of different locations. Many people believe that most of these stories were fabricated, but the truth remains that Kidd did, in fact, bury treasure. In one case, he cached a hoard of gold on Gardiners Island, a small island located in Gardiners Bay on the eastern end of Long Island. In 2015, explorers found a treasure in gold in Madagascar, believed to be part of a cache that Kidd left there. Other treasure experts are convinced he also cached treasure at Delaware's Indian River Bay.

Many decades after Kidd's death, on an afternoon in June 1932, a black Ford panel truck pulled into the only gas station in Millsboro, Delaware, on the Indian

River. Jimmy Butler, the son of the owner, filled the gas tank while the driver and passenger asked about lodging. Butler recommended a room that his mother rented out to travelers and gave them directions to the house.

The following morning, as young Butler busied himself with his job at the filling station, the two strangers returned and asked him about directions and certain landmarks. As Butler responded to their questions, they occasionally referred to a map they had unrolled and laid across the hood of the vehicle. In particular, the strangers were interested in the location of a large oak tree that they believed could be found near the southern shore of the upper reaches of Indian River Bay. Butler knew the tree well, as he had often played near it when he was younger. He told the two men he would lead them to it the next day, since it was his day off.

At 9:00 a.m. the following day, the two strangers arrived, and Butler climbed into the panel truck. As the driver steered the vehicle out of town toward the bay, Butler directed him along a series of seldom-used dirt roads. A half-hour later, they arrived at the edge of a broad meadow, where a large oak tree stood at the far end. The driver headed for it.

The oak tree grew at the top of a low bank that graded gently toward the bay some 50 yards away. Stopping the truck, the two men got out and walked toward the tree, the driver carrying the map. Butler remained in the vehicle. The men slowly walked around the large trunk of the tree as if searching for something. Presently, one of them cried out that he had found what they were looking for. Butler got out of the truck, walked up to the tree, and saw them staring at something chest-high on the trunk of the tree.

Stepping closer, Butler saw that it was a crude diamond-shaped figure that had apparently been carved into the wood many years earlier. It had been partially obscured by new bark growth, but it was clearly man-made.

The two men spread the map out on the ground next to the tree and examined it. Butler noted that the map was very old and made of heavy parchment. As Butler watched and listened, the men looked around, pointed to features on the map, and matched them with existing landmarks. Butler asked the two men if it was a treasure map. He was told that it was, and that it had been found in an old trunk in North Carolina several years earlier.

As the story unfolded, Butler learned that the map had been prepared by one of Kidd's crewmen who had helped bury the treasure at Indian River Bay. The map also described the wooden trunks and what each of them contained. The two men told Butler that if he would keep their activities secret, they would cut him in for a percentage of the treasure when they found it.

Pointing at the map, one of the men noted that the location of the treasure cache was indicated by the placement of a cannonball. Butler explained that a cannonball was, indeed, found near this location several years earlier. The finder carried it home and later donated it to a museum in Washington, D.C.

Expressing disappointment and frustration at the missing maker, one of the men began pacing off distances from the tree in various directions. After considerable discussion, they eventually agreed on one particular location and commenced digging. By 3:00 P.M., they had excavated a hole seven feet deep before giving up for the day.

Each day over the next two weeks, the two strangers returned to the oak tree. They would discuss possibilities, pace off in another direction, and dig another hole. Each time, they failed to locate any treasure. Finally, they decided to try another approach to locating the cache.

It took three days, but they finally located the man who had found the cannonball. They asked him to return to the tree with them and indicate the spot at which it was found. Since the discovery had taken place many years earlier, the man could not recall the exact distance or direction from the oak tree. After a few more days of searching and digging, the two men finally gave up and returned home.

A few days after the men left, Butler returned to the oak tree. He had grown fascinated with the tale of Captain Kidd's buried treasure and became captivated by the notion of perhaps discovering it on his own. On several occasions, Butler excavated holes near the tree but found nothing. After days of digging with no success, he felt defeated and gave up.

Over the years, others treasure hunters have arrived in the Indian Bay area to undertake a search for Captain Kidd's treasure. One major obstacle is that the oak tree is no longer standing. Having succumbed to age, it was removed many years ago. Today, no one in Millsboro can recall where it once stood.

In 1999, a team of electronics experts who were experimenting with a state-of-the-art metal detector decided to try to locate Captain Kidd's Indian Bay treasure. The detector could apparently locate precious metals to a depth of eight feet. On arriving in the general area of the treasure cache, the team employed the instrument along the top of the bank, where many believe the treasure is buried. Though they spent three days searching, nothing was found. It was later determined that the metal detector was faulty, but another search was never scheduled.

Another pair of professional treasure hunters insisted that if they had access to the map presented by the two strangers in Millsboro many years ago. However, no one remembers the names of the strangers, where they came from, or what became of the map. Nevertheless, there is solid evidence for Captain Kidd's buried treasure as well as the fact that the pirate never returned to the site to retrieve his fortune, and very few experts question the evidence. That means the treasure, estimated to be worth tens of millions of dollars today, is most likely still buried somewhere near Millsboro.

-16-

William Neub's Buried Treasure

A New Castle constable organized a posse of fifteen armed men and plans were made to travel to the Neub farm and arrest him.

William Neub was one of several pirates who, though enjoying a successful career raiding and plundering merchant ships and coastal communities, somehow has managed to elude the attention of historians and enthusiasts. Thus, though little is known of this brigand, the tale of his buried treasure has not only survived but thrived as it has been passed down over the generations.

Sometime during the mid-1720s, pirate William Neub, the so-called "Scourge of the Atlantic," decided to retire from his long career. Neub sported a mane of gray hair and by pirate standards was considered elderly at the age of 50. He had a variety of scars, plus a multitude of broken bones that caused him pain and he found it difficult to climb out of bed some mornings. Neub also grew weary of the constant pursuit by British and American warships and found it increasingly challenging to evade them.

Neub longed to settle down and lead a quiet life without interference from his neighbors. Passing himself off as a cattleman, he arrived at a location between the northern Delaware towns of New Castle and Newark and purchased a farm with some of his treasure. After securing his property, he moved his treasure – consisting of chests filled with gold coins and ingots, jewels, and precious stones – to the property and began to ponder the best site to bury it.

Neub lived a quiet and peaceful life, rarely interacting with his neighbors or the nearby townsfolk. When he arrived in New Castle to purchase supplies, he remained only long enough to stop at a tavern for a pint of ale before returning home.

Neub's nearest neighbor was a man who had lived in the region for several years. The neighbor had been suspicious of Neub from the day he moved in, since the farm didn't have any cattle, and no crops were planted. In spite of having no obvious income, Neub always seemed to have plenty of money.

The neighbor, who often observed Neub from a distance, somehow recognized him as the pirate he had once been. The neighbor was also aware that, though Neub had apparently retired from piracy, authorities in New Castle were still searching for him. The neighbor recalled that a reward had been offered for the capture of Neub, and he lost no time in relaying this information to officials. A New Castle constable organized an armed posse of 15 men and made plans to travel to the Neub farm and arrest him.

Neub somehow learned of the impending raid and hastened to cache his treasure, which had been stored in his house since his arrival. He selected a location on his farm, excavated a deep hole, placed the treasure chests within, and refilled it. Then he carefully marked the location by scratching the image of an anchor and chain on a nearby rock. The end of the chain pointed directly to the treasure trove.

On the day the authorities arrived at Neub's farm to arrest him, they found the place abandoned. The ex-pirate had fled the previous day. It's believed that he intended to eventually return for his treasure, but he was never seen again.

The story of Neub's buried treasure, along with the "anchor and chain" marker, made the rounds of the area over the next several generations and, as a result, hopeful treasure hunters arrived at the site of the old Neub property to search for it. On at least two occasions, records show that the marker was found.

In 1842, a man who introduced himself as Mr. Thomas arrived in Newark and made inquiries about the old Neub farm. Because more than a century had passed since Neub had lived there, no one remembered the pirate. Thomas immersed himself in a search through old courthouse records and eventually found the information he wanted.

While in New Castle, Thomas kept to himself and

rarely engaged in conversation with any of the residents. Each evening, he retired to his rented room. On occasion, he rented a horse and buggy and traveled out to the old Neub property. There, he would park the vehicle and walk around as if searching for something. This behavior attracted the attention of neighbors who reported him to a Newark constable. Under questioning, Thomas confessed that he was searching for the lost treasure of Captain William Neub, the pirate.

The constable remained suspicions and doubted Thomas's story. In response, Thomas pulled an old, yellowed, rolled up parchment from his coat pocket and showed it to the constable. Thomas explained that William Neub had drawn the map himself. On examining it, the constable recognized familiar landmarks. In fact, the outline of an anchor and chain could be found in the section of the map that held the boundaries of the old Neub property. Thomas explained that Neub had carved the image into a rock not far from the treasure cache.

The constable grew more interested, and on subsequent visits to the old Neub property, he accompanied Thomas on his searches. For the next eight months, the two men walked back and forth across the property. They never found the marker and, consequently, never found the treasure. Thomas left Newark with the map, and as far as we know, was never seen again in the area.

Then, in 1888, two strangers arrived in Newark and were soon observed exploring the old Neub property. As with Thomas nearly a half-century earlier, neighbors grew concerned at the presence of the newcomers and reported their activities. Lawmen arrived and arrested the two men. After being interrogated for two hours, the strangers admitted that they were searching for a lost pirate treasure they believed was buried on the property. As proof, they unrolled a large parchment map that they had in their possession and showed it to the police. From a recorded description of the map, it was apparently the same one employed by Thomas years earlier. The two men claimed they had purchased the map at an estate auction.

Arrangements were made that would allow the two newcomers to continue searching the Neub property. After several weeks of effort with no results, they decided to visit area residents and ask them questions. The men asked residents whether or not any of them knew of a rock with the image of an anchor and chain carved on its face. No one admitted recognizing the rock until the two men questioned an elderly man named Bradley.

During the visit at Bradley's home, the old man said that, indeed, he had seen such a rock on numerous occasions while he was hunting rabbit. He described the rock as he remembered it, and his description matched the information on the map. With the help of Bradley, the two strangers conducted several more searches but were never able to find the rock.

Later, in the 1970s, a man named Gerard arrived at Newark with yet another map purporting to show the location of William Neub's buried pirate treasure. Instead of investing the time to search for the rock with the marker, Gerard placed an ad in the local newspaper, describing the anchor and chain carving.

Within two days, Gerard received a visit from a local man named Benson. Benson claimed he had worked for a road construction crew that performed maintenance on roads and highways in the area. Benson told Gerard that one day, while he and his crew were undertaking some roadwork a short distance south of town, he encountered a rock fitting the description in the newspaper ad. Benson said the rock had been pushed at least 50 feet from its original location by a bulldozer in order to facilitate some roadwork. During the process, he said, the rock had fractured into several pieces. Unfortunately, Benson was unable to recall the exact location of the rock before it was moved. Gerard received no further responses to his ad, and he left town disheartened.

From time to time, professional treasure hunters have expressed interest about undertaking a search for the lost treasure of pirate William Neub. Some people have arrived in the area to investigate but admit that so much time has passed it may be impossible to determine even a general location of the treasure cache.

Some 300 years after William Neub buried his immense treasure, the notion of finding it still attracts interest and people continue to arrive at this picturesque part of Delaware, believing they will be the one to locate the riches. Occasionally a search is undertaken, but to date, the treasure has never been recovered.

-17-

Captain Charles Morgan and the Secret Tunnel Treasure

All of Whitlock's success attracted the attention of Captain Charles Morgan... Whitlock feared the pirate Morgan and was intimidated by his style.

Captain Charles Morgan, noted privateer and part-time pirate, is often confused with Captain Henry Morgan, a pirate of greater fame. Henry Morgan spent most of his pirate career preying on ships in the Caribbean Sea and along the coasts of Europe and Africa. As with pirate William Neub, history has not recorded a great deal of information regarding the exploits of Charles Morgan. What is best known about this mysterious buccaneer is his relationship with a businessman named Thomas Whitlock and the treasure that linked the two men.

Located on the north shore of Raritan Bay, in the town of Port Monmouth, New Jersey, stands a history museum known as the Seabrook-Wilson House. It was originally built by Thomas Whitlock in 1663 and is nicknamed "The Spy House." Ongoing rumors have convinced many people that the house is honeycombed with secret passageways, many of which have never been located. According to legend, within some of these passageways lie a number of caches of gold and silver ingots, jewelry, fine china, and emeralds, all placed there by the pirate Charles Morgan.

Historians consider Thomas Whitlock to be one of the first official residents of New Jersey, having arrived on the north coast of what would eventually become Monmouth County. Whitlock was born in England to a father who had once sailed with Sir Francis Drake. The elder Whitlock first settled on Long Island, New York with his family. As his son Thomas Whitlock grew into young adulthood, he had his mind set on developing his own businesses and growing wealthy. To that end, he decided to sail from Long Island to the New Jersey shore. Once there, he established a trading business with the Native American Indian residents.

Whitlock was a successful trader and at the same time, grew fond of this coastal countryside. He decided he wanted to live there forever. During his free time, he explored the area and mapped much of it, hoping to create a suitable location for a settlement. Eventually, Whitlock, along with a number of investors, purchased a large parcel of land from the natives. The land comprised much of the north coast of New Jersey, and Whitlock planned to establish a number of farms and a small community.

Whitlock constructed a modest, one-room log cabin to serve as his residence along with his wife and children. It is believed to be the first house built in the state. Between expanding his trading business, planting crops, and making plans for the future, Whitlock enlarged the cabin. He also constructed a large root cellar* as well as a garret* for storage. During this process, his family grew, and his children eventually numbered seven.

As a result of his commitment and success, Whitlock developed a reputation as a competent and forward-thinking entrepreneur. His trading enterprise grew, and his farms produced crops that were sold and transported to New York. Numerous customers and other businessmen traveled to Port Monmouth to meet with him.

Sadly, Whitlock's wife died several years after settling in Port Monmouth, leaving him to raise his children. Following a suitable period of mourning, Whitlock married Mary Seabrook, a widow with three children of her own. In need of more room for his growing family, Whitlock constructed a second house less than 20 feet from the first. As he worked on his new home, Whitlock built a series of secret passageways and underground tunnels as well as a corridor connecting the new house to the old.

Whitlock's reason for constructing the secret tunnels was based on his concern for the safety of his family. As a result of increasing Indian raids, he was convinced that the tunnels would afford some measure of protection for his wife and children. Carefully concealed trap doors led from the house to the passageways that stretched beneath the floors. In addition, some of the walls had hidden openings. It was also rumored that Whitlock had excavated a tunnel that extended from his house to a boat dock several dozen yards away.

Whitlock called his home and the surrounding property the Whitlock-Seabrook Estate. He named his plantation Shoal Harbor. In addition to his trading business and his farms, Whitlock established a shipping company, which flourished. As his reputation as an astute businessman grew, he was honored in New York social circles.

All of Whitlock's success attracted the attention of Captain Charles Morgan. Morgan had initially gained fame and notice as a successful privateer, but once he realized that piracy was more fruitful, he oriented his career in that direction. Morgan arranged a meeting with Whitlock and informed the businessman that going forward, he would provide protection for his shipping business. For a reasonable fee, Morgan explained that pirates would not attack Whitlock's ships ever again. In the past, one of Whitlock's ships had been attacked and plundered by pirates.

Whitlock feared the pirate Morgan and was intimidated by his style. He was also fearful of turning down the proposal and eventually agreed to it. Several months passed, and not a single ship belonging to Whitlock suffered a pirate attack. When he thought the time was right, Morgan scheduled another meeting with the businessman. During this exchange, Morgan demanded the deed to Whitlock's house and property. At first, Whitlock refused, but as the meeting wore on and he crumbled under Morgan's threats, he finally complied. The transfer was made, and Morgan was pleased. Unfortunately for the pirate, however, officials did not recognize the transaction.

On learning that his plan had been thwarted, Morgan and several of his crewmen moved onto the Whitlock-Seabrook Estate, commandeering the house and forcing Whitlock and his family to move into one of the outbuildings. In effect, the Whitlock family was held hostage on their own property.

While living in the house, Morgan grew fond of one of the Seabrook daughters. When the pirate returned from raids at seas, he often brought gifts for the young girl – expensive china, jewelry, gold and silver coins, and emeralds. Morgan carried the booty from his raids into the house but, after several voyages, started running out of sufficient room to store it.

During one of his earlier meetings with Whitlock, the businessman had told Morgan about the secret tunnels under the house and showed him how to access them. Morgan began caching some of his treasure in these passages.

As Morgan's treasure cache grew, he ordered several of his crewmen to enlarge the narrow passageways in the house and the underground tunnels. In time, the pirate created a vast and intricate network of tunnels. Morgan mentioned to Whitlock that he was expanding the tunnel system, but he did not reveal that the reason was for caching his treasure within.

Taking a break from working on the secret tunnels, Charles Morgan gathered his crewmen and set out on another voyage to acquire more treasure. However,

Morgan would never return to the Whitlock-Seabrook Estate to reclaim his treasure cache. During what later became known as "Morgan's last voyage," he was met with resistance and was killed in battle, along with most of his crewmen.

Weeks later, Whitlock learned of Captain Charles Morgan's death and, relieved, made plans to move back into his home. By this time, the Indian raids had ceased, and since Morgan's obsession with the tunnels had come to a mortal end, Whitlock decided to immediately seal off the passageways. He never ventured into them and was unaware of the wealth that had been stored there.

Many years later, David Seabrook, the oldest Seabrook stepson, developed an interest in farming, so Whitlock arranged for Seabrook to purchase 200 acres of prime agricultural land and assisted him with the initial planting. Over the next few years, David's harvests yielded substantial profits. With his growing income, David had a house constructed just 25 feet from the home of his mother and stepfather. When Thomas Whitlock passed away in 1703, David connected his house with the others via yet another passageway.

Time passed, and one of David Seabrook's nephews inherited the property. During the time he lived there, he invested considerable effort into enlarging the oddly evolving set of interconnected houses. A generation later, William Wilson, a minister, married into the Seabrook family. He was named the first postmaster of Port Monmouth. The post office was located in what is now referred to as the Whitlock-Seabrook-Wilson House.

While living in the complex, Wilson heard tales of secret tunnels and hidden treasures related to him by neighbors. While he regarded these as mostly tall tales, he was intrigued with the notion of secret passageways under the houses. A curious man, Wilson invested time in digging under the floors and pulling down walls. In the process, he exposed a few of the tunnels, and retrieved several artifacts. Captain Charles Morgan's treasure, however, eluded him.

Many years later, in 1993, a stranger arrived at Port Monmouth. He carried with him a blueprint of the original two houses, which he claimed had been drawn by the pirate Captain Charles Morgan, allegedly showing the system of secret passageways running throughout the houses and underground. Along one side of the map, according to the stranger, was an inventory of all of the treasure stored in the passageways by Morgan.

When the map-bearing stranger arrived in Port Monmouth, no one lived in the old Whitlock-Seabrook-Wilson home. He spent several days trying to locate someone who could grant him access to the property and the house. However, in a strange twist of events, the stranger was killed in a freak accident, run over by a horse-drawn wagon, before he could obtain permission. Unfortunately, the map was never found.

Today, the Whitlock-Seabrook-Wilson house serves as a museum. On display are a number of photographs and artifacts of the historical period associated with the surrounding area. Beneath the floors and between some of the walls, many believe, runs a system of long lost secret passageways connecting the houses. Cached in some of these passageways, as the legend goes, are a number of wooden chests filled with gold, silver, china, jewelry, and precious stones, still waiting to be discovered.

-18-

Pirate Charles Wilson's Lost Treasure

When news of his execution reached American shores, there was a collective sigh of relief.

As a result of his piratical activities, Charles Wilson developed the reputation as a cruel and greatly feared brigand; his name was whispered in coastal communities up and down the Atlantic coast from New York to Florida, and residents lived in fear that he and his fleet of ships would arrive at their ports. Despite his reputation, however, Wilson tried, sometimes in vain, to maintain a low profile, preferring to remain as anonymous as possible. Wilson had little use for the more flamboyant and notorious pirates such as Blackbeard and Captain Kidd, believing that they attracted far too much attention from British and American warships.

As with a number of pirates who frequented the North American coast, little is known about Charles Wilson. Most researchers believe that he was from South Carolina, but the documentation is questionable. More credible documents indicate that during his career as a pirate, Wilson accumulated several wooden chests filled with treasure: gold and silver coins, gems, and jewelry. His hoard was estimated to weigh hundreds of pounds.

Despite Wilson's desire to remain somewhat obscure, he was eventually captured and shipped to England, where he would stand trial. He was found guilty of a number of crimes and sentenced to death by hanging. When news of his execution reached American shores, there was a collective sigh of relief.

During the pirate era, it has been estimated that hundreds of millions of dollars' worth of treasure had been buried at various locations up and down the Atlantic coast. In most cases, the locations of these treasures were never written down, since the pirates preferred to trust their memories until they could return to collect their caches. In some cases, the pirates would construct maps or write down directions in a journal or diary. A few of these documents have been recovered, but most of them have been lost.

In the case of Charles Wilson, no one had an inkling of where he had hidden his great treasure. None, that is, until specific directions to its location, written down in a letter by Wilson himself, were found 198 years after he was hanged.

While he was awaiting his execution, Wilson was confined to a small cell in an English prison. There, he wrote a letter to his brother, George, who was a resident of Charleston, South Carolina. Before it could be mailed, the letter was confiscated and filed among stacks of official documents. Most of these documents were later thrown into a trunk – the typical filing system of the day. After the trunk was filled with dated documents, it was carried away and placed in storage.

For 198 years, the trunk remained untouched, until 1948, when it was found and opened. Among stacks of official documents was the letter Wilson had written to his brother from prison. (One account claims the trunk was found in an attic in Germany, but this seems unlikely.) The letter read:

The Year 1750
London, England

To my Brother, George Wilson,

There are three creeks lying 100 paces or more north of the second inlet above Chincoteague Island which is at the south end of the peninsula. At the head of the third creek to the northward is a bluff facing the Atlantic Ocean with three cedar trees growing on it, each about one-and-one-third yards apart. Between the trees I buried ten iron-bound chests, bars of silver, gold, diamonds, and jewels to the sum of 200,000 sterling. Go to the woody knoll and remove the treasure.

The peninsula described in Wilson's letter is

Assateague Island, not Chincoteague. It is unlikely that he knew the difference in 1750. For reasons unknown, Wilson's letter was printed in newspapers throughout England and America. Within days, hundreds of treasure hunters descended on the area, each one hopeful of recovering the chests and becoming wealthy overnight. But no one was successful. A significant challenge to locating the treasure, using Wilson's description, was the fact that nearly two centuries of storms with high winds and waves had reconfigured the island's landscape.

Assateague Island is a long barrier island widely known for its herds of tiny wild horses. It extends along the Atlantic Coast from Ocean City, Maryland, in a south-southwesterly direction, to a point east of Wallops Island, Virginia. The northern three-fourths of Assateague Island belong to the state of Maryland, while the southern one-fourth belongs to the state of Virginia.

It is estimated that since Wilson cached his huge treasure, as many as 11 new inlets have been cut through Assateague Island, some by men and others by nature. In addition, some of the inlets that existed during Wilson's time have been filled in with sand and are now impassable. The cedar trees identified in the letter were either cut down or simply died and rotted away over time. According to geographers, Assateague Island has actually migrated westward as a result of continual erosion accompanied by sand disposed from ocean currents and storm waves. It is estimated that portions of the island that were once above the waterline 200 years ago are now underwater and exposed only at low tide.

During the 1950s, there was a renewed effort by a treasure-hunting group to locate and retrieve Charles

Wilson's buried treasure. For unknown reasons, the group primarily concentrated on the portion of the island that belonged to Virginia. Their efforts spurred a closer examination of evidence related to Wilson's letter, a study of old as well as contemporary maps, along with an investigation of his known activities. These studies led researchers to conclude that Wilson's chests were most likely buried at some location on the island just north of the Maryland–Virginia border and close to the eastern shore. A number of other researchers who have studied the documents are convinced that the location is now under water.

During the early 1960s, a young enlisted man assigned to the Assateague Island Coast Guard Station was taking a stroll along a stretch of the island's beach. During his walk, he found a sand-encrusted colored stone near the water's edge. Believing it to be a unique rock, he placed it in his pocket and continued on his walk. After several steps, he found several more. When he returned to his living quarters, he soaked the stones in soapy water and carefully brushed away the loosened sand grains. What was left were stones of a bright red color and almost glass-like in appearance. The largest one was as big around as a quarter.

Weeks later, when he returned home on leave, the soldier gave the stone to his mother. Fascinated by the beauty of the object, she placed it on her mantelpiece, where she could look at it from time to time. Several more weeks passed, and the mother carried the stone to a jeweler, with the idea of having it mounted for a more professional-looking display. The jeweler immediately identified the stone as a ruby.

As soon as she returned home, the mother contacted her son and told him what he had found. At the first opportunity, the young Coast Guardsman went to find more stones. Regrettably, so much time had passed since he found them that he was not certain of the exact location. Though he spent hours looking for the spot, he never found it.

Veteran searchers for lost pirate treasure have arrived at a theory. First, they are convinced that Wilson's original cache is now under at least two feet of seawater, perhaps more. Second, there is a great possibility that the wooden trunks in which the treasure was placed have long since rotted away and the contents have been scattered along the bottom sands. Third, and most likely, the contents of the chests are now at the mercy of the waves and currents. For these reasons, and given the prevailing currents of this area, some of the treasure has no doubt been carried along and deposited around Assateague Island's shore and in the adjacent shallow waters. Fourth, given the inconsistency of the currents, the treasure is likely to have been scattered for miles along the beach.

Because Charles Wilson's treasure is estimated to be worth approximately $20 million, a number of professional treasure hunters have expressed a great deal of interest. Since 1990, more than a dozen organized searches have been conducted, a few of them funded by corporations. To date, no discoveries have been reported.

Despite the attention of historians, folklorists, and treasure-hunting enthusiasts, there are still some skeptics who insist that the entire story of Charles Wilson's treasure is fabricated. One blogger maintains that individuals selling real estate concocted the notion of a great treasure on Assateague Island as a marketing scheme. However, people who have spent time researching and investigating Wilson's tale are unanimous in their conclusion that it is authentic. Wilson existed, his piratical activities are well documented, and it has been established that he did, indeed, accumulate a significant amount of treasure during his piracy days. Wilson's presence on Assateague Island has likewise been established.

Thus, there is a great chance that a huge treasure was buried at some location on Assateague Island in 1750. Those who are discouraged by the fact that no one has reported finding the treasure are countered by others who continue to believe that it is still lying somewhere in the sands of an island beach, and that their chances for finding the treasure grow every day.

-19-

Blackbeard's South Carolina Treasure Cache

In leaving the area of Charleston, however, Blackbeard left untold millions of dollars' worth of buried treasure that, as it turned out, he would never return to recover.

The first pirate we met on this journey was Blackbeard, one of the most infamous and busiest pirates of that time. Many rumors claim that he's hidden treasure in various locations, and many of these caches have been found. What is known for certain is that this notorious brigand cached a vast fortune in gold and silver coins and ingots, along with chests filled with gems and jewelry, in the tidal marshes near Charleston, South Carolina.

Blackbeard favored the Charleston harbor and often retreated there to repair his ships and give his crew a break for rest and relaxation. It was said that he fell in love with the location for its pristine, calm bay waters and reveled in everything that the waterfront environment had to offer. Though Charleston's citizens were aware that Blackbeard was a pirate, he always treated them kindly and with respect. As a result, they found him quite amicable. Historians suspect that the townsfolk welcomed Blackbeard's presence in order to deter more ruthless pirates from visiting their city.

One account has Blackbeard purchasing a house in Charleston, with the intent of eventually retiring to the city. Between raids, Blackbeard often retreated to Charleston to relax in his fine home filled with handcrafted furniture and fine silk curtains. Other accounts maintain that he enjoyed the company of several women in the town.

However, Blackbeard was still a pirate at heart, and in May of 1716, he set up a blockade at the entrance of the harbor and captured every vessel that arrived and departed. Most of the seizures, however, amounted to little of value to the pirate and consisted mostly of barrels of rice and tar. The always-enterprising Blackbeard, however, fixated on another idea. He captured the crewmen of the ships, imprisoned them, and held them for ransom.

Despite what he thought was a brilliant idea, Blackbeard was ultimately disappointed with the response, for very little ransom was forthcoming. Likewise, his disappointed band began abandoning the pirate leader in search of greater adventures with more opportunities for plunder. With only a skeleton crew, Blackbeard decided it was time to find a new sanctuary, and to that end he steered his ship to Topsail Inlet at Fish Town, North Carolina. (The name Fish Town was eventually changed to Beaufort.) In leaving Charleston, however, Blackbeard left untold millions of dollars' worth of buried treasure that he never returned to recover.

The Atlantic coastal town of Charleston, South Carolina is located on a point of land extending between the Ashley and Cooper Rivers. Originally called Charles Towne, it was a bustling port, one of the busiest along the coast. From the time it was settled, Charleston evolved into one of the most influential business and trading centers in the Americas. A prominent geographic feature known as the tidal marsh lay to the west of Charleston Bay.

The tidal marsh is a vast, swampy area with mostly shallow water. Dotted throughout the region are small islands of silt, held together by clusters of densely growing vegetation. Most people generally avoided the tidal marsh: It was difficult-to-impossible to navigate and was densely populated with aggressive mosquitos and poisonous snakes. In addition, quicksand was an ever-present danger. This region of lowland South Carolina is replete with stories of people entering the tidal marsh and never being seen again.

Given these considerations, it is indeed curious that Blackbeard expressed a keen interest in the tidal marsh. Apparently, he thought that the forbidding nature of this primitive and hostile habitat was ideal for hiding his great fortune in treasure. Following successful raids up and down the Atlantic coast, as well as throughout the Caribbean Sea, Blackbeard repeatedly returned to Charleston Harbor to hide his plunder.

Blackbeard had his gold and silver ingots and coins and jewels sealed into waterproof casks. The casks were loaded into rowboats and taken out into the tidal marsh where they were hidden in locations pre-selected by Blackbeard himself. It's estimated that, at today's values, the pirate cached several hundred million dollars' worth of treasure in the tidal marsh.

After pulling out of Charleston Bay, Blackbeard headed for another sanctuary he was familiar with – the tiny community of Bath, North Carolina, a day's sail from Beaufort and up a small tributary to Pamlico Sound. Here, Blackbeard met with North Carolina Governor Charles Eden.

Bath seemed an unlikely place to serve as a residence for the governor. The small community consisted of low-lying tracts of occasionally flooded cypress forests, swamps, and muddy creeks. Most of the settlers in the area barely sustained a living and were out-numbered by the Indians who, six years earlier, had attacked the settlement and killed a large percentage of its population.

During his meeting with Governor Eden, Blackbeard, with a desire to quit piracy and settle down, requested a pardon. In exchange, Blackbeard would offer his crewmen, all of whom were experienced and armed fighters, to defend the settlement should another confrontation with the Indians occur. In addition, Blackbeard said he would infuse the settlement with money and assist in transforming the town into a significant trading center. He also suggested that more money could be forthcoming. The politician Eden, his eyes on the potential fortune that could be made in Bath, freely granted a pardon.

With his pardon completed, Blackbeard and his men started constructing homes for themselves in Bath. A document exists that testifies to the fact that Blackbeard married a Bath woman. As the men appeared to be intent on settling down and removing themselves from their piratical ways, Blackbeard made plans to occasionally slip away and resume his attacks on merchant vessels. To that end, Blackbeard and his pirates established a camp on Ocracoke Island, a long, narrow stretch of land separating Pamlico Sound from the Atlantic Ocean. From this location, the pirates would set out on their raids. With newly accumulated booty, they would return to the island and divide the plunder. Some of the treasure would go to the crewmen, some to Bath, and some was destined for Blackbeard's secret caches in the Charleston tidal marsh.

On one of their predatory raids, Blackbeard and his crew encountered two French ships, looted both, and took possession of one, the Rose Emelye, which they sailed back to Ocracoke Island. Some of the ship's contents – sugar and chocolate – were presented as gifts to Governor Eden and Tobias Knight, North Carolina's chief justice and customs collector.

While Blackbeard had successfully aligned himself with Eden and Knight, Alexander Spottswood, the North Carolina Lieutenant Governor, had kept his distance and remained keenly suspicious of the pirate and his relationships with state officials. In fact, Spottswood had been spying on Blackbeard for several months.

Spottswood's clandestine activities likely stemmed from a sense of jealousy towards Eden and Knight, who were receiving significant monetary benefits from Blackbeard's exploits, while he was being left out. Though Spottswood was no model of virtue. In fact, he had demonstrated questionable ethics while in office, and the North Carolina state legislature was building a case to have him removed from office. While serving as Lieutenant Governor, Spottswood had awarded himself 85,000 acres of North Carolina land. In addition, he had been reprimanded for recklessly spending tax revenues. Convinced that Blackbeard was engaged in criminal activity related to piracy, Spottswood alerted the captains of two naval brigades, and together they concocted what author Colin Woodard called "an audacious and illegal plan to wipe out the fearsome pirate."

Uncertain of whether Blackbeard would be at Bath or on Ocracoke Island, the naval officers organized a two-pronged invasion: One group traveled overland on horseback and arrived in Bath. The second group, led by Lieutenant Robert Maynard, consisted of 60 armed sailors on two small, swift sloops, headed for Ocracoke Island, where they spotted Blackbeard's vessel at anchor. The next morning, Maynard's force attacked.

Blackbeard only had a crew of 20 men, all of whom had spent the previous night drinking heavily and were sleeping past dawn. So it should have been easy for Maynard's troops to surprise the unsuspecting pirates, but one of the naval sloops ran aground while deciding on a suitable anchorage. The commotion made while trying to free the ship aroused Blackbeard and his pirate crew.

Experienced at traveling light and fleeing pursuit, Blackbeard raised anchor, hoisted sails on his own ship and prepared to flee toward the open sea. Before departing, however, he fired a broadside that damaged the naval ship and killed a number of sailors. Bravely, Lieutenant Maynard was determined to fight the brigand and ordered his men to fire cannons and muskets at the escaping ship. A musket ball severed a halyard* on the pirate ship, causing one of the sails to drop, which in turn caused the vessel to slow down dramatically. Minutes later, the naval ship caught up with Blackbeard, only to be greeted by a hail of grapeshot and hand grenades. Twenty more of Maynard's sailors were killed or wounded in the barrage.

Angered by the attack from the navy, Blackbeard ordered his ship to come alongside the vessel so that his crewmen could seize it. Blackbeard tied the two ships together and was the first to step on board. At that moment, Maynard, along with a dozen armed sailors, broke from hiding and launched an offensive directed at the pirates. Taken by surprise, Blackbeard's forces were quickly overwhelmed. During the brawl, Blackbeard suffered numerous sword cuts and five bullet wounds. He dropped to the deck, bleeding heavily. As he tried to rise, he was attacked by more of Maynard's men, who slashed and hacked away at him. Moments later, one of the most notorious pirates to plague the Atlantic Coast died.

By this time, the second naval sloop arrived at the scene, took control, and captured 14 of the surviving pirates. They were bound and later taken to Virginia to stand trial. Blackbeard's head was severed from his body and hung from the bowsprit*. His body was later tossed overboard into Pamlico Sound.

Later, Blackbeard's head was presented to Spottswood, who had it mounted on a pole. Four years later, Spottswood was unceremoniously removed from office. Around the same time, Eden died from Yellow Fever. Very few people remember either Eden or Spottswood, but the exploits of Blackbeard, the pirate, continue to fascinate people.

With his death, along with the imprisonment and subsequent execution of his crewmen, no one was left alive who knew the location of Blackbeard's treasure cache in the Charleston, South Carolina tidal marsh. Nothing in the way of a map or written directions relative to the location was found among Blackbeard's effects on his ship. Over the years, many people have been attracted by the lure of Blackbeard's treasure, but no one has ever determined so much as a starting point for a search. As far as anyone knows, this fabulous treasure is still lying somewhere in the Charleston tidal marsh.

-20-

Mary Anne Townsend, Lady Pirate

Townsend more than proved herself a capable pirate, and soon gained a reputation of being fearless, and even dangerous.

Other than the recorded information that Mary Anne Townsend's uncle, a prominent and wealthy government official, raised her in Jamestown, very little is known about her life. Much of her life as a pirate remains shrouded in legend and mystery.

Mary Anne was reportedly well educated and often seen at important Virginia society functions. Many eligible bachelors frequently tried to court Mary Anne, but her streak of independence and sense of adventure kept her from committing to any of them. She was more attracted to rogues than to the "soft," less adventurous sons of wealthy families.

As a young lady, Townsend accompanied her un cle to Bermuda one summer. For him, it was a business trip, but for Mary Anne, it was an opportunity to remove herself from what she regarded as the dull and stifling environment of elite Virginia society. By the time Mary Anne turned 20, she stood at over six feet tall with a statuesque build and long, flaming red hair.

The trip to Bermuda would change Mary Anne's life forever, for it was on the way home from there that she met the infamous Blackbeard, when the pirate attacked and captured the ship on which she and her uncle were passengers.

While in Bermuda, the uncle had engaged in and completed several business transactions. With his negotiations completed, he and Mary Anne sailed away on the Shropshire Lass, bound for Virginia. The vessel had not been out of port for more than two hours when it was seized by Blackbeard and his band of fearsome pirates. While the crew of the Shropshire Lass fought valiantly, they were no match for the experienced brigands. Mary Anne watched in horror as the pirates overran the ship; yet at the same time, she was fascinated. In a short time, however, the crew of the Shropshire Lass was subdued and they, along with the passengers, were taken prisoner.

As Blackbeard walked among the captives, the stunning Mary Anne Townsend caught his attention. He beheld her exquisite beauty but was also struck by her poise and spirit as she held her head high and glared defiantly at any of the pirates who approached her. Such a woman no doubt would have appealed to Blackbeard.

On approaching Mary Anne, Blackbeard removed his hat, executed a deep bow, and introduced himself. He had her bonds removed and bade her to follow him. The pirate leader escorted Mary Anne to his cabin, placed her within, and returned to the other prisoners. After taking whatever goods of value from the Shropshire Lass, Blackbeard released all of the prisoners except for Mary Anne and sailed away. He had another cabin on the ship prepared for his new prisoner, and before the day was over had her moved into it. The room was furnished with hand-carved furniture and silk curtains. Blackbeard instructed the ship's cook to prepare meals at Mary Anne's request. He gave her gifts of gold, silver, jewels, and fine cloth, all taken during raids on ships and Atlantic coastal communities.

In the days that followed, Mary Anne Townsend followed Blackbeard everywhere as he went about his duties commanding the ship. It became clear to the other pirates that Blackbeard was courting the young lady. Following the passage of a few short weeks, according to legend, Blackbeard asked Mary Anne to marry him.

Mary Anne was intrigued by Blackbeard, but she was just as keen on exploring the opportunities for adventure that he presented. After giving his marriage proposal several days of concentrated thought, she finally agreed to his offer. Following a brief honeymoon, Townsend committed herself to a life of piracy and she began to accompany Blackbeard on his raids.

It took no time at all for Mary Anne Townsend to adapt to the life of a pirate on the high seas. She begged Blackbeard to teach her all that he knew, and she anticipated capturing treasure from merchant ships and coastal towns and villages. For his part, Blackbeard encouraged the willing Townsend and tutored her. After a year of participating in a number of raids, Townsend had more than proved herself a capable pirate and soon gained a reputation of being fearless and even dangerous. When she was convinced that she was ready, Mary Anne asked Blackbeard for a ship of her own to command. Always agreeable where she was concerned, Blackbeard gave her the Odyssey, an extremely swift vessel captured during an earlier attack.

With her reputation as a competent seafarer and a fearless fighter, Townsend had no trouble attracting a crew of her own, one composed of experienced sailors and fighters. In a short time, she was capturing and plundering ships throughout the Atlantic Ocean and the Caribbean Sea.

In addition to teaching her all he knew about piracy, Blackbeard introduced Townsend to the charms of Charleston, South Carolina, a port long favored by the pirate leader. It was reported that the two were often seen walking through the town arm-in-arm, going from tavern to tavern drinking ale and rum, and swapping tales with other pirates.

During one trip to Charleston, Blackbeard told Townsend about his treasure cache in the nearby tidal marsh and even offered to show it to her. On a number of occasions, the two were seen rowing out into the marsh. Many believe that Townsend was the only other person alive who had seen Blackbeard's fabulous treasure.

As Townsend accumulated treasure of her own during the ensuing months of raids, she, like Blackbeard, carried it back to Charleston and selected a secret location in the tidal marsh in which to hide it. Many estimate that she accumulated millions of dollars' worth of gold, silver, and jewels. Unlike Blackbeard, Townsend seldom entered the tidal marsh alone. Instead, she employed two stout sailors to row two boatloads of treasure at a time to her hiding place. It was rumored that, while Townsend and the two sailors were often seen entering the tidal marsh together, she always returned alone.

During one long season of raiding in the Caribbean Sea, Townsend received word that Blackbeard had been killed. Several weeks later, on arriving at the Jamaican port of Kingston, she learned that a fleet of privateers had sailed out of South Carolina and was in pursuit of her. A huge reward had been offered for Townsend - dead or alive.

Townsend realized that her life as a successful pirate was drawing to a close. Instead of returning to Charleston to retrieve her immense treasure, she set sail for South America, where she believed she would be safe from pursuit and capture. The only treasure she carried with her was what was stored in the hold of the Odyssey at the time.

For years, no one knew of Mary Anne Townsend's whereabouts. In time, however, rumors drifted northward, eventually arriving at Charleston. The most commonly related tale was that Townsend had arrived in Lima, Peru. There, it was said, she had married a wealthy Spanish landowner and businessman.

Residents of Charleston waited many years to learn something about Mary Anne Townsend, and they anticipated her return to claim the treasure she had hidden in the tidal marsh. As time passed and it became clear that this was not going to happen, the treasure was eventually forgotten.

100 years following Mary Anne Townsend's disappearance, some men began to arrive in Charleston to undertake a search for her treasure. Where and how they had learned of it is unknown, for most residents of Charleston were not aware of it by this time. The newcomers were warned of the hazards presented by the tidal marsh, but they were undeterred and ventured forth in the hope of locating and retrieving a vast fortune. Frustrated, they all returned empty-handed. Her treasure cache, potentially worth millions of dollars, still remains unclaimed somewhere in the tidal marsh.

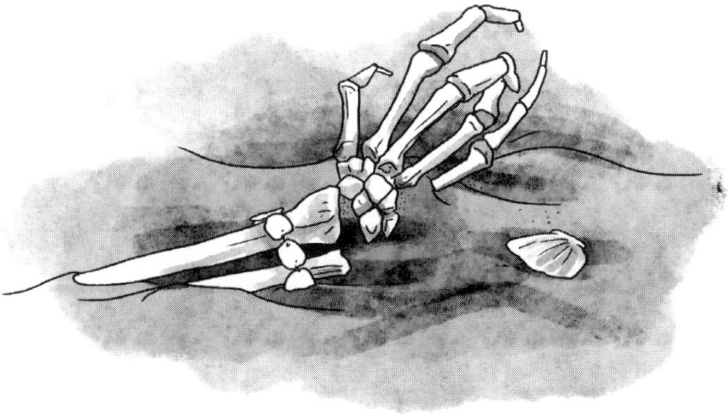

-21-

Blackbeard's Georgia Treasure

Realizing that he could not outrun the privateers and that it was only a matter of time before they caught up with him, Blackbeard instead chose to outwit them.

The tidal marshes in Charleston Bay and Ocracoke Island were not the only locations on which the pirate Blackbeard was reputed to have cached great amounts of treasure. As this most notorious freebooter sailed up and down the Atlantic coast, he became intimate with a number of locations and landscapes, some of which he deemed suitable for hiding more of his treasure. One such location was Ossabow Island, a low, swampy isle separated from the Georgia mainland by Bear River and the Florida Passage. Though less known than Blackbeard's other treasure caches, the one on Ossabow Island may be the largest of them all.

So much time has passed since the glory days of piracy along the Atlantic coast that concrete facts are sometimes hard to come by. What we have in abundance, however, are legend and folklore, stories that have been passed down over the generations, sometimes exaggerated, but almost always with a basis in truth. It may be argued that more legend and lore surround the pirate Blackbeard than any other pirate, and many of the tales focus on his buried treasures. The legend of hidden treasure on Ossabow Island falls into this category and the actual truth may never be known. The story, however, bears all of the earmarks of truth, and the treasure has attracted dozens of professional fortune hunters to the area over the decades.

As the tale goes, Blackbeard, in command of three ships and following a series of successful raids on several merchant vessels along the Carolina coast, eventually found himself in the position of being pursued by four privateers. The officers and crew of these well-armed ships, commanded by a corporation of businessmen and traders who had suffered significant losses to pirates, were paid an impressive amount of money to eliminate piracy in and around their preferred shipping lanes. The ships employed by the privateers went by the same name: They were swift, sleek, and capable of moving through the sea with sufficient speed to catch up to and engage the pirates.

Blackbeard, aware of the pursuit and the fact that the privateers were gaining on him and his fleet, initiated a tactic he believed would confuse them. He signaled for two of his ships to split off and set out in a southeasterly direction into the Atlantic waters while his ship continued southwestward following the South Carolina coastline. Two of the privateers followed the Atlantic-bound ships while the other two continued after Blackbeard.

Though Blackbeard's vessel was the fastest of his fleet, it was no match for the swift privateers that were closing in. In addition to being a much larger and heavier ship, Blackbeard's vessel was densely packed with booty taken during the raids. The hold of the ship was loaded with 15 wooden casks filled with gold and silver coins and ingots. The weight of these and other goods caused the ship to ride precariously low in the water.

Realizing that he could not outrun the privateers and that it was only a matter of time before they caught up with him, Blackbeard instead chose to outwit them. Blackbeard waited until two hours after sunset, when he was certain he would not be seen by privateers. As he was sailing along the northern part of the Georgia coastline, Blackbeard ordered his ship to be turned into Ossabow Sound, a shallow body of water that separated Pine Island from Ossabow Island. Deep into the sound, Blackbeard ordered that the sails be lowered. Unaware of the pirate's maneuver, the pursuing privateers sailed by, continuing along the Georgia coast.

The following morning, Blackbeard had the sails raised, and the ship headed toward Bradley Point, the northeastern tip of Ossabow Island. Blackbeard had anchored off Bradley Point in the past and had explored the island. He knew of a freshwater pond located 200 yards inland from the point, and as his ship was in need of fresh water, he decided to take the time to refill the barrels. After anchoring offshore, Blackbeard and a selected crew rowed to the island to obtain water.

As the crewmen carried the barrels to the pond, Blackbeard stood on the shore and regarded his ship. He was concerned about the weight it was transporting and how deep it lay in the water. Should he encounter the privateers again, he feared the great weight would slow him down such that he would be overtaken. At that point, the pirate decided it was in the best interest of survival if the treasure were offloaded from the ship and cached at Bradley Point.

With the help of several crewmen and two prisoners, 15 heavy casks, each filled with precious metals and coins, were lifted from the hull, loaded into several rowboats, and transported to shore. From there, according to the legend, they were carried to the highest point of the beach. As the sun was setting on this day, the two prisoners were put to work excavating a trench five feet deep and 20 feet long. When the trench was completed, the casks of treasure were rolled in, but before the excavation could be refilled, the two prisoners were shot and buried in the trench, along with the treasure. The next morning, Blackbeard's ship, considerably lighter, sailed out of Ossabow Sound in search of more merchant vessels to capture. According to research about the life and exploits of this famous and daring pirate, Blackbeard never returned to Ossabow Island to retrieve his treasure. In time, Blackbeard was killed in battle. The story of his treasure on Ossabow Island, however, lived on.

Ossabow Sound has long been a favored fishing destination for residents of nearby Savannah, Georgia. In

1957, two Savannah men were fishing in the sound when they decided to take a break and put in at Bradley Point. Cramped and stiff from sitting for four hours in their boat, they decided to stroll around and explore that part of the island. After two hours of hiking, they were returning along the beach to their boat when they encountered a skeleton that lay partially buried in the sand. Curious, the two fishermen brushed the sand away from the remains and in the process, found another skeleton.

The two fishermen decided that they had accidentally stumbled onto an Indian gravesite. Thy began to search for artifacts but found nothing. As it was getting late in the day, they pushed sand back atop the skeletons and returned to their boat.

Several months later, the two fishermen related their discovery of the two skeletons to an acquaintance who, in turn, told it to another. In a short time, the story made the rounds and found its way to a historian who was steeped in Atlantic Coast pirate lore. The historian immediately connected the two skeletons to the tale of Blackbeard's buried treasure. If the tale was true, the immense treasure of gold and silver-filled casks lay in the ground only a short distance beneath the bones.

Within a few weeks, the historian arranged to be taken by boat from Savannah Harbor to Ossabow Island. After landing at Bradley Point, he undertook a search for the site where the two skeletons were found, based on third-hand descriptions he had obtained from others. Though he explored, as he said, every inch of Bradley Point, he was unable to find them. During an interview with a Savannah newspaper, the historian explained that storm winds and waves continue to modify beach landscapes over the years, and the possibility was great that the bones and treasure had been either covered up by more sand or carried away completely.

Given the weight of the treasure-filled casks, the possibility that they might have been carried away by wave action is not likely. What is more probable is that the casks are still there, still buried under a few feet of beach sand at Bradley Point, Ossabow Island, Georgia.

-22-

Pirate Louis Michel-Aury and the Amelia Island Treasure Cache

Amelia Island has, on occasion, given up her treasures to the fortunate who chance upon them.

Louis Michel-Aury was born in Paris, France in 1787 to a family of fishermen. Growing up in poverty, the young man had been fascinated by the sea. He longed to board a ship and explore the world's oceans. (Some accounts have his name as Louis d'Aury, and others have his birthplace listed as Calais, France.) When he was 15 years old, Michel-Aury obtained passage on a trading ship that crisscrossed the Atlantic Ocean and visited a number of ports along the eastern seaboard of the United States. During the early nineteenth century, he served in the French navy as a sailor on a ship stationed primarily in the West Indies, but in 1802, his career shifted – he began serving on a French privateer throughout much of the Gulf of Mexico and the Caribbean Sea. By 1810, he was commanding his own ship.

During the early 1800s, the Spanish colonies in South America were fighting for their independence from Spanish rule, and Michel-Aury decided to side with them. He sailed to the region and engaged in attacking Spanish ships. He was subsequently commissioned as a commodore in the navy of New Granada (now Colombia). In 1815, Michel-Aury's ships ran a Spanish blockade and assisted in evacuating hundreds of people from the war-torn city of Cartagena.

Later, Michel-Aury accepted an appointment as "resident commissioner" of Galveston Island, Texas by the Republic of Mexico. Mexico had declared Galveston Island as a Mexican port. In 1816, Michel-Aury established a privateering base on the island. It was here, many believe, that Michel-Aury buried a chest containing an estimated $60,000 worth of gold coins.

Michel-Aury sailed from Galveston Island on April 6, 1817 to assist Mexican officials in defending a town that had been threatened by the Spanish. While he was away, the noted pirate Jean Lafitte arrived at Galveston Island and took control of it. A number of researchers believe that Michel-Aury and Lafitte were acquainted and that Aury may have once served as a member of his crew, participating in several raids on merchant vessels, but this has never been substantiated. In any case, when

Michel-Aury returned, he saw that he would be unable to wrest the island from Lafitte, so he made an attempt to establish another station at Matagorda Bay, a Texas port approximately 100 miles to the southwest. However, his attempt was unsuccessful, and he left the area in 1817.

Time passed, and Michel-Aury aligned himself with a Scotsman, Gregor McGregor, who had been commissioned by a number of South American countries to assist in fighting the Spaniards. Together, they attacked a Spanish contingent at Amelia Island, Florida. Then on September 12, 1817, the Republic of Mexico annexed Amelia Island. On December 23, 1817, Michel-Aury surrendered the island to U.S. forces under the command of Captain J. E. Henry.

When he arrived at Amelia Island, Henry found Michel-Aury in residence and ordered him to vacate in 24 hours. Out-manned and out-armed, Michel-Aury had little choice but to pack up and leave. As Michel-Aury and his crew hastily gathered their belongings and loaded them onto the ships, Henry's troopers watched them closely. As a result, there was no opportunity to dig up the treasure chest. Michel-Aury decided he would return to the island another time to retrieve it.

Captain Henry had somehow learned about the caching of Michel-Aury's treasure on Amelia Island, and as soon as the privateer disappeared over the horizon on his way to the Caribbean, Henry ordered a search for it. He never found it. While historians disagree on the ultimate fate of Louis Michel-Aury, it remains a fact that he never returned to Amelia Island.

Today, Amelia Island, located in the northeastern corner of Florida, is a popular resort area and tourist destination. Few vacationers to the island are aware that it was at one time a favored destination for pirates and other seafarers, who had used it as a hiding place. In addition, many of them, like Michele-Aury, buried treasure on the island.

In 1748, the Spanish vessel Halcon, transporting a shipment of gold and silver coins, sank in the nearby waters of Nassau Sound. In recent years, the sunken ship has been located, but archeologists state that it is almost completely covered with sand and silt and that the costs of removing the debris are expensive. In 1795, another Spanish ship, the Santa Barbara, was carrying several kegs of gold coins when it sank within two miles of Amelia Island. Its location has never been determined.

Documents record the sinking of the British ship Betsey a short distance off the eastern shore of Amelia Island in 1812. The same documents reveal that the ship was carrying $10,000 worth of gold coins. If the gold coins were found today, they would be worth considerably more.

The Nicholas Adolph, a Swedish merchant vessel, went down in shallow water not far from the island's north shore. The ship was carrying a safe filled with money intended to purchase sugar in the Caribbean Islands. The wreck of the ship has been found, but the safe has yet to be located.

At the northern end of Amelia Island is what today is known as Fort Clinch State Park. Not far from old Fort Clinch is Egan's Creek. During the 1890s, three men sailing a small schooner arrived in the nearby harbor and dropped anchor. The following morning, they came onto the island carrying shovels. When asked by the locals what they were up to, the men explained that they were searching for buried pirate treasure. One of the newcomers possessed a map, which he referred to on occasion.

For more than a week, the trio explored that part of the island. During that time, one of them died. Area residents insisted the circumstances were mysterious, but no one launched an inquiry. The dead man was buried, and the others wasted no time in continuing on with their search, which was now concentrated near Egan's Creek. Curious observers, who often followed the men on their explorations, claimed that the two would walk no more than 20 paces before stopping to consult a map. This was repeated many times.

The map proved to be accurate. After arriving at a certain point, the two men bent to the task of excavating a deep hole. Two hours after they started, they pulled from the hole a heavy wooden chest. On opening it, they reportedly discovered $170,000 worth of gold coins, along with jewelry studded with pearls and emeralds. Within hours, the two transported their newfound fortune to their schooner and sailed away.

In 1920, a man walking along the beach near the town of Fernandina came across a metal pot partially buried in the sand. It was filled to the top with silver coins bearing eighteenth-century dates, and in 1922, two children playing in a grassy field above the beach found several gold coins, all dated in the 1700s. When the owner of the field was notified of the discovery, he excavated several holes near where the children found the coins. He eventually recovered over $20,000 dollars worth of coins. Then, in 1923, two men found a cache of 400 gold coins on the beach near Fernandina. The coins were dated from the mid-1500s and originated in England, France, and Spain.

In addition to the buried treasures located on the island as well as those associated with sunken ships, every year the beaches of Amelia Island continue to yield coins and a variety of artifacts. Following severe storms, hobbyists with metal detectors descend on the beaches in hopes of finding items washed up by the surging waves and currents. Over the decades, hundreds of thousands of dollars' worth of coins have been found. Amelia Island has, on occasion, given up her treasures to the fortunate who chance upon them, but Louis Michel-Aury's cache of gold coins remains undiscovered, elusive to the treasure hunters.

Louis Michel-Aury was not the only pirate attracted to Amelia Island. During the era of pirates in North America, many pirates, whose identities remain unknown to this day, visited the island. A favorite refuge on the island was at the extreme northeastern tip. Today, the location is known as Fort Clinch and is a Florida State Park. Evidence for pirate habitation has been found in the form of buried treasure and period artifacts.

Construction of Fort Clinch began in 1847, but prior to that time, primarily fishermen and explorers favored the island. This location saw the establishment of a number of campsites over a number of generations, and recovered artifacts provide evidence of occupation by Indians, French, Spanish, and English. In 1861, Confederates took over the fort from the Union forces, but in 1862, Union troops took it back by launching a combined land and sea raid.

In 1932, two men, lured by tales of buried treasure at Fort Clinch, visited the island. After spending several days searching, they discovered and retrieved a cache of over 400 gold coins that had been buried between the fort and the old nearby town. The coins had dates from the 1500s, and consisted of pieces from France, England, and Spain. Most who have examined the coins agree that they likely represent money that was taken during pirate raids.

Another tale of pirate treasure on Amelia Island identifies the cache site near a point where the Amelia and Nassau Rivers come together. One morning in 1950, two strangers arrived at this location. Like the trio of men who came in the 1890s, these newcomers were in possession of a map. The map indicated that a great treasure, buried long ago by pirates, lay at the base of a very old oak tree. Because they were unfamiliar with the island, the strangers enlisted the help of a resident named Booth.

After swearing Booth to secrecy, the two men showed him the map in the hope that he could decipher it and locate pertinent landmarks. They allowed him to study it closely. A short time later, the three undertook a hike to the alleged location of the buried treasure. At this point, some difficulties ensued. The two strangers seemed reluctant to heed Booth's suggestions regarding critical landmarks and directions. After what seemed like days searching and retracing their steps, no treasure was found. The two men, discouraged, folded their map and departed the island, never to be seen again.

Booth, however, was able to recall the specific details of the map. After the two men left the island, he obtained paper and pen and reconstructed the map from memory. If Booth ever located any treasure, he never told anyone. Within only a few weeks of the departure of the two strangers, however, Booth mysteriously came into a great deal of money. Booth left Amelia Island and was never seen again.

-23-

More Treasures of Louis Michel-Aury

The Mexicans were providing Michel-Aury with a license to steal. He accepted the offer.

Aside from the buried treasure he was forced to leave behind on Amelia Island, Louis Michel-Aury was known to have multiple caches elsewhere. Once such cache was a buried hoard estimated to be worth $14 million at a location near Clearwater Bay, and another large cache lay buried on a little-known mass of land called Anclote Key.

At one time, Michel-Aury commanded a pirate vessel belonging to the noted brigand Jean Lafitte. Michel-Aury conducted a number of successful raids on Gulf Coast villages and merchant ships, and in the process, accumulated several wooden chests filled with gold and silver. Following one series of successful raids, Michel-Aury noted his ship was running short of fresh water, so he dropped anchor in Clearwater Bay on the west coast of Florida. The bay was named after a freshwater spring that flowed from a small bluff above the beach. While taking on water, Michel-Aury decided this location was a fine place to bury his treasure chests. Selecting a location not far from the spring, he supervised the caching of 11 treasure-filled chests.

The consensus of pirate historians who have studied Michel-Aury claim he never returned to Clearwater Bay to retrieve his treasure. There exists a story, however, that at least one of the chests was found.

After the end of the Civil War, it was a few years before boiling tensions between the North and South subsided. During the early 1870s, a retired sea captain named Benjamin Roberts moved to the settlement of Clearwater on Florida's west coast. He intended to spend the remainder of his years in the peaceful environs of this coastal town. Roberts was not a wealthy man, but during his time at sea, he had accumulated a sufficient amount of money to get by on, if he was frugal enough.

It was said that Roberts spent his mornings exploring the location of Clearwater Spring, a place where he liked to hike. Those who saw him, however, suggested that he always seemed to be searching for something. Others claimed the old man always carried a map with him on these morning walks, and that he would pause from time to time to consult it.

One day, much to the surprise of his neighbors, Roberts came into possession of a quantity of gold coins, which he used to pay his bills and improve his standard of living. In 1882, he passed away, and when relatives went through his belongings, they found six leather bags filled with more gold coins, all dated from the early nineteenth century. When word of this find spread throughout Clearwater, most citizens were convinced that Roberts had found at least one of Michel-Aury's treasure chests.

At one point in his pirate career, Michel-Aury established a headquarters at Anclote Key, an island located in the Gulf of Mexico near the present-day town of Tarpon Springs. This location soon attracted other pirates to the area, and over time, Michel-Aury built a hotel, a tavern, and a mercantile. As he continued to experience success with his raiding and plundering, Michel-Aury constructed two warehouses in which to store his accumulating booty, which included not only treasure in the form of gold, silver, jewelry, and precious stones, but also cloth, silk, spices, tools, and rum. Much of the accumulated merchandise was shipped to New Orleans, Louisiana, and Havana, Cuba, where it was sold or traded. The notorious pirate Captain William Kidd reportedly purchased a significant percentage of Michel-Aury's stolen goods, which he, in turn, sold in New Orleans.

While Michel-Aury maintained his headquarters at Anclote Key, he was said to have buried more of his treasure at a location on the bank of the Anclote River. Reputedly, he also buried some on Honeymoon Island, located a few miles to the south on tiny Seahorse Key. Over the years, treasure hunters have arrived in this area in search of Michel-Aury's caches, but as far as anyone knows, they have come away with only a handful of coins found on the beach near the pirate's old headquarters.

While Michel-Aury was living on Anclote Key, he received a visit from a Mexican emissary* representing an official named Arturo Valdez. The emissary explained that the government of Mexico was in the process of declaring independence from Spain. One advantage Spain had that Mexico did not have was a navy. The emissary offered Michel-Aury the position of commander of the fleet of the Mexican Republic and waging war on the country's enemies. In essence, Michel-Aury was officially granted permission to prey on Spanish ships. In return, he was to deliver a percentage of the plunder to the Mexican government but was allowed to keep a huge share for himself and his men. When the separation of Mexico from Spain was completed, Michel-Aury was to be given the title of Military Governor of the Province of Texas. In effect, the Mexican government provided Michel-Aury with a license to steal, and he gladly accepted the offer.

Michel-Aury was now more anxious than ever to return to the sea and conduct his raids on Spanish vessels. In a hurry to abandon his Anclote Key headquarters, he buried two more gold- and silver-filled treasure chests at the northern end of the island. He then sailed his fleet of ships westward to Galveston Island, Texas, where he established a new headquarters.

From this new location, Michel-Aury's success improved far beyond his expectations. So abundant were the opportunities to seize and plunder Spanish vessels that the pirate found himself filling even more chests with treasure. These were buried on Galveston Island's beaches. Other confiscated cargo was transported to New Orleans to trade with Lafitte. Several of the Spanish ships seized by Michel-Aury became part of his own pirate fleet, which flew the flag of Mexico. Michel-Aury invited the captured Spanish seamen to become part of his crew. Those who joined were treated fairly and shared in the rewards, and those who refused were put to the sword.

In 1817, Michel-Aury formed an alliance with a mercenary soldier who, with his force of 200 men, had been hired by the Mexican government to conduct an invasion to end Spanish rule in one particular area. Michel-Aury contributed a number of his crewmen to assist the force. By the time the fighting was over, the invasion had been successful, and Michel-Aury and the mercenary set about to divide the spoils. A disagreement ensued, and the pirate decided to return his men to the ships and depart for Galveston. As it turned out, Michel-Aury left Mexico just in time – a counterstrike commanded by the Spanish forces captured the mercenary a short time later and executed him.

On returning to Galveston Island in 1818, Michel-Aury was faced with a surprise. While he was away in Mexico, his old friend and one-time fellow pirate Jean Lafitte, finding the island headquarters deserted, took possession of it. When Michel-Aury arrived at the island, Lafitte refused to return it to him. Instead, he had dozens of cannons aimed at Michel-Aury's ships. Lafitte commanded his old friend to leave the area immediately. Seeing that he was clearly out-numbered and out-gunned, Michel-Aury gathered his fleet and departed. However, Michel-Aury was more bothered by the fact that he was forced to leave his buried treasures.

Michel-Aury quickly returned to attacking and capturing merchant vessels that he encountered along the coasts of Florida, eventually arriving at Amelia Island, where he would establish yet another headquarters and cache even more treasure.

-24-

The Adventures of Billy Bowlegs

Most of the pirates prowling the Atlantic Ocean and Gulf of Mexico avoided the escorted and plated ships. Bowles, however, viewed them as a challenge, and attacked them with impunity.

Many people debate the identity of pirate Billy Bowlegs, and in the end, very few facts have been determined. One account claims that William Rogers in England was Billy Bowlegs and that he was of noble blood. According to this story, Rogers was forced to flee England because he was caught in a series of crooked business deals. Another story identifies William Augustus Bowles from Fredericksburg, Maryland as pirate Billy Bowlegs.

This tale describes Bowles as a "charismatic, egotistical schemer." Odd as it may seem, there is evidence to suggest that both of these men, Rogers and Bowles, went by the nickname "Billy Bowlegs."

The nickname may have come from a Seminole Indian chief named Holata Micco. The English who entered this area called Holata "Billy Bolek," for unknown reasons. "Bolek" became "Bowlegs" over time. He died in 1858. Not long after his death, another Seminole – Sonuk Micco – took the name "Billy Bowlegs" for himself. He enlisted in the U.S. Army during the Civil War and rose to the rank of Captain.

Then, in 1862, Billy Fewell, the son of a black father and a Seminole mother, was born. As a young adult, he adopted the name "Billy Bowlegs." He became a prominent Seminole historian and passed away at 103 years of age.

At the age of 13, William Augustus Bowles joined the Maryland Loyalist Battalion, where he was promoted to the rank of lieutenant and sent to Pensacola, Florida as part of a garrison reinforcement. Upon arrival, Bowles resigned his commission, left the protection of the fort, and was later captured by the Creek Indians.

While Bowles was living with the Creeks, Spanish naval forces began attacking British forts along the coast of the Gulf of Mexico. Bowles somehow convinced the Indians to rally behind the British garrison at Pensacola and fight the Spaniards. The year was 1781, and Bowles was 17 years old. The heavy armament of the Spanish proved too overwhelming for the British forces, and the garrison fell. Survivors were captured, but Bowles fled into the wilderness with his Creek allies.

A short time later, Bowles re-enlisted with the British army and was sent to the Bahamas. After a few months there, the British Governor, Lord Dunmore, sent Bowles back to Florida to live among the Creeks and establish a trading center. He did so, and in the process, took two wives – one Cherokee and the other Muskogee. Bowles self-titled his position as "Director General of the Muskogee Nation." Soon afterward, Bowles formed an army and began to lead raids into Spanish territories in Florida. In 1800, he declared war on Spain. By then, he commanded two ships with a total crew of 400 sailors and fighting men.

Spain offered a reward of $6,000 and 1,500 kegs of rum for the capture of Bowles. He was eventually captured and sent to Spain, where King Carlos IV tried to convince him to join the Spanish Army. Bowles declined, escaped, commandeered a ship and then returned to the Gulf of Mexico. Following a period of raids on merchant ships, Bowlegs accumulated enough money to purchase a plantation where he would grow sugar cane, located 75 miles north of Crescent City, Florida. Bowles refused to reveal information regarding his origins to any of his neighbors.

Growing tired of farming, Bowles soon found himself doing business with two familiar brothers: Jean and Pierre Lafitte. The Lafitte brothers made significant profits fencing* stolen goods that were plundered by themselves and other pirates. Jean Lafitte had his own fleet of pirate ships and raided across the Gulf of Mexico and the Atlantic Coast. Bowles decided to join the two brigands. After a time of successful pillaging, Bowles decided to go out on his own and built his own fleet. He was very successful, and in time, accumulated shiploads of goods as well as chests filled with treasure. Bowles concentrated on attacking and pillaging Spanish ships. He learned early in his pirate career that the Spanish vessels transported more gold and silver than the French, British, or American ships.

The Spanish ships were often commissioned to transport gold from Mexico and South America across the Atlantic to Spain. They were referred to as "plate ships," so named because they were plated with sheets of metal that served as armor and were often escorted by one or more armed frigates* to guard against pirate attacks.

Most of the pirates prowling the Atlantic Ocean and Gulf of Mexico avoided the escorted and plated ships. Bowles, however, viewed them as a challenge and attacked them with impunity. Every ship that Bowles seized and plundered was either burned or scuttled after all of the crewmen were slain. The pirate didn't want any survivors to return to shore and incriminate him for his deeds.

Along the way, Bowles acquired the name Charlie Bowlegs and was referred to by that nickname for the rest of his life, and it wasn't long before no one could remember Bowles's real name. Over the years, pirate researchers and enthusiasts mistakenly referred to Charlie Bowlegs as Billy Bowlegs, who turned out to be a different pirate altogether.

As Bowles (Charlie Bowlegs) and his officers and crew grew older, the work of running ships and fighting became too much for them. Bowles decided to retire. After two years of idleness, however, he began to miss the thrill and adventure of piracy. He reassembled several of his comrades, recruited some new crewmen, and returned to attacking and plundering ships. Along the way, Bowles filled more chests with treasure and cached them at different locations along the Gulf Coast. The one that he is most often associated with is a shipload of gold that went down in the shallow waters of Choctawhatchee Bay near the present-day town of Destin in the Florida Panhandle.

Earlier, Bowles had traveled to the Yucatan Peninsula in Mexico and robbed a pack train, along with a number of cargo wagons, of an immense fortune in gold. This story relates that Bowles had gathered so much gold – tons of it, it has been estimated – that he was forced to toss his cannons overboard to allow for easier transportation of the loot.

In 1803, Bowles attended a tribal council and declared himself "Chief of All Indians Present." He was eventually betrayed, captured, and handed over to the Spanish. He was imprisoned in Havana, Cuba, where he died in 1803 following an extended hunger strike.

In the meantime, the pirate referred to as "Billy Bowlegs," William Rogers, was having great success attacking and plundering Spanish merchant vessels and filling the holds of his ships with booty, including several chests containing gold, silver, and jewelry. Rogers was referred to as "Billy Bowlegs" because he allegedly resembled the Seminole chief, Holata Micco, who had gone by that name in earlier years. Rogers had been successful in eluding the warships patrolling the Atlantic, but as he was heading for one of his favored hideouts, bad luck finally caught up with him.

On returning to his hideout at Choctawhatchee Bay, Bowlegs encountered a severe storm. While he was fighting strong winds and high seas, he spotted a heavily armed British Man-of-War* that had taken up pursuit of the pirate vessel. Since Bowlegs had no cannons, he was defenseless. With his options limited, he attempted to outrun his pursuers.

By the time Bowlegs reached the Florida coast and the location of Camp Walton near Choctawhatchee Bay, the British, fighting the rough seas, were almost upon him. The pirate steered his vessel, the Mysterio, through East Pass and into the calmer, shallow bay, knowing that the hull of the British ship was too deep to pursue. As he sheltered in the bay, Bowlegs decided he would wait there until the British grew frustrated and sailed away.

Much to the pirate's surprise, the commander of the British ship ordered longboats lowered and filled them with marines who continued the pursuit. Fearful that the British would confiscate his treasure, Bowlegs sailed his ship as close to Alaqua Bayou as he could and then abandoned it in the shallow water. When the waters were up to the deck of the sinking ship, Bowlegs ordered the masts to be sawed off so that the vessel would be totally submerged and not easily located. As the masts were being removed, Bowlegs had four cypress chests that were filled with gold and silver coins and jewels brought up from the hold, placed in rowboats, and transported to the shore. As Bowlegs and his crew rowed to safety, the ship containing the bulk of his Mexican treasure settled onto the sands below.

A few moments later, the pirates stood along the shore and watched as the marines turned the longboats around and returned to the Man-of-War. When he was convinced that they were no longer being observed, Bowlegs decided to leave his crew at the location to guard the treasure while he set out overland to New Orleans, where he hoped to obtain another ship and return with the equipment to retrieve the treasure that had gone down with the ship.

Bowlegs arrived back at Choctawhatchee Bay a few weeks later in a small schooner. He brought along some diving equipment to assist in the recovery of the treasure. He also brought his wife and children. When Bowlegs arrived on shore, he discovered all but four of the crewmen he left near the bayou to guard the treasure had died of fever or were killed during an Indian attack. The four survivors were weak, sickly, and in no condition to dive for the treasure.

Bowlegs had a rude cabin constructed nearby. He was determined to wait for his men to recover from their sickness before undertaking a recovery operation. When they were well, Bowlegs intended to recruit others to assist him in bringing the treasure up from the bottom of the bay. A few weeks later, however, a fever struck the area again, this time claiming additional crewmembers as well as Bowlegs's wife. Discouraged, the old pirate began to lose interest in the sunken treasure, believing it was cursed.

Years passed, and Bowlegs built a more substantial house not far from the point where the Mysterio sank. In time, Bowlegs was the only man left alive who knew the location of the scuttled treasure ship, as well as the four buried cypress chests filled with coins and jewels.

Bowlegs's children, having grown weary of living

close to the edge of poverty, once approached the ex-pirate and requested that he inform them of the locations of the buried treasures. Bowlegs refused, flew into a rage, and chased them way. For the rest of his life, he never revealed to them any of the secret locations of his buried caches.

For 48 years, Bowlegs lived more or less as a pauper*, even though he was only a short distance from several treasures. Before he died at 93 years of age in 1888, he provided information on the location of the treasure ship, as well as where the four chests were buried, to a close friend and neighbor, a man named Moses Hudson.

A few months after Bowlegs died, Hudson found the sunken ship. Unable to salvage the treasure by himself, he hired seven men to assist in the recovery. As the hired hands were working at trying to bring the gold and silver up from the sunken ship, Hudson, in a moment of poor judgment, revealed to them the locations of the four cypress chests and indicated he also needed their help to dig up the treasure. The far-too-trusting Hudson was double-crossed in a matter of days. The men dug up the chests and fled, leaving not a single coin for Hudson.

The deception caused Hudson to be more cautious. As a result, he never revealed the location of the sunken ship to anyone ever again. For years, he kept the secret to himself. One day, however, he revealed the location to his son, Edward. Edward, along with a friend, attempted to recover the treasure but had little luck. They were able to locate only a few loose gold coins in the area of the wreck, but the main treasure eluded them.

With the passage of more time, the story of Billy Bowlegs's sunken treasure ship made the rounds throughout much of Florida. Strangers arrived in the area of Choctawhatchee Bay from time to time to try to locate the sunken ship. One of the arrivals, with a keen interest in recovering the pirate treasure, was a retired physician named H. H. Humphreys. Humphreys spent weeks exploring various parts of the bay. With the aid of a Texas oil field engineer, Humphreys constructed a dam and partially drained the bay. At a point where Alaqua Creek formed a bayou that entered the bay, he found what he was convinced were the remains of the Mysterio.

The partially rotted vessel was 75 feet long and held together with wooden pegs. Parts of the stern were visible, but the remainder of the ship was buried under 20 feet of silt. Humphreys's state-of-the-art metal detecting equipment found evidence of dense metal beneath the silts, but nothing was ever recovered save for an anchor chain. Given the rather basic equipment available during that time, removing the silt and sand from the bulk of the wreck proved to be an overwhelming task.

Dedicated research over the years leaves little doubt that the pirate Billy Bowlegs sunk his ship, the Mysterio, with what is estimated to be in excess of $65 million worth of gold aboard. The remains of the ship have been found at a point in Choctawhatchee Bay where Alaqua Creek drains into it. It is possible that with the employment of modern salvage and recovery equipment, the pirate's long lost treasure could be recovered. It would require a significant investment in time, energy, and money to do so, but finding a quantity of gold that large would make the effort worthwhile. Currently, a recovery group has solicited investors to fund such a project.

Other treasures cached by Billy Bowlegs have

proven more accessible. It has long been rumored that when the pirate was buried, he secretly had a large portion of his treasure buried with him. Late one night in 1901, William Lee and Alex Moore made their way to the secluded gravesite. After riding their horses through miles of rough terrain and thick undergrowth, they attacked the grave with shovels. The wet soil made digging easy, and in a short time, the two men lifted two iron cooking pots out of the grave. Each of the pots was filled to the top with gold and silver coins. The coins were estimated to be worth $80,000 in 1901 values.

Several months later, another man traveled to Bowlegs's gravesite in search of more treasure. Acting on a lead, he chopped into a tree located only a few steps from the grave. After breaking into a cavity in the tree, he stepped back and watched as a number of silver coins spilled out onto the ground.

Other Florida sites have served as caches of Billy Bowlegs's treasure. One particularly large hoard, estimated by some to be worth close to $5 million, was buried on the beach near the old town of Franklin in Franklin County, located in the Panhandle. Many believe that Bowlegs buried at least one wooden chest filled with gold and silver coins on the north side of Santa Rosa Island, located near Pensacola. Yet another treasure site is a place called Bald Point near Alligator Harbor, east of Apalachee Bay.

According to legend, a secret cave is located beneath the old Spanish bastion* at Fort San Carlos. In this cave, Bowlegs allegedly hid more than $3 million in gold and silver plundered from Spanish vessels.

Now and then, someone claims to have found one

of Billy Bowlegs's buried treasure caches. The biggest one, however, the one worth tens of millions of dollars and lying deep in the mud of Choctawhatchee Bay, continues to elude the searchers. Perhaps one day the bay will yield its treasure to an enterprising and fortunate treasure hunter.

Now and then, portions of what some claim to be one of Bowlegs's treasures have been found at a number of different Gulf Coastal locations. Markings on the coins indicate they were plundered from Spanish vessels around the time Bowlegs was active. What has been found represents only a tiny fraction of the total treasures buried by Bowlegs. It is likely no exaggeration that hundreds of millions of dollars' worth of treasure remain hidden in shallow caches in a number of locations along Florida's coast.

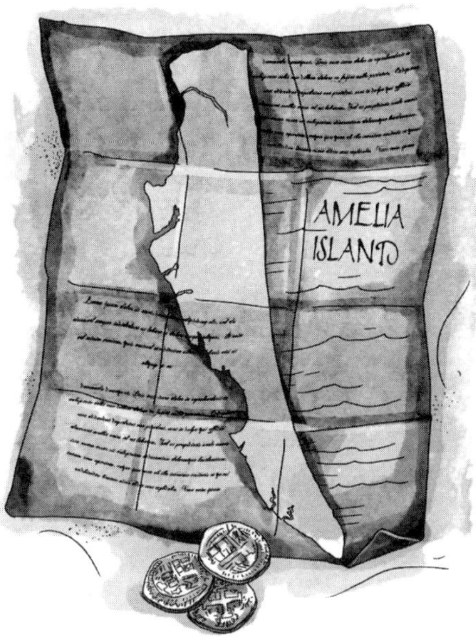

-25-

Gasparilla

"Gasparilla dies by his own hand, not the enemy's!"

Of all the pirates who roamed the coastlines of the Gulf of Mexico, one of the most mysterious is Jose Gaspar. Known as Gasparilla, this pirate's career is so clouded with myth and legend, along with the absence of any legitimate archival evidence, that some have suggested that he never existed at all. Furthermore, the so-called details of Gasparilla's life and adventures vary widely from publication to publication.

For example, one version has him being born in Spain in 1756. As a youth, he allegedly kidnapped a girl and held her for ransom. When he was caught, he was given the choice of serving an extended time in prison or joining the Spanish Navy. He chose to go to sea. According to this tale, Gaspar served with distinction, proving to be a competent seaman and fighter until 1783, when he led a mutiny against an abusive captain and fled to Florida where he turned to piracy.

Another version has Gaspar being born into a family of nobility, rising to a high rank in the Spanish Navy, and serving as an advisor to King Charles III. He was allegedly charged with stealing the crown jewels. When faced with arrest for this crime, he decided to flee.

A third version describes Gaspar as having a wife and child. While he was serving as a court advisor, the queen attempted to seduce him. When he refused her advances, she was insulted and in retribution had his wife and child, along with his mother, killed.

Whichever is true, if any, Gaspar, with the help of friends, stormed a nearby prison, killed the guards, and released all of the prisoners. With the newly freed men, he organized a ship's crew. The following week, Gaspar commandeered one of the king's warships and sailed away to Florida. His mind was filled with revenge, and he satisfied himself by preying on Spanish merchant vessels.

Gaspar established a base of operations on what is known today as Gasparilla Island. From this location, he ventured out and attacked Spanish ships. The captains and crew of these vessels feared him, for they knew that, should Gasparilla succeed in capturing a ship, all would be put to death. In the process of plundering these ships, on those occasions when Gasparilla encountered women, he captured them and relocated them to his headquarters at Gasparilla Island or to another called Captiva Island, where they were forced to serve as concubines for his crew. A few were held for ransom. Over the months of successful raids, Gasparilla accumulated a fortune in gold and silver coins and ingots as well as precious stones and jewelry.

Gasparilla's adventures were considerably more hazardous and difficult than those of the pirates who had come before him decades earlier. When Gasparilla practiced piracy in the late 1700s, it was very common for warships flying the flags of England, Spain, France, and the United States to hunt down pirate vessels. A number of pirate strongholds along the Atlantic and Gulf coasts, as well as in the Caribbean Islands, were attacked and cleaned out one by one. These bases of operations were important to the pirates. From there, they often obtained supplies and disposed of much of the loot and merchandise they captured. Furthermore, these were locations where the pirates could rest and see to the repairs and maintenance required for their ships.

Gasparilla chose to operate one such base on the west coast of the Florida mainland, at the time a Spanish territory. The warships seldom visited this location, now known as Charlotte Harbor near Port Charlotte and Fort Myers, and it afforded a sheltered location with a deep-water harbor. The entrance to the harbor was hidden from all but the most experienced sailors. It was also easy to defend, should the need arise.

At this location, Gasparilla founded a town called Alta Puebla. It was located at the end of a long, narrow peninsula and at the entrance to the harbor. Today, it is known as Boca Grande. Here, Gasparilla relocated his headquarters, often shared with other sea-going cutthroats, including Caesar LeGrande (known as Black Caesar) and Brewster Baker (known as Brubaker), as well as others. This loosely organized band of pirates referred to themselves as "The Brotherhood of the Seas" and often conducted raids together, always with Gasparilla in command.

For years, Gasparilla and his companions ranged out from the stronghold to raid and plunder, attacking ships, sacking and looting coastal towns, and occasionally taking prisoners they held for ransom. While any and all merchant vessels were considered fair game for the pirate, Gasparilla took great pleasure in seizing ships belonging to Spain.

In time, Gasparilla and his gang established trading centers along the coast and on a few islands, where they dealt goods to mainland merchants. They even carried merchandise and contraband to larger cities such as New Orleans.

In 1819, the United States acquired Florida from Spain. One of the first major decisions made regarding this new territory was to rid the region of pirates once and for all. The federal government established the United States Revenue Service (USRS), a forerunner to the Coast Guard. The USRS operated in conjunction with the U.S. Navy, and armed ships were occasionally sent out to eliminate the pirate menace from the Gulf of Mexico. A fleet under the command of Commodore David Porter was ordered to capture or kill all pirate crews they encountered.

Gasparilla learned of the approaching USRS warships and realized he was about to be out-numbered and out-gunned. He decided he did not want to tangle with the federals. Instead, he decided it was time to depart from Charlotte Harbor and find a better location from which to conduct his piratical operations. He considered Central or South America. In the time he had before sailing away, the pirate leader converted all of his wealth into gold coins and jewels and had them loaded aboard his ship, the Gasparilla. His treasure was estimated to be worth well over $1 million at the time, an immense fortune.

As he was preparing the flagship for departure, one of his crewmembers informed him that a ship was positioned just outside the entrance to the harbor at Boca Grande Pass. After examining the ship through his telescope, Gasparilla decided it was a trading vessel and that he would seize it, along with whatever goods and treasure it carried, before leaving the area.

Unknown to the pirate leader, the ship was the U.S.S. Enterprise, camouflaged to look like a merchant vessel. As the Gasparilla closed in on the stationary ship, Commodore Porter had his cannons brought to the fore and ordered bombardment. Too late, Gasparilla realized his mistake. In less than five minutes, the pirate ship was riddled with cannon shot and already sinking onto the bottom sands at the mouth of Boca Grande Pass.

Today, researchers debate about what really happened to the Gasparilla. While most maintain that the vessel was destroyed by cannon fire, there are those who insist that the pirate leader himself set fire to the ship so that his treasure could not be seized. There exists additional controversy over the manner in which Gasparilla died. Many claim that he simply went down with his ship, but there are those who defend a version in which Gasparilla wrapped himself in a length of anchor chain and jumped overboard to his death. As he jumped from the bow, he is reputed to have screamed, "Gasparilla dies by his own hand, not the enemy's!" The latter makes for a more dramatic ending and certainly fits the colorful life of the pirate.

The members of the ship's crew who did not drown managed to swim to nearby La Costa Island on the south side of the pass. Most were captured or killed by the troopers aboard the U.S.S. Enterprise. Those who were captured were subsequently hanged. Those who managed to escape from the federals were the source of the stories related to Gasparilla's suicide.

Although the location the Gasparilla's remains is known, aside from a handful of freelance recovery efforts, not a single organized attempt has been made to retrieve the treasure that went down with it. Other sunken treasures along the coast of Florida have attracted a number of professional treasure hunters, but the Gasparilla remains relatively untouched. In the years that have passed since the sinking, coins from its cargo have been found washed up on the nearby beaches following storms.

In addition to Gasparilla's gold and silver, there is even more reason for treasure hunters to reach the cargo transported by the pirate ship. Research reveals that among the treasure transported by the Gasparilla was a quantity of U.S. silver dollars minted between 1799 and 1804. These coins were in favor with the pirates when conducting business on the mainland. They are extremely rare and the collector value quite high.

-26-

Calico Jack

After assembling a new crew, Rackham stole a sloop and once again took to attacking and seizing merchant vessels in the Caribbean.

John Rackham was born in England on December 26, 1682. There are few records about his family or youth, but we do know that he served as a quartermaster* on the sloop Ranger commanded by Charles Vane, operating out of New Providence Island in the Bahamas. New Providence Island was also known at the time as the "Pirates' Republic" and served as a well-known base of operations for pirates.

Rackham (also seen in the literature spelled as

Rackam and Rackum) earned the nickname Calico Jack from the clothing he preferred. While his fame as a pirate does not come near that of Blackbeard or Billy Bowlegs, he is noted for two important pirate-related things: He designed the famous skull and crossbones flag known as the Jolly Roger, and he had two female crewmates on his ship – Mary Read and Ann Bonney – both of whom went on to even greater pirate fame than Rackham.

While serving on Vane's ship, Rackham, along with most of the crewmembers, grew angry when the captain retreated from a French Man-of-War. Rackham argued that if they captured the ship, it would give them a much larger and better-armed vessel at their disposal. In addition, it was believed that the ship was carrying valuable cargo. On November 24, 1718, Rackham accused Vane of cowardice and called for a vote among the crew. The resulting vote removed Vane from the captaincy and installed Rackham as the new leader. With Calico Jack at the helm, the pirates successfully attacked ships throughout much of the Caribbean.

Rackham, along with most of his crew, appeared before Bahamian Governor Woods Rogers in Nassau to request a pardon. Rackham stated that Captain Vane had forced them into piracy against their will. Rackham knew that Rogers despised Vane, and by the time the hearing was over, the men were granted pardons. Calico Jack's time of peace did not last long.

While in Nassau, Calico Jack was involved in an affair with Ann Bonney, the wife of James Bonney, a sailor who was employed by Governor Rogers. James learned about the affair and brought the issue before Rogers. The governor charged Ann with adultery and ordered her to be whipped. When Rackham learned of this, he met with Rogers and offered to buy Ann in what was called a "divorce by purchase." Ann refused to be bought, but she agreed to flee the island with Rackham.

After assembling a new crew, Rackham stole a sloop and once again took to attacking and seizing merchant vessels in the Caribbean. Ann Bonney cut her hair short and dressed in the manner of the crewmen. No one suspected that she was a woman, and that was the way Calico Jack wished it. Most seamen believed that a woman aboard a vessel was bad luck, but Ann eventually changed their minds and proved herself to be skilled with both cutlass* and pistol, participating in battles alongside the men.

Eventually, Calico Jack arrived at Oyster Bay on the west coast of Florida. From this location, he ranged out into the Gulf of Mexico attacking everything he encountered, and in the process, acquired an impressive amount of gold and silver. When the pirate had amassed around $2 million worth of coins and ingots, he decided it was time to cache it in a secret location rather than continue to carry it aboard his ship, the Fancey. He did not want to risk losing it should his ship be captured. Loading his treasure into several small rowboats, Calico Jack had it transported 10 miles up the deep and wide Lostman's River in the Florida Everglades, where it was buried on a high bank.

After a year aboard the Fancey, Bonney became pregnant. Calico Jack anchored in a Cuban harbor long enough for Bonney to give birth. At night when no one was around, he placed her in a rowboat and took her into town, where they met with a doctor. The baby was delivered, and two days later, Jack snuck the newborn and mother back aboard the ship. A few days later, the Fancey set sail and headed out to sea. There are no records in history relating what became of the baby.

After a few more months at sea, Bonney became enamored of another crewman. He had been captured earlier from a Dutch ship and agreed to serve aboard the Fancey. Bonney began meeting secretly with the young and handsome sailor, and one night she took him aside and revealed her gender. Much to Bonney's surprise, the sailor, on revealing "his" own gender, disclosed to Bonney that she was also a woman. Her real name was Mary Reed.

Over time, Reed became as skilled with a cutlass as Bonney. The two women began a long affair that they tried to keep secret from Rackham, but he eventually found out. At first, he threatened to kill them both but declined and admitted that they were two of the best "crewmen" on his ship.

After months of successfully preying on ships, Governor Rogers issued a proclamation declaring Calico Jack and his entire crew pirates. The year was 1720. Noted pirate hunter Jonathan Barnet was commissioned by the governor to hunt down Calico Jack. Mere days after Barnet set out to search for the pirate, Calico Jack steered the Fancey into Jamaica's Dry Harbor Bay. There, he encountered a small ship crewed by nine English pirates and invited them to come aboard for drinks. In a short time, they were all drunk and unaware of Barnet's approach. The pirate hunter's sloop attacked the Fancey, and after a spirited yet hopeless resistance put up mainly by Bonney and Reed, Rackham and his crew were placed in chains and transported to Spanish Town, Jamaica, where they awaited trial for crimes related to piracy, all punishable by hanging.

Both Ann Bonney and Mary Reed claimed to be pregnant during the trials. When appearing in court, the two women dressed demurely in feminine clothes. The judge took some amount of pity on what he regarded as the unfortunate plight of the two helpless women and granted them a stay of execution.

Calico Jack and the rest of the crew were found guilty. One week after the sentencing, Calico Jack was marched toward the gallows at Port Royal. He was permitted a few moments to be alone with Ann Bonney. Rather than offering a tender goodbye, Bonney scorned the pirate for being careless and stupid, for getting caught, and for not putting up a fight. Moments later, Rackham was hanged. It was November 18, 1720. His body was gibbeted* and placed on display on a small island at the entrance to Port Royal to serve as a warning to other pirates. Today, the location is known as Rackham's Cay.

According to the few documents available, both women were released. Reed died in 1721; the cause of death was recorded as "fever related to childbirth." Ann Bonney disappeared and was never heard from again.

Time passed, and the tale of Calico Jack's buried treasure somewhere along the banks of Lostman's River made the rounds throughout much of southern Florida. Searching for a long lost treasure like this is not easy, given the passage of so much time and the meandering ways of slow moving rivers such as Lostman's. To add to the difficulty, some researchers have suggested that Calico Jack did not bury his treasure along Lostman's

River at all, but instead somewhere along the Shark River. Both rivers are in the same general area and of the same general appearance.

None of these challenges, however, has deterred treasure hunters. Over the generations, they have arrived in this region to search for the millions of dollars' worth of gold hidden long ago by one of history's most colorful pirates.

-27-

Captain Henry Ross and the Ross Island Treasure

So many complaints had arrived at the Department of the Navy in Washington, D.C. that the newly formed Anti-Piracy Squad was ordered to chase down and apprehend or kill Ross.

Captain Henry Ross was relatively unknown until 1812, when he began serving as a commander for one of pirate Jean Lafitte's ships operating out of Barataria, Louisiana. Lafitte, for reasons debated to this day, aligned himself with the forces of General Andrew Jackson to help defeat the British at the Battle of New Orleans. As a result, Lafitte, along with all of his seamen and officers who joined in the campaign, were granted full pardons by President James Monroe for their crimes on the high seas, but only if they would publicly renounce their immoral tendencies and become honest, law-abiding citizens.

As far as anyone knows, most of the pirates agreed to this proposition. A few, however, wasted little time, returned to their ships and resumed raids on merchant vessels that worked on the waters of the Atlantic Ocean and the Gulf of Mexico.

At first, Henry Ross made an attempt to settle down on land and pursue honest work, but there were few work opportunities available for a former pirate. By the time he was close to running out of what money he had accumulated, Ross began thinking about a small island he thought would be ideal for establishing a pirate headquarters. The island had a natural lagoon and a deep-water channel that was ideal for his piratical comings and goings and for hiding his ship when he chose to spend time there. Once he set his course, Ross wasted little time recruiting a number of ex-pirates who had also grown bored with settled life. He told them that, once he had established himself on the island and completed the necessary construction of piers, homes, and warehouses, he would allow his crew to bring their wives, children, and girlfriends. Longing for adventure and anticipating wealth from raids, the seamen readily signed on with Ross and were eager to raise the sails.

Ross acquired a three-masted schooner, a fast, sleek vessel with only a five-foot draft. Once his crew was in place, he set sail for his chosen island hideout in 1817. In a short time, a dozen crude houses were constructed from timbers salvaged from old shipwrecks that had washed up on the beach. A well was dug to provide fresh water, and rainwater was collected in barrels. A dock was built, extending out into the lagoon on the eastern side of the island. As a bit of protection from potential attacks from other pirates or the United States Navy, a fortification was constructed on the northern side of the lagoon. The fort, also built from abandoned ship timbers, housed three brass cannons. In anticipation of the amount of plunder to come, Ross ordered the construction of two large warehouses. When this work was completed, the pirates brought their loved ones to the island, which soon became known as Ross Island.

Ross and his crew returned to the high seas in full force. Not only were they involved in piracy, but Ross also discovered opportunities for profit in smuggling and trading. So successful were these enterprises that Ross was soon devoting most of his attention to them.

When Ross had filled his ship with stolen loot and merchandise, he set sail for New Orleans, which offered the best markets for the goods he had obtained. The Crescent City was also the best place to unload and sell his smuggled merchandise. Whenever Ross captured a slave ship, he would take it to Weedon Island, located a short distance northwest of his own stronghold. Here, the slaves were unloaded and kept in a pen until Ross accumulated enough to take to market.

The United States government had outlawed the importation of slaves in 1808 and Ross was aware that many plantation owners were constantly in the market for workers and were willing to pay high prices. After a particularly remote bayou along the Gulf coast was selected, Ross would load the slaves onto his ship, transport them to the location, and make a deal with the buyer, who would be waiting for him.

During one of his voyages, Ross came upon a Spanish vessel sailing from Mexico and bound for Cuba. With little effort, the ship was seized, and when Ross inspected the cargo, he discovered a large wooden chest filled with gold coins. Next to it was a stack of several dozen silver ingots.

Instead of sinking the Spanish ship, as was his practice, Ross decided he would put it to use as a pirate vessel and ordered the crew to sail the ship back to Ross Island. When the pirates arrived at the island, it became clear that the deep draft of the Spanish vessel would inhibit it from entering the lagoon. The ship was taken to nearby Riviera Bay, where the chest of gold was transferred to Ross's vessel. During the trip to the bay, Ross decided that the Spanish ship would not serve him well as part of his fleet, so he scuttled it in the relatively shallow waters of Riviera Bay. Knowing that he could return and retrieve the silver ingots any time he wished, Ross decided to leave them on board. When the ship had settled onto the bottom sands of the bay, Ross, not wanting to leave any clear evidence of its location, had his crew saw down the masts that were still protruding from the water.

When Ross's vessel returned to the stronghold, he had the chest that was filled with gold coins unloaded. With the help of four trusted crewmembers, he carried the chest to a location just above the beach a short distance from the village and buried it.

Ross's raids and smuggling operations were so frequent and successful that he began to attract the attention of the federal government. So many complaints had been received by the Department of the Navy in Washington, D.C. that the newly formed Anti-Piracy Squad, stationed in Key West, was ordered to chase down and either apprehend or kill Ross. Before long, a sleek sloop named the Hornet began patrolling the area around Tampa Bay. (At least one historical document claims the sloop was named the Spark.)

Ross was apparently unaware that he had attracted the notice of the government, for he did not reduce his piratical activities at all. In fact, he increased them. One day Ross encountered a merchant ship just outside the Egmont Channel. The pirate brought his ship alongside the other and, when he was close enough, tossed grappling hooks over the gunwales* to secure the captured vessel to his own. The fighting men among the sailors and crew then clambered aboard the merchant ship and subdued all of its personnel. Ross and his men were in the process of looting the ship when they were surprised by the sudden appearance of the navy sloop.

After the sloop fired a warning shot from one of its cannons, Ross decided to make a run for it. He ordered his crew to cut the grappling lines and set full sails. He then undertook a flight toward his stronghold at Ross Island.

Ross's ship stayed ahead of the navy sloop, but the pursuing vessel kept in sight. When Ross reached the island, he steered his ship into what he expected to be the safety of the lagoon. He reasoned that the draft of the sloop would keep it from entering the still body of water.

While Ross gloated over his narrow escape, one of his crewmembers rushed up and informed him that the sloop was positioning itself in the mouth of the lagoon so that it would be able to fire its cannons at Ross's vessel. At the same time, several longboats filled with armed troops were being lowered into the water from the sloop.

Moments later, the naval warship let loose with a barrage of cannon fire. Ross's ship suffered several direct hits, and the deck was blasted into splinters in a matter of minutes. As the pirate ship began to sink into the lagoon's waters, Ross and his crew jumped overboard and made for shore. There, they led their families deeper into the island, where they believed they would be safe from the troops.

The longboats arrived at the beach, and the soldiers stormed the village. In a short time, every building was set afire. Seven pirates who were hiding in the buildings were taken prisoner. Before the day was over, they were all hanged from a nearby tree. A search for Captain Ross was initiated, but he was never found. In fact, Captain Henry Ross was never heard from again, and what became of him remains one of the more compelling pirate mysteries.

Ross Island has occasionally been inhabited since the days of the pirate stronghold in the 1820s. Over the years it has served as a home for smugglers, rumrunners, fugitives, and fishermen. During the 1950s and 1960s, squatters settled on the island but were evicted during the early 1970s.

Every now and then, a treasure hunter will arrive at Ross Island in search of the pirate's cache of gold coins, but so far none have been successful. A number of items from the days of its occupancy by pirates have been discovered on the island: cannon balls, bottles, nails, swords, and a musket. Every now and then, a gold or silver coin is picked up from the sands.

The lagoon that Ross so highly prized as a suitable hiding place for his ship has filled in and long since become overgrown with mangrove trees. As a result of a mosquito control program undertaken during the 1960s, a series of drainage ditches traverse the island and have left the lagoon disheveled.

While carving a ditch across a portion of the old lagoon, a dragline operator hooked onto an object several feet below the surface. Following some difficulty, he eventually brought up an old, heavy, and badly rusted ship anchor. Experts are convinced it was the anchor to Ross's pirate vessel. If the ship was transporting gold and silver when it was sunk by the U.S. Navy, as many believe it was, then there is little doubt that the treasure still lies in the same area, covered by sand, silt, and vegetation.

Then there is the matter of the dozens of silver ingots that went down with the Spanish ship in Riviera Bay. The remains of the ship have long since been covered over by the shifting sands of the bottom, and there is no record of any recovery attempt.

-28-

Pirate Brubaker

The old man told of the treasure chests filled with riches. There was more wealth, he explained, than 10 men could spend in their lifetimes.

Brewster Baker was born in 1758 in the seaport town of Avonmouth, England. As a boy hanging around his father's tavern, Baker often heard stories of sailors and the sea. Naturally, he found himself longing to pursue the high adventure offered on the ocean. At 15 years old, Baker joined the British Navy, hoping that life at sea would prove far more adventurous and fulfilling than living and toiling in Avonmouth. Working his way through the ranks, Baker achieved the status of midshipman* in 1780 while serving aboard the H.M.S. Warnock.

In 1782, while the Warnock was being overhauled on the island of Martinique, Baker struck up a friendship with a young Spanish naval officer named Jose Gaspar. Gaspar, who later became known as Gasparilla, went on to become one of the most famous and notorious pirates to sail the Atlantic Ocean and the Gulf of Mexico.

Baker remained in the British Navy until 1791. He had achieved the rank of lieutenant, but every day he was growing more dissatisfied with his salary, as well as with the tedium of his job. Baker craved certain luxuries that he could not afford on his officer's pay. He also longed for the romantic adventure he had heard about as a boy. Unfortunately, his experience as a military officer lacked a sense of adventure and failed to offer opportunities for gaining riches.

Baker decided not to wait any longer to pursue his dreams. While serving aboard the H.M.S. Heather, he organized a mutiny while the ship was anchored off the island of Barbados in the Caribbean Sea. Assembling the entire crew on the deck, he informed those who were loyal to the British crown that they were free to go ashore. To the remaining crewmembers, he offered the adventure and plunder of piracy.

By now, Baker was an experienced seaman. Under his leadership, his band of pirates attacked merchant and cargo ships, regardless of national affiliation. Before long, the hold of the Heather was filled with the loot from dozens of ships. One day, Baker captured a French vessel, the Andre Follet, near the Caribbean island of Guadalupe. Baker so admired this ship that he transferred all of his belongings onto it and abandoned the Heather.

Baker's newfound career of piracy inspired him to take on a new name. He shortened "Brewster" to "Brew" and later simplified the spelling to "Bru." Finally, with a combination of his nickname and his last name, "Brubaker" was born.

During his achievements as a pirate, Brubaker learned that his old friend Gasparilla was having success raiding up and down the Florida coast. Brubaker sought an audience with Gasparilla, and the two men eventually had a meeting at Boca Grande. Although they liked and respected one another, their crews did not get along. As a result, the two pirate leaders agreed to go their separate ways.

Brubaker eventually established a pirate headquarters on the tiny Bokeelia Island at the mouth of Charlotte Harbor, not far from the town of Fort Myers. Here, the crew constructed basic houses, and Brubaker utilized the location as a business center where he could conduct his affairs, most of them related to the disposition of his stolen cargo via the pirate Jean Lafitte, who had captured the black market in New Orleans, the largest trading center in the area.

Brubaker's piratical enterprises remained successful and profitable for several years. Then, something happened in 1819 that marked the beginning of the end for him and his peers. In that year, the United States initiated government negotiations with Spain for the purchase of Florida. Spain had been the benign, passive owner of Florida, and as such, governance and law enforcement was little more than an afterthought. On the other hand, the U.S. had an established army, navy, and set of laws that it intended to enforce in the newly acquired territory.

Before the final details for the transfer of Florida to the U.S. could be worked out, the U.S. Navy sent gunboats into the area to begin cleaning out known pirate strongholds. Many long-time buccaneers, seeing the writing on the wall, sailed for other locations in the Caribbean where they thought they might be able to pursue their activities. Others, knowing defeat was imminent, simply abandoned their adventurous way of life and settled into the routine of making their livings any way they could. A number of them re-emerged as businessmen, honest and otherwise.

In preparing for the inevitable, in 1820, Brubaker dug up all of the treasures he had buried on various islands with the intent of moving his entire operation to Cartagena, a Caribbean port in the South American country of Colombia. It has been estimated that Brubaker possessed $3 million worth of gold and silver coins and ingots, along with a quantity of emeralds, diamonds, pearls, and opals.

As he was traveling along the west coast of Florida in the Andre Follet, Brubaker stopped at small settlements along the way to replenish his supplies. At one settlement, he received word that U.S. Navy vessels were in the area searching for pirates. Concerned about his treasure, Brubaker steered his ship into Lemon Bay, a relatively small, narrow inlet near the present-day town of Englewood on the west coast of Florida. After darkness had fallen, Brubaker lowered a longboat. He then transferred all but two of his chests of treasure into the boat. Securing the services of four crewmen and some shovels, Brubaker ordered the crew to row the boat to the mainland shore in the dark.

After lighting some lanterns, Brubaker examined the beach and selected a particular location, where his men excavated a hole, placed the treasure chests into it, and filled it in. As it was past midnight and the pirates were tired, they decided to sleep on the beach and return to the ship in the morning for the remaining treasure chests.

At sunrise, Brubaker assigned two of the sailors to begin excavation of another hole while he and the others returned to the ship to retrieve the remaining chests. Just as Brubaker and the two sailors arrived at the Andre Follet, one of the crewmen spotted a U.S. Navy vessel entering the bay. Before defensive preparations could be undertaken, the swift navy ship moved in and seized the pirate vessel. The officers immediately recognized Brubaker, and he along with his crew were immediately placed in irons. With little to no formal proceedings, all of the pirates were hanged. Thus, Brubaker's life as a successful and free-living buccaneer came to an end.

As the capture of the Andre Follet and the subsequent hangings took place, the two crewmen left on a nearby shore witnessed the events. Fearing that the navy troops would come to the mainland and find them, they fled deeper inland.

The navy officers in charge were convinced that the two chests filled with treasure found on board the Andre Follet were the total of Brubaker's wealth, and it was seized. They were unaware that the greatest portion of the pirate's fortune actually lay buried in the sand less than a quarter mile away.

Many years later, two fishermen, who were trying their luck in the waters of Lemon Bay, decided to go to the nearby shore and take a break. There they encountered an elderly man living in the nearby woods. The old fellow appeared thin, with long, shaggy hair that had not been cut in years, and he shuffled along as though he were infirm. He approached the fishermen and asked if they had any food to spare. After sharing what they had, one of the fishermen asked the old man how he came to live in such a wild state.

The old man explained that he lived in the mangroves and pointed inland. In a mumbling and rather incoherent tone, he explained that it was his responsibility to guard the treasure. When the two fishermen invited the old man to explain what he meant, they were rewarded with a most amazing story.

As it turned out, the old man was one of the crewmen who had come to shore years earlier with Brubaker to bury the chests of gold. He related that he and his partner had witnessed the seizure of the pirate ship and the subsequent hanging of Brubaker and his entire crew. He explained that he and the other crewman had decided to remain at this location to guard the treasure, afraid that if they returned to civilization, they would be hanged for crimes of piracy. After a few years, his companion had died, leaving him to live alone on the beach.

The old man told of the treasure chests filled with riches. There was more wealth, he explained, than 10 men could spend in their lifetimes. When the two fishermen asked the old man if he could show them where the treasure was buried, he waved a hand across a vast expanse of beach and said, "It's around here somewhere."

It was clear that he had forgotten the exact location.

And there the treasure remains today – millions of dollars' worth of gold, silver, and jewels lying in what are likely rotted wooden chests. Only a few treasure hunters have ever searched for this cache over the decades because the story of Brubaker's treasure is not well known and the island has never been a major destination for treasure hunters.

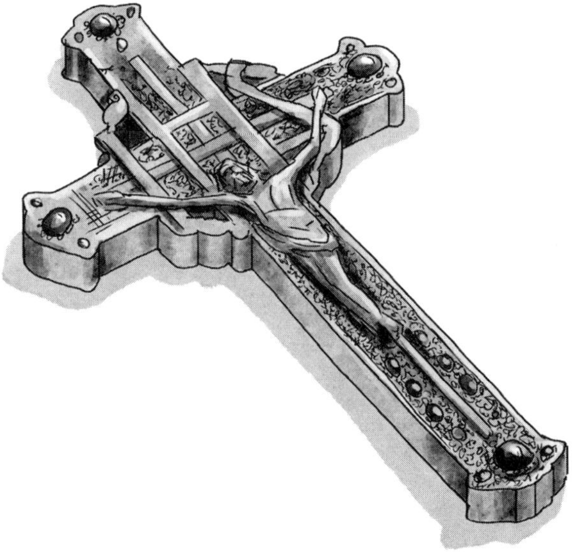

-29-

Jan Van Oss and the Treasure of Cudjoe Key

Van Oss harbored an extreme bitterness toward the Spanish, and lived only for revenge. His fight with them was personal, and he wanted to engage them in battle on his own terms.

Buried somewhere in the sands of Cudjoe Key are three separate treasures, their total worth estimated to be in excess of $20 million in today's values. Cudjoe Key is located near the far southeastern end of Florida's Keys. In generations past, Cudjoe, as well as many other keys in this area, saw significant pirate activity. Cudjoe Key was a favorite location for the pirate Jan Van Oss, who was responsible for burying the treasures.

Van Oss was born in 1551 to Dutch parents in the Netherlands. His father was a humble fisherman, and Jan began to assist him in this occupation at an early age. As a result, young Jan came to love the sea. He decided that he wanted to be a fisherman just like his father and looked forward to the day when he could command his own fishing boat; but certain events would prevent him from doing so.

The region of the Netherlands where Jan and his family lived came under the control of Spain and its cruel ruler, Prince Philip II. Before long, Spanish forces occupied Jan's country, beginning a period of stern and ruthless rule, plagued with suspicion and accusation. Jan's parents were arrested and tortured into confessing to crimes that they never committed. A short time later, they were executed.

Filled with hatred for the Spanish and vowing to avenge his parents' deaths, Jan escaped northward into a portion of the country that was under their reign. There, Jan joined the army of William the Silent, also known as the Prince of Orange. Not long before, William had successfully routed the Spanish from his domain. Shortly after Van Oss arrived in the region, William learned of his tragedy and took the lad into his inner circle.

In the years to follow, Jan served admirably in William's somewhat small and ineffective fleet of warships. Van Oss convinced the prince of the importance of having a strong navy and encouraged him to organize and expand his seagoing force in order to achieve some prominence in the region. As a result, William ordered the purchase of a number of high-quality vessels from Portugal. On his thirtieth birthday in 1581, Van Oss was given command of one of the vessels, the Wolvega.

In a short time, Van Oss was offered the position of Commodore, or commander of the entire fleet of warships. He declined. For years, he had harbored an extreme bitterness toward the Spanish and lived only for revenge. His fight with them was personal, he said, and he wanted to engage them in a one-on-one battle on his own terms. He requested permission to sail the Atlantic Ocean in search of Spanish vessels to capture and plunder.

Later that same year, William the Silent completed the Union of Utrecht which officially declared the northern provinces independent of Spain. After being granted an audience with William, Van Oss explained the importance of cutting off Spain's flow of wealth from the Americas: gold and silver that was used to finance their military and governmental campaigns. Van Oss proposed that he be granted the freedom to search for and seize Spanish ships, confiscate any cargo, and sink the vessels. William the Silent was impressed with Van Oss's proposal and granted him authority to carry out his plan with the full endorsement of the government.

Van Oss left immediately for the Caribbean Sea. He spent a great deal of time exploring the region, making maps, and establishing locations from which he could launch his raids. He also observed, from a distance, the deployment of Spanish ships into the area and made note of trade routes.

In searching for a harbor for his center of operations, one sufficiently far from Spanish traffic, Van Oss sailed to the Florida Keys and selected Cudjoe Key. He reasoned that it was unlikely that the Spanish would sail this far to the west and stumble onto his stronghold.

By the beginning of summer 1582, Van Oss was ready to put his plans into action. He returned to the Caribbean island of Hispaniola, the area's center of Spanish government, and ordered some of his sailors to infiltrate the main city. Once in town, they hung around the wharves and taverns, gathering information about the comings and goings of Spanish cargo ships as well as warships. On returning to the Wolvega, the spies provided Van Oss with the information he needed to wreak havoc on his enemy's shipping operations and warship deployments.

Over the next several months, Van Oss raided and sacked three Spanish settlements. He captured and plundered 15 Spanish ships. Van Oss decided not to sink any of the ships, but he never left any of the sailors or officers alive. In venting his hatred for the Spanish, Van Oss had their legs cut off and left them to bleed to death on the decks of their ships. To serve as a warning, he then set the ships adrift so they would be discovered by other Spanish vessels.

From the 15 ships Van Oss plundered, it's been estimated that he accumulated a total of $6 million worth of gold and silver, along with golden religious artifacts such as crucifixes, chalices, and goblets. Van Oss also seized chests of precious stones such as diamonds, emeralds, opals, and pearls. A portion of the booty was divided among his men and another was sent back to the Netherlands. The largest share, however, went into Van Oss's own chests.

Following a series of successful raids on Spanish

ships, Van Oss returned to Cudjoe Key to undertake some maintenance and repairs on the Wolvega. While there, he buried his treasure in three separate locations.

A short time later the Spanish crown placed a large reward on the head of Van Oss. As a result of pursuit by the Spanish government, as well as by bounty hunters, he was forced to flee Cudjoe Key. Because he left in such a hurry, he was unable to recover the three buried treasure chests. Fearing he would be caught and executed, Van Oss never returned to the area.

The exact locations of Van Oss's treasure caches on Cudjoe Key have remained a mystery. Although it's not a big island, very few attempts have been made to find his treasures. With a bit of patience and commitment, along with the correct kind of treasure hunting gear, it is possible that the island may soon yield Van Oss's fortune.

Cudjoe Key was not the only place where pirate Jan Van Oss left treasure. After leaving that small island, the pirate remained busy attacking merchant vessels and seizing cargo of gold and silver coins, along with ingots, as well as precious stones.

During the first week of April in 1583, Van Oss waited in ambush along the coast of Cuba for the arrival of the Espada de Plata, a Spanish ship reputed to be transporting a rich cargo of silver ingots. The captain of the Spanish ship must have had suspicions about the notorious Van Oss being in the area, because just as one of the pirate's crewmembers sighted the vessel, the Espada de Plata turned and sailed back in the opposite direction.

Not to be deterred, Van Oss set off in pursuit of the ship and finally caught up with it a short distance off the Inagua Islands. The ship was seized and the silver-filled chests transferred to the pirate ship, the Wolvega. As was his practice, Van Oss ordered the legs cut off all of the Spaniards on board the ship. Then he turned the vessel loose to drift in the open sea and set sail for Florida.

Unknown to the pirate, a group of three Spanish warships was sailing among the straits of the Florida Key in search of him. Because of the damage Van Oss had inflicted on Spanish shipping over the years, the Spanish government attempted to trace his movements in order to find a pattern in his activities and then set a trap for his ship. Over time, the Spanish learned of his base of operations at Cudjoe Key, so they narrowed their pursuit to focus on that area.

Van Oss decided that he wanted to cache the three chests of silver ingots, as soon as possible. Since he had already buried three others on Cudjoe Key, he considered another location. He set sail for a group of small islands known as Snipe Keys, not far from Cudjoe Key. As he sailed through the clear shallow waters, the sun was setting. Selecting one of the islands, Van Oss dropped anchor in a small cove. He had a longboat lowered and sent four of his crewmen ashore to select a suitable place to bury the treasure. Van Oss decided to spend the night on his ship and carry the three chests of silver to the beach in the morning.

At dawn, as Van Oss was preparing to load the chests into a second longboat, one of his crewmen called out that he had sighted three Spanish warships heading toward their position from the south. Van Oss observed the ships through his telescope. It was obvious that they had not yet spotted the Wolvega in the tiny cove, since they were only engaged in surveillance. Van Oss knew, however, that it was only a matter of time before they found him.

Assessing his options, Van Oss decided his only chance was to outrun the three Spanish ships, and he needed to get moving before he was discovered. As the sails were being raised, Van Oss ordered the ship's load to be lightened in order to gain maximum speed. In addition to several cannons and other heavy equipment, he decided to toss the three treasure chests overboard. As the last of the chests sank to the bottom of the shallow cove, the Wolvega, picking up a wind, sped through the water, away from Snipe Keys.

Once the Wolvega was moving, it was easily spotted by the Spaniards, who immediately took up the chase. None aboard the Spanish warships was as skilled a seaman as Van Oss, and soon the pirate ship eluded the pursuers.

For several more years, Van Oss fought the Spanish with great success, but he was never able to return to Snipe Keys to retrieve his fortune in silver ingots. His ultimate fate remains a mystery. As far as anyone knows, the three chests still lie in the bottom of one of the small coves today.

-30-

Black Caesar

Legend has it that while Black Caesar resided in Elliot Key, he buried a total of 26 tons of silver ingots in wooden chests somewhere on the island.

As with many pirates who carried on their trade throughout the waters off the North American continent, the pirate captain known as Black Caesar is surrounded by myth and legend, since verifiable facts are hard to come by. He was known throughout the Gulf of Mexico for his huge size, great strength and cunning, as well as his fearless and bloodthirsty demeanor.

One story has Black Caesar born in Africa and rising to the position of tribal war chieftain. There, it is said, he and some companions were lured aboard a slave ship and placed in chains. As the ship neared the coast of Florida, an oncoming hurricane threatened to destroy the ship, so a friendly sailor set Black Caesar free. The two men escaped in a longboat and rowed to shore just as the hurricane struck, sending the doomed ship to the bottom of the sea.

The two men landed on Elliot Key. There, they posed as shipwrecked sailors and lured passing ships close to shore to provide assistance. On boarding the vessels, Black Caesar and his companion produced weapons and threatened to sink the ship if supplies and valuables were not turned over to them. In this manner, Black Caesar and his partner accumulated a sizeable trove of treasure, which they buried. In time Black Caesar acquired a ship, recruited pirates and crewmen, and began attacking ships in the area.

Another tale has the famous pirate being born as Henri Caesar on the island of Haiti to slave parents. Henri soon became a favorite of the wealthy French plantation owner, a man named Arnaud. So impressed was Arnaud with Caesar's charm and intelligence that he employed him as a houseboy. Because Arnaud liked to make a good impression on his neighbors, as well as the numerous businessmen with whom he traded, he made sure that all of his house servants received an education. Thus, young Caesar learned not only how to read and write, but was conversant in history, politics, and economics. The position of a house servant carried with it a certain status, one much higher than that of a field hand. For a time, life was good for young Henri Caesar – but not for long.

As Henri grew into a tall, muscular, and somewhat intimidating boy, he frightened the sheltered and pampered children of the Arnaud household. As a result, at 16 years of age, he was transferred to a job in the lumberyard. For 12 hours each day, Caesar, along with another man, cut logs into planks under the watchful eye of a cruel overseer who was fond of applying his whip to the backs of the workers when he thought they weren't moving fast enough. Caesar often thought how satisfying it would be to kill this man, but he was only a slave and conditioned to do what he was told. In the meantime, Caesar continued to grow, and his body filled out, his confidence and physical strength increasing daily.

In his early twenties, Caesar was still working in the lumberyard when the island's slaves organized a revolt. Tired of the inhumane treatment, unsanitary conditions, and poor food they were subjected to, the prisoners armed themselves and went on a rampage that encompassed the entire island. At the Arnaud plantation, every member of the French family was killed, and all of the buildings were set on fire. During the revolt, Caesar cornered the overseer, killed him, and dismembered his body.

For the next 10 years, Caesar, along with dozens of other ex-slaves, lived in hiding on the island and waged a guerilla* war on French officials and their attendant military troops. Caesar, leading his small army of fighters, armed with primitive weapons, ambushed patrols and occasionally attacked the military encampments, killing many in the process. Soon, officials offered a large reward for the capture of Henri Caesar, dead or alive.

In the end, Caesar and his forces proved to be too much for the French government. The officials, along with the military, abandoned the island, and it soon fell under the rule of the former slaves. Though they were now free and able to make decisions for themselves, the slaves soon encountered difficulties. Because no crops had been planted during the revolution, there was little food left to eat. The slaves, accustomed to stealing and living off of the provisions imported by the French, now went hungry.

Caesar was growing weary of living in Haiti and struggling with the obstacles that he continued to encounter. During the revolution he had felt alive, invigorated, and infused with a passion to defend his newfound freedom. Now, life on the island was back to planting and cutting timber. Caesar wished for more and he longed for adventure.

One morning, during the late spring of 1805, Caesar, along with a band of followers, spotted a Spanish ship that had anchored just outside the harbor at Port de Paix. Seeing his opportunity, he devised a plan. Around midnight, a group of former slaves under Caesar's leadership rowed out to the ship, quietly boarded it, and killed all of the crew save three sailors. They also spared the captain.

Neither Caesar nor any of the former slaves knew how to sail a ship. Caesar explained to the captain and the captive crewmembers that if they taught him and his men how to operate the vessel, they might live another day. Thus, Caesar entered his new life, one of piracy, raiding, pillaging, and growing wealthy from the accumulation of cargos of gold, silver and jewels.

Weeks later, when Caesar and his men felt competent enough to sail the ship, they killed the captain and the three crewmen, then tossed their bodies overboard. At first, Caesar attacked small, defenseless villages that he encountered along the coasts of Cuba and the Bahamas, as well as small ships that possessed little or no armament. In this manner, Caesar came to learn and grow more efficient in the business of piracy. During this time, he became known as "Black Caesar."

Because of the increasing pirate menace in the Caribbean, British warships began to converge on the area after the War of 1812. The increased vigilance and pressure caused Black Caesar to look for other waters to conduct his raids. He began exploring many of the small islands and keys he found near Florida in the Gulf of Mexico.

During a series of raids along the western coast of Florida, Black Caesar met Gasparilla. For a time, the two men spoke of joining forces and splitting the take from their respective pillaging, but in the end decided against it. They remained friends, however, and often met with each other.

At the time, Gasparilla had established his headquarters at the Boca Grande peninsula at the mouth of Charlotte Harbor. Black Caesar also desired to establish a stronghold in this area, and Gasparilla agreed that he could occupy Sanibel Island some 20 miles to the south.

Where Gasparilla and his crew lived in well-constructed and sometimes ornate houses at Boca Grande, Black Caesar and his men chose to live simply in palm-thatched huts. It was during the time of the settlement of Sanibel Island that Black Caesar had three wooden chests of treasure in the form of gold and silver ingots, along with emeralds, pearls, and more, transferred from his ship to the island. Then he had the chests buried in three different locations.

For years, Black Caesar and Gasparilla remained friends, but an incident occurred in 1817 that divided the two men forever, and many believe it led to the end of Black Caesar's reign as a pirate. Not far from Sanibel Island was Captiva Island. On this small strip of land, Gasparilla built a small prison, where he kept captives being held for ransom. Most of the captives were women taken from ships seized by the pirate and most were from wealthy families. At Captiva Island, they were kept in somewhat acceptable conditions until a ransom was paid.

During the summer of that year, Black Caesar and his crewmen, following a night of hard drinking, traveled the short distance from Sanibel Island to Captiva Island and stormed the prison. They killed at least one of the guards and took several of the women back to Sanibel Island, where they abused them. When Gasparilla learned of the incident, he instructed his men to arm themselves. Moments later, they boarded a ship and sailed to Sanibel Island. There, Gasparilla told Black Caesar to return the women immediately and to vacate the island. Seeing that he was out-manned and out-armed by a factor of three, Black Caesar had no other choice but to abandon Sanibel Island. As Gasparilla and his forces watched, Black Caesar and his men boarded their vessel and sailed away. Black Caesar had neither the time nor the opportunity to retrieve his three buried treasure chests.

With the increase in British warships in the area, Black Caesar found it difficult to pursue his piratical activities in the Gulf of Mexico and along the Atlantic Coast. Following a long period of searching, he finally selected a new location for his headquarters – Elliot Key. Elliot Key was a long and narrow strip of land. Today, it separates the Intracoastal Highway and Biscayne Bay from the Straits of Florida. The location is now part of Dade County.

Prior to Black Caesar's arrival, numerous ships carrying treasure were run aground there or sunk in the nearby waters by hurricane-force winds and waves. A ship that sank off Elliot Key in 1733 yielded hundreds of silver coins, clay pottery, jars of olive oil, and other artifacts, all of which had been carried to the beach by subsequent storm waves.

Legend has it that while Black Caesar resided here, he buried a total of 26 tons of silver ingots in wooden chests somewhere on the island. Allegedly, the fortune was buried near a location known today as Black Caesar's Rock. The rock juts out into Caesar's Creek, which runs around the south end of the island.

One morning, Black Caesar and his crew broke camp and boarded their ship. They sailed away in search of more ships to plunder but, according to some researchers, were never seen or heard from again.

More recent investigations into what happened to this fascinating pirate yield the information that he may have joined forces with Blackbeard and sailed with him for a few years. One version of the tale of Blackbeard's battle with Lieutenant Robert Maynard at Ocracoke Island has Black Caesar attempting to ignite the powder magazine and blow up the ship, per orders, when he was stopped. Another version has Black Caesar, along with other crewmen, arrested and taken prisoner by Virginia authorities. Tried for piracy, he was found guilty and hanged in Williamsburg, Virginia.

The three treasure chests that Black Caesar buried on Sanibel Island are still there, as far as anyone knows. Over the years, some treasure has been found on the island in the form of gold and silver coins washed up on the beaches, as well as artifacts likely left over from the time the pirate resided there. The wooden chests have likely rotted away, spilling the contents into the sand. Perhaps another hurricane will arrive someday, blowing and washing away a portion of the beach to expose them. Until then, people keep searching.

In addition to Sanibel Island, Elliot Key has also attracted treasure hunters. During the 1970s, a fisherman's anchor accidentally hooked onto an object in shallow water near the southern shore. The fisherman pulled on the line, struggling with the resistance, until he noticed a curious object in the water. On closer inspection, he saw that it was a wooden chest. He attempted to haul it to the surface and into his boat, but the line broke. He raced home and returned with a heavier line, but was never able to locate the chest again. It is very likely that the fisherman had located one of Black Caesar's treasure chests.

-31-

Jean Lafitte

As a pirate, Lafitte gained the reputation of a gentleman. He always treated captured crewmen well, and freed them at the first opportunity.

Of all the pirates that sailed the Gulf of Mexico and frequented that coast, none garnered more recognition than the colorful, dashing Jean Lafitte. Much of what has been written about this buccaneer over the years has been consigned to legend, but many of his exploits, as well as his buried treasure, have been documented. Jean Lafitte was indeed noteworthy and notorious, and he left behind rich treasures in gold, silver, jewels, and precious stones. Although the pirate was born "Jean Laffite" in

France, most English language documents and resources spell his surname "Lafitte." Since that remains the most common usage, it is the name that is used in this book.

At one point in his life, Lafitte claimed to have been born in Bordeaux, France in 1780. According to Lafitte, his parents were Sephardic Jews whose ancestors had fled Spain for France during the 1760s. On another occasion, Lafitte, along with his brother Pierre, claimed to have been born in the French city of Bayonne. Research into Lafitte's origins have also have yielded additional claims that he was born in the French towns of Brest and St. Malo. One of Lafitte's biographers suggests that it was convenient to claim France as a birthplace during this time, for it provided some element of protection from American law. Yet other accounts provide Orduna, Spain, and Westchester, New York as his place of origin.

To add to the confusion of Lafitte's origins, author Jack C. Ramsey introduces the notion that the pirate was born in the French colony of Saint-Domingue, the former name of present-day Haiti. A number of French plantation owners migrated from Haiti to Louisiana, where they established expansive farms. An examination of population records from the 1760s reveals a number of families with the surname "Lafitte." Ramsey suggests that Lafitte, along with his brother and widowed mother, left Saint-Domingue for New Orleans in the 1780s.

Another Lafitte biographer, William C. Davis, claims that Jean Lafitte was born in Pauillac, France, in 1782, one of nine children. Davis also claims that the noted pirate and entrepreneur Pierre Lafitte was Jean's half-brother. According to Davis, Lafitte's father was a trader who owned ships and spent much of his time at sea, and the young Jean learned his seamanship by serving aboard these vessels.

As a young man, Lafitte was fascinated with the bayou country of Louisiana and spent days exploring as much of it as possible. In time, this interest led to the exploration of inlets, harbors, and other locations eastward along the Mississippi coast and westward along the Texas coast. While Jean was learning much about the geography of the Gulf Coast, his older brother Pierre was operating as a privateer out of Saint-Domingue. Evidence suggests that Pierre brought captured merchandise to New Orleans to sell and that Jean assisted him in his endeavor.

By 1812, Jean Lafitte had grown tired of his role as a broker of stolen cargo. He saw some advantage in capturing the cargo himself and eliminating the middleman. With that in mind, he and Pierre purchased a schooner and employed a man named Trey Cook to captain it. As the schooner did not apply for a commission from the government, it was therefore operating illegally. According to the law, such a vessel was regarded as a pirate ship.

In January 1813, the Lafitte brothers captured a Spanish slave ship. They later sold the slaves, along with some of the additional cargo, and pocketed $18,000. The brothers converted the slave ship into a pirate vessel and named it the Dorada. After capturing another ship using the Dorada, the Lafitte brothers deemed it a less than useful pirate vessel and returned it to its owners. As a pirate, Jean Lafitte gained the reputation of a gentleman. He always treated captured crewmen well, and freed them at the first opportunity. Captured goods were taken back to New Orleans and sold.

Acting governor of Louisiana Thomas B. Robertson was irritated by the piracy activities of the Lafitte brothers. While the residents of the Louisiana coast appreciated the Lafittes for providing them with goods at a low cost, Robertson referred to them as "brigands who infest our coast and overrun our country." When Governor William C. C. Claiborne returned to office and sent Robertson back to his previous duties, he relieved the official pressure on the Lafittes.

On June 18, 1812, the United States declared war on Great Britain despite having a naval disadvantage, with only a few ships to fight Great Britain's powerful navy. In order to fortify the navy, the U.S. government offered letters of marque to private vessels. A letter of marque authorized a private citizen, a privateer, to attack and capture enemy vessels and bring them before admiralty courts for possession and sale. One such letter was granted to Jean Lafitte. While Lafitte turned over some of the booty he had captured to the authorities, most of it was sold illegally through his and Pierre's operation. When authorities learned of Jean's activities and realized how much revenue they were losing as a consequence, they set out to prevent him from continuing his operation.

On November 10, 1812, U.S. District Attorney John R. Grimes filed charges against Lafitte for "violation of revenue law." Three days later, Jean and Pierre Lafitte were captured along with 25 of their crewmen. While the authorities were distracted with confiscating contraband, the Lafittes escaped.

In March 1813, Jean Lafitte registered as the captain of a brig. While he listed his job as piloting the vessel on a trip to New York, he was, in truth, establishing himself as a privateer. Not long afterward, he obtained a letter of marque from the country of Colombia. Although he captured ships and seized cargo, he never returned any of it to Cartagena in northern Colombia, directing it instead to the port of New Orleans, where he and Pierre continued to sell it.

This blatant disregard for the laws angered Governor Claiborne, who began making plans to capture the bandits. He appointed his revenue officers to prepare an ambush. In addition, a $500 reward was offered for the capture of Jean Lafitte. In response, Lafitte printed dozens of handbills offering a $500 reward for the governor, which he handed out and tacked up on walls.

In January 1814, Lafitte arranged for an auction of a large amount of contraband outside of New Orleans. Federal authorities attempted to break up the operation, but in the process, one of the revenue officers was killed, and two others were wounded. In addition to these difficulties, New Orleans merchants put pressure on the governor to do something about Lafitte, because the pirate was charging lower prices for the same goods. In response, Claiborne approached the state legislature, requesting to establish a militia company with the sole purpose of removing pirates from Louisiana once and for all. The legislature appointed a committee to study the matter, but in truth, they were in no hurry to get rid of Lafitte, as many of their constituents benefitted from the pirate's sales. A short time later, Pierre Lafitte was arrested, convicted, and jailed on charges related to acts of piracy.

The jailing and conviction of Pierre did not deter

Jean one bit. While his brother was incarcerated, Jean operated the piracy and smuggling business with ease. In response to Lafitte's activities, as well as those of other pirates, the British Navy increased patrols throughout the Gulf of Mexico. By August 1814, they had established a naval base in Pensacola, and in September, a British ship fired at one of Lafitte's vessels and gave pursuit. Lafitte took to shallow water, where the larger British ship could not follow. The British commander raised a white flag and indicated that he wanted to talk; he ordered several officers to deploy a dinghy and row towards Lafitte's ship. Likewise, Lafitte lowered a rowboat and met the British crewmen halfway.

The captain of the British ship, Nicholas Lockyer, along with Royal Marine Infantry Captain John McWilliam, had been transporting a package, with orders to deliver it to Lafitte. Lafitte, who had not yet revealed his identity, invited the men to row to the nearby island. On arriving at the island, the pirate's men surrounded the officers, and Lafitte finally identified himself. The British officers had no choice but to hand over the package.

Inside was a letter from King George III, who offered Lafitte and his pirates full British citizenship, as well as land grants in the British colonies in the Americas, if they promised to assist in the naval fight against the United States. The letter stated that if Lafitte refused, they would bombard Barataria, a known pirate haven south of New Orleans and a base of operations for Lafitte. The second letter was from Lieutenant Colonel Edward Nicholls of the Royal Marines, urging the pirate to accept the offer.

Lafitte realized that he would eventually have to fight either the U.S. or the British. He felt that he had a better chance of eventually defeating the U.S. forces as a pirate, so he decided to align with them in the fight against the British. Lafitte sent a message to U.S. officials informing them that some of his men wanted to side with the British, but that they would side with the American forces if Pierre was released from prison. The U.S. accepted his offer.

On September 13, 1814, U.S. Navy Commodore Daniel Patterson led a warship, six gunboats, and a tender* into Barataria Bay and began shelling* ships and the settlements on the shore. Ten of the pirate ships formed a battle line in the bay and returned fire, but it became clear that the U.S. forces were winning. Lafitte, realizing what the battle's outcome would be, ordered his men to abandon the ships. Several of the vessels were set afire. When Patterson's troopers arrived on the shore, they met no resistance, took 80 captives, and captured eight pirate ships along with $500,000 worth of stolen goods, but they could not locate Lafitte, who had escaped into the nearby forests and swamps.

Governor Claiborne wrote letters to U.S. Attorney General Richard Rush and General Andrew Jackson. Claiborne requested a pardon for the Baratarians and implied that Commodore Patterson had erred in destroying the "first line of defense for Louisiana."

In mid-December 1814, Andrew Jackson arrived in New Orleans and met with Jean Lafitte. Lafitte offered to help defend New Orleans against the British if the United States would pardon any of the men who agreed to join in the fight. Jackson agreed to the terms, and on December 19, the state legislature recommended a full pardon. Encouraged by Lafitte, many of the pirates joined the New Orleans militia or volunteered to serve as sailors on the ships. The rest formed three artillery companies.

On December 23, several ships of the British fleet sailed up the Mississippi River toward New Orleans. Lafitte noted that the American line of defense did not extend far enough to keep the British from encircling the American troops. Lafitte told Jackson it was necessary to extend the line into the swamps, and Jackson gave the order to do so. The British commenced firing on the Americans on December 28 but were driven off by an artillery company manned by two of Lafitte's former lieutenants.

During the ensuing battles, Lafitte's men distinguished themselves by helping defeat the British. Even Jackson voiced praise for the bravery and skill of the former pirates. With Jackson's recommendation, the U.S. government granted full pardons to Jean and Pierre Lafitte as well as to all of the men who had served under them. Pardons were granted on February 6, 1815.

Almost a year later, in January 1816, Jean and Pierre Lafitte made an agreement with Spain to serve as spies. At that time, Spain was involved in a war with Mexico, which was fighting for independence. Jean received the order to travel to Galveston on the Texas Gulf Coast, which at that time belonged to Spain, along with the entire state of Texas. Galveston also served as a headquarters for the pirate Luis Michel-Aury, the French privateer who sympathized with the Mexican side of the war. Shortly after arriving, Lafitte assumed command of Galveston Island. Lafitte found the island ideal for his needs: It was essentially uninhabited save for his own men and the Karankawa Indians, and it was outside the authority of the United States. He lost no time in establishing it as a base for his smuggling operations. Lafitte's crewmen tore down the house previously constructed by Michel-Aury and built 200 new ones.

By the end of 1817, Lafitte's colony, which he deemed Campeche, boasted a population of almost 200 men and women. Newcomers to the island were required to sign a loyalty oath to the pirate. Lafitte remained busy attacking and capturing merchant and slave ships. The Galveston Island location served Lafitte well until a series of mishaps arose. After some of his men kidnapped a Karankawa woman, the Indians attacked the colony and killed five men. Lafitte's gunboats rained fire on the Karankawa encampment, killing most of the inhabitants. Not long afterward, a hurricane devastated the island; most of the houses were destroyed, along with several ships. Nonetheless, Lafitte continued to use the island as a base from time to time, but it was never the same. As a result, he often operated out of Matagorda Bay, 100 miles to the southwest.

In 1820, Lafitte reportedly married Madeline Regaud, the daughter of a French colonist. They had a son – Jean Pierre Lafitte. In 1821, the U.S.S. Enterprise was ordered to Galveston Island to remove Lafitte and his pirates once and for all because of the pirate's attack on an American merchant ship. Lafitte met with the captain of the Enterprise, a man named Kearney. After several days of discussions and negotiations between the pirate and Kearny, Lafitte ordered the hanging of two men he said were responsible for the attack on the American ship, in the hope that this would appease the captain. Kearney was not impressed with Lafitte's gesture. He ordered the guns of the Enterprise aimed toward the island and gave Lafitte 30 days to vacate. Lafitte agreed to depart without a fight.

Several days before the period was to expire, one of Lafitte's ships, the Pride, was somehow forced aground near the mouth of the Lavaca River in Matagorda Bay, and a number of hull planks were fractured, sinking the vessel. The Pride carried a great quantity of treasure taken during raids of several Spanish ships in the Gulf of Mexico. Lafitte, in the company of several crewmen, sailed to the site and recovered a wooden chest filled with treasure, along with two canvas sacks containing silver ingots. The booty was carried to shore. After dividing much of it among his crew, Lafitte assigned two men to ready the remainder for burial. Lafitte and his men hauled the treasure several hundred yards across the salt marsh, selected a suitable location, and buried it.

Lafitte took a compass reading and a bearing on two nearby mottes, or groves of trees – Kentucky Motte and Mauldin Motte. The pirate made some notes in his journal, and when he was finished, he took a long brass rod that he had carried from the ship and shoved it deep into the ground just above the treasure until only eight inches remained visible. Lafitte then told his two companions that if they returned to the site after three years and found the treasure still there, they could have it. Lafitte then sailed back to Galveston Island.

However, before vacating the island, Lafitte and his men burned all of the standing structures and buried most of the stolen cargo. Several of the crewmen were arrested and later convicted of piracy. Those who were not captured joined Lafitte aboard one of his ships.

When Lafitte informed them he was returning to piracy, half of the men refused to accompany him. He allowed them to depart and told them they could take his other ship, the General Victoria. That night, Lafitte, apparently in a vengeful mood, led his pirates aboard the General Victoria, where they crippled the ship by destroying the masts and spars. Lafitte sailed away, never to return to Galveston Island.

For the next several months, Lafitte preyed on Spanish ships in the Gulf of Mexico. When he had filled his hold with stolen cargo, he returned to the barrier islands near New Orleans, where he would unload his treasure and replenish his supplies. Brother Pierre handled the sales of the contraband. As this was going on, the congressional delegation of Louisiana petitioned the federal government to do something about Lafitte and put an end to the piracy and smuggling. In response, ships from the U.S. Navy were sent to the Gulf.

During the ensuing weeks, a number of pirates were put out of commission. In November 1821, Lafitte was fired upon, pursued, and captured. On February 13, 1822, he escaped. Once free, Lafitte acquired more ships and established a pirate base on the island of Cuba by bribing local elected officials. In April, as he set his sights on seizing an American merchant ship, he was captured again. The Americans turned him over to the Cuban authorities, but Lafitte was promptly released.

Lafitte continued to prey on ships in the Caribbean. Unfortunately, several of the ships he captured and pillaged were carrying important and necessary goods to Cuba. This angered Cuban officials, who sought to put an end to Lafitte's destruction. With the increased pressure,

Lafitte made an arrangement with Colombia to raid Spanish ships.

On February 4, 1823, Lafitte's ship engaged in a battle with two Spanish merchant vessels. The Spaniards were heavily armed and inflicted great damage to the pirate ship. During the onslaught, Lafitte was severely wounded. According to reports, he died on the morning of February 5 and was buried at sea. Whatever the truth, Jean Lafitte was never seen again.

Lafitte has been gone a long time, but the treasures he cached in various locations have yet to be uncovered. According to legend, one of Lafitte's trusted companions helped him cache the Lavaca River treasure, but he died from malaria within a few months of Lafitte's departure from the island. Before the companion died, however, he related the account of the burial to a friend. Using the directions provided by the late pirate, the friend made several unsuccessful trips to locate the chest and the silver ingots.

The second pirate who assisted with the burial of the treasure never returned to the site, choosing instead to remain in New Orleans and raise a family. As an old man, the former buccaneer told the story of the buried chest of gold and jewels to his two sons. With great enthusiasm, and certain of their ability to find the treasure, the sons organized an expedition to the Lavaca River marsh, only to fail like their father.

More time passed, and a man named Hill sought to establish a ranch on the land at the junction of the Lavaca River and stocked the grassy marshes with fine horses and cattle. One of Hill's employees was a man named Ward, who was placed in charge of the livestock. Ward's responsibilities included running horses and cattle out into the marsh during the day to graze and returning them to the pens each night.

While the livestock were grazing in the marsh during the day, Ward would sometimes lie down on the grassy pasture and take a nap. One afternoon, as he was tending the stock on horseback, he grew drowsy and searched for a good spot to stretch out on the soft ground. Dismounting, he looked around for something to tie his horse. Nearby, he found the tip of a brass rod sticking out of the ground. After hitching the horse to the rod, Ward lay down a few paces away and dozed off.

The horse Ward was using on this day was unaccustomed to being staked. He pulled at the rod, bending it and extracting almost its entire length. When Ward awoke from his nap, he pulled the rod completely out if the ground and carried it back to show his employer.

Rancher Hill was familiar with the tale of Jean Lafitte's buried treasure, and when he saw the long brass rod, he knew it immediately for what it was. Hill told Ward he wanted to be taken the next morning to the spot in the marsh where the rod had been found. The two men searched throughout the marsh the following day, but Ward was unable to locate the spot where he had lain down to nap.

In 1870, a man was turkey hunting near the mouth of the Lavaca River. On spotting a flock of birds several dozen yards away, he got down on his hands and knees and crawled toward his game. As he was slowly creeping along on all fours, the turkey hunter's knee struck hard against something partially buried in the ground. When he turned to examine what had caused his pain, he saw what he thought was a low pile of small bricks. Wondering why bricks would be in this remote location, he placed one in his pouch, intending to examine it later.

On returning home, the hunter removed the heavy brick from the pouch and showed it to his brother. The brother scratched the surface of the object with his penknife and discovered it was almost pure silver. Familiar with the story of the pirate Lafitte, the turkey hunter deduced he had stumbled onto a portion of the lost pirate cache.

When the brothers sought to return to the location of the pile of silver the next day, they could not find it. The two men searched several miles of the grassy marsh, but the uniformity of the landscape made it difficult to pinpoint a specific location. They also searched in the area of Mauldin Motte and Kentucky Motte, but neither man was aware of the relationship of the mottes to the treasure cache.

Another man may have actually found Lafitte's treasure cache, but it seems likely that he only removed a few gold coins. A rather eccentric local resident known as Crazy Ben was familiar to most people in the area but was seldom taken seriously and remained unfriendly to all. The old man was never known to hold down a job, and he lived in squalor in an old shack near the mouth of the Lavaca River. Crazy Ben was different from other area residents because he always paid for his drinks with gold Spanish coins.

Crazy Ben often told stories about serving as a cabin boy to the pirate Jean Lafitte. He said he would secretly follow the famous buccaneer across the salt marsh and watch as he buried his chests filled with treasure. The pirates fled the area when Ben was no more than 10 years old, and he decided to remain on the south bank of Clear Creek near Galveston Bay. He worked as a fisherman and handyman, and when times were tough, he would beg for handouts. After several years had passed and Ben was certain that Lafitte was never going to return for his buried treasure, he went to the site, dug up the chest, and helped himself to a handful of coins. After pocketing the coins, he reburied the chest. With the few coins in his pocket, Ben was able to purchase meals and drink his fill for several weeks. When he finally ran out of money, he simply returned to the cache and retrieved more coins.

An unambitious man, Crazy Ben preferred to drift around the bay area visiting a number of different taverns and spending his coins on ale. During his common, alcohol-fuelled conversations with fellow drinkers, Ben would admit to deriving his income from the buried treasure chest of the pirate Jean Lafitte. Word of the old man's source of wealth spread throughout the region, and from time to time, men would attempt to follow him into the marsh, but Ben always managed to elude them.

One evening, after a full day of drinking at a local tavern, Crazy Ben staggered out of the establishment and headed down the street toward his shack. Moments later, two shadowy figures left the tavern and followed him into the night. That evening was the last time anyone saw Crazy Ben alive. The following morning, Crazy Ben's body was found washed up on the shore of the bay near Clear Creek, his throat slashed. Most people believe he was murdered because he refused to reveal the location of the Lafitte treasure.

A number of attempts to locate Jean Lafitte's treasure

cache have been made during the past century and a half. During the 1920s, a man arrived from Oklahoma with what he claimed were the original handwritten notes from Lafitte's journal describing the location of the buried treasure chest. Although the newcomer had no trouble locating the two prominent mottes, he was unable to find the cache. No one has been able to locate the treasure, yet people still take their chances. The search continues to this day.

-32-

Jean Lafitte and the Neches River Treasure

Before leaving the cache site, the pirate stood over the excavation and placed a curse on the treasure, vowing that anyone who tried to recover the treasure would be stricken with unnamed horrors.

The buried treasure cache near the Lavaca River is not the only one associated with the pirate Jean Lafitte. There are, in fact, so many stories of lost treasure associated with this fascinating buccaneer that they could fill an entire book. However, many of these tales are undoubtedly exaggerated. As the reputation and mystique of this daring and adventurous pirate grew, so did the number of legends and accounts associated with him, particularly those regarding lost treasure. In spite of the various buried treasure stories associated with Lafitte, a number of these tales possess elements of truth, and deep investigation yields compelling evidence pointing to the notion that many of these treasure tales are based in fact.

Another, and important, truth is that Lafitte himself cultivated this mystique. He was an elusive, sly, and enterprising adventurer to be sure, but he was also a highly skilled self-promoter who understood the value of possessing a reputation as a notorious and feared freebooter.

One of the more intriguing tales of Lafitte's buried treasures is one that is said to have a curse associated with it. According to the curse, anyone who attempted to remove the treasure, other than Lafitte himself, would be struck down and rendered helpless or even put to certain death.

Sometime during 1820, Jean Lafitte and his crew piloted a treasure-laden ship to a location near where the Neches River of Texas enters the secluded bay of Port Arthur near the Texas–Louisiana border. Steering the vessel as close to shore as possible, Lafitte selected a site to bury several chests filled with gold and silver coins and jewels recently taken from a Spanish ship on its way to Cuba. As he was searching for a suitable cache site, Lafitte was also concerned about pursuit from a second Spanish galleon*, whose captain was intent on exacting revenge on the pirates.

Lafitte had his ship moored* by stretching a long, heavy iron chain to a stout tree near the river. The pirate leader then had his men bury the chests in the shadow of the tree. After lowering the chests into the excavation and as the pirates were refilling it, the pursuing Spanish vessel sailed through the bay with the pirates in sight. Lafitte ordered his men back on board the pirate ship, but before leaving the cache site, as the tale goes, the pirate leader stood over the recent excavation and placed a curse on the treasure. He vowed that anyone unworthy who tried to recover the treasure would be stricken with unnamed horrors. On returning to the ship, the pirates hoisted the sails, primed the cannons, and unfastened the heavy chain, tossing it into the water and leaving the other end still attached to the tree.

As the pirate ship moved out into the bay, Lafitte challenged the Spanish galleon. For over an hour, the two ships exchanged fire, but it soon became clear that Lafitte's ship was getting the worst of it. Realizing his dire situation, Lafitte eluded the Spaniards and sailed out of the bay into the Gulf of Mexico. However, Lafitte's relief at escaping was short-lived, for the Spanish ship fell into pursuit once again and was closing in. Approximately two miles out into the Gulf, Lafitte's ship took two direct cannon hits and started to sink. Most of the crew went down with the vessel, but Lafitte and a few crewmen escaped and made their way back to the nearby shore. Weeks later, the pirate obtained another ship and was back in the business of sailing the Gulf of Mexico to prey once again on Spanish merchant ships. According to the legend, Lafitte never returned to the Neches River to retrieve his treasure.

Decades later, when Jean Lafitte was just a distant memory to many Gulf Coast residents, a curious map surfaced. It was of crude construction, and with some difficulty one could make out the description of the pirate vessel chained to the tree, the story of the buried treasure worth millions of dollars, and a description of the battle with the Spaniards. Though inexpertly drawn, anyone familiar with the area could easily recognize the Neches River and related landmarks.

Right after the Civil War, this odd map came into the possession of a Mexican peasant who later moved to Texas. According to the man's widow, he followed the map, found the tree with the heavy chain still attached to it, and started digging. To this day, no one knows what he found, if anything, for when he returned home the following day, he was in a state of shock and unable to speak. Whatever happened to him during his attempt to recover the treasure caused him to lose his voice. Within a week, he was dead from unknown causes.

Several years later, the Mexican's widow passed the map on to a neighbor. The Mexican woman did not tell the neighbor of the fate of her husband. The man, a farmer with a small family, grew excited at the prospect of locating one of Jean Lafitte's treasures. He began making plans for a trip to the mouth of the Neches River.

The farmer obtained a shovel and pickaxe, then traveled to the location on the river described by the map. Like the man before him, he found the tree with the chain attached and began excavating. According to his version of what transpired, after excavating a hole around two feet deep, the farmer suddenly jerked upright as if seized by something unseen. He flailed his arms and grasped at his throat as if trying to ward off strangulation. With difficulty, the farmer climbed out of the hole and made his way home. Like the Mexican before him, the farmer lost the ability to speak. Before the week was over, he died. All of his belongings, including the treasure map, were stored away and forgotten.

Many years later, the farmer's widow cleaned out many of her late husband's belongings and gave them to a neighbor named Meredith, who had recently moved into the area. When Meredith asked the widow about the old map, she explained what had happened to her husband when he searched for the treasure, as well as what had happened to the man before him, and related that she thought they were victims of Jean Lafitte's curse. Meredith placed little confidence in curses and was skeptical of the widow's tale. He decided to try his hand at recovering the treasure and recruited a partner, an old friend named Clawson, to assist him in the search. After studying the old map, the two men made their way to the mouth of the Neches River.

With little difficulty, Meredith and Clawson located the tree near the river. The long, heavy chain was still attached to it. Next to the tree was a shallow cavity where the hole had been excavated years earlier. Nearby was a rusted shovel and pickaxe.

Meredith and Clawson began to excavate the site of the cavity. They had removed about three additional feet of soil when they encountered a skeleton, carefully laid out and wrapped in what had once been sail canvas. The metal buttons and buckles, along with the remains of leather boots, suggested it was the skeleton of a pirate. Very carefully, the two men removed the skeleton and placed it aside, with the intention of reburying it later.

As the hole deepened, Meredith and Clawson,

growing tired, decided to alternate digging chores. After a stint in the hole, Meredith climbed out and leaned against the tree for some rest as Clawson took a turn. Meredith was on the verge of falling asleep when he was jarred awake by Clawson's screams. Jerking upright, Meredith saw a wide-eyed Clawson frantically scrambling out of the deep hole. He looked as if he had aged 20 years, and his eyes were wide with fright.

Clutching Meredith, the terrified Clawson begged to leave the place immediately. Meredith tried to look into the pit to see what his partner had seen, but Clawson held tight to his friend and prevented him from approaching the hole. Pulling Meredith's face close to his, the quivering Clawson stated that he had just stared into the depths of hell and seen all of its horrors.

Clawson's terror was so overwhelming and his hold on Meredith so unyielding that there was nothing to do but leave the place at once. The men ran down the trail and away from the site, abandoning all of their tools. When they finally arrived home the following day, the still frightened Clawson begged his friend never to return to site of the pirate treasure.

In spite of Clawson's experience at the treasure site, Meredith went back to the site two weeks later – alone. With caution he approached the tree and the recently excavated hole. He spotted the skeleton lying where he and Clawson placed it earlier. The hole had been partially filled in with mud as a result of recent rain. Feeling somewhat nervous, Meredith carefully placed the skeleton back into the hole and filled it in. He gathered up all of the tools, departed, and never returned to the site for as long as he lived.

Clawson never completely recovered from his frightening experience. Although he did not die like the others associated with the treasure site, he lived the remainder of his life in terror, jumping at the slightest sound. He eventually moved to Beaumont, Texas. Several years later, Meredith was in Beaumont on business and looked up his old friend, Clawson. During their conversation, Meredith tried to get his friend to describe what he had seen in the treasure pit years earlier. His friend refused to discuss it and begged Meredith never to ask him again.

Whatever the Mexican, the farmer, and Clawson saw in the treasure pit will probably never be known. The stories have endured and have been passed down through the years, all the while contributing to the notion of a curse. If, indeed, such a curse was effectively placed on the huge treasure cache, it adds another dimension to the mysteries associated with the complex and elusive pirate, Jean Lafitte.

-33-

Buried Pirate Treasure on the Oregon Coast

As the crewmen commenced digging, several elders of the tribe approached the pirate leader and told him to stop, for they were digging into a sacred burial ground.

Most people associate historical pirates and pirate activity with the Atlantic Ocean, the Caribbean Sea, and the Gulf of Mexico, and for good reason. During the eighteenth and nineteenth centuries, the trade routes throughout those geographic areas were filled with merchant ships from France, Britain, Spain, and other countries, all carrying valuable cargo including gold, silver, and precious stones. Almost no one associates pirate activity with the Pacific Ocean or the west coast of North America, since the level of pirate activity was so much lower. However, one case of Pacific Ocean piracy involves the coast of Oregon.

Sometime during the first half of the nineteenth century, a Spanish pirate ship sailed into a small bay on the Oregon coast near present-day Three Rocks Beach in Lincoln County. Months earlier, the ship had departed from a Mexican port and made its way up the west coast of North America. According to the legend, the hold of the ship was filled with goods and treasure gleaned from successful raiding expeditions along the California coast. The ship limped into the bay, suffering from a significant leak in the hull.

Observing the arrival of the pirate ship were the residents of a small Indian village located on a grassy flat above the shore. During the next several days, as the pirates made repairs to the vessel, the Indians watched from a distance. From time to time, crewmembers came to shore in rowboats to fill casks with fresh water, and the friendly Indians led them to springs. In time, the Indians were providing fresh meat to the pirates in exchange for blankets, tools, and beads.

Days passed, and the repairs went poorly. At one point, the leak became worse, and their ship began taking on water, causing it to list to one side. It was beginning to look hopeless. When it was certain that the ship was going to sink, the pirates loaded a large wooden chest filled with gold coins and jewels into one of the rowboats and transported it to shore. Three other rowboats accommodated the rest of the pirates and crewmen, who arrived minutes later.

The leader of the pirates was a tall, bearded man wearing a long crimson cape. After examining the area, he led a contingent of crewmen to a particular location beyond the beach and onto a level, treeless field. He then directed his men to dig a hole large enough to accommodate the chest. As the crewmen commenced digging, several elders of the tribe approached the pirate leader and told him to stop, for they were digging into a sacred burial ground. Unmoved by the request, the pirate leader ordered several of his men to chase the Indians away. With swords and muskets pointed at them, the elders were herded back to their village.

After the chest was buried and the hole filled in, the pirate appointed two men to stand guard over it, in the event that the Indians returned to dig it up. One of the men was of slight build with a long mustache that extended well below his chin. Though somewhat frail-looking, the pirate carried a long sword, which he would pull from his belt. He would also engage in fights with mock opponents from time to time. The second guard was a large man, well-muscled, and standing close to seven feet tall. It is believed that this man was mute, for he never uttered a word. He remained expressionless save for when his skinny companion jabbed at him with his sword, pestering him with jokes and simulated jousting.

Two days later, the pirate vessel, unable to be repaired, sank beneath the waters of the bay. Before the ship went under, crewmen removed several rowboat-loads of goods and transported them to shore. Following several trips, the pirates, along with the crew, stood on the beach awaiting instructions from the captain.

The captain learned from the Indians that other men

were living with tribes located several miles inland. In the hope of making contact with these men and obtaining overland directions back to Mexico, the captain led his crew across the dunes and into the woods beyond. Before leaving, he informed the two men guarding the treasure – the frail man and the large man – to remain at the site until summoned by a runner. He left a case of provisions for the two men.

One week passed, and the two guards faithfully remained at their post, watching over the cache of buried gold and jewels. With each passing day, however, the large man grew increasingly annoyed with the antics of his trickster companion. Every now and then, the smaller man, brandishing his sword, would jab violently at him. Once, he drew a trickle of blood from a resulting wound. Unable to endure the stabbings any longer, the large man, enraged, seized the frail man and rained heavy blows onto his skull, killing his partner. With his hands, the large man dug a shallow hole above the treasure, placed the dead man into it, and covered him over.

Several Indians had observed the large man killing his smaller companion. They ran back to the village and informed the elders. Following a brief council, it was decided that the tribe could no longer tolerate the desecrations of their burial ground at the hands of the newcomers. They decided to drive the remaining guard from the area.

The next morning, a group of armed warriors approached the large guard and, employing sign language, ordered him away. When the guard refused to move, one of the Indians hurled a lance, the point piercing the ground near his feet. The guard pulled the lance from the ground and broke it in half across his knee. Grabbing the nearest Indian, he snapped his neck with his powerful hands and threw him aside. Almost immediately, a rain of arrows and lances fell upon the guard, and seriously wounded, he collapsed to the ground. Seconds later, the warriors were upon him, kicking and beating him until he eventually died. The Indians buried the remains next to the other dead pirate.

As a result of the bad experience with the Spanish pirates, the Indians were convinced that bad luck had befallen them and that their land was cursed. During the following week, they packed their belongings and departed, eventually settling in a new coastal location several dozen miles to the north. Behind them they left the remains of their tiny village – several shell mounds, cooking fire rings, crude dwellings of brush and log, and the graveyard. In subsequent years, the violent winter storms that arrived from the Pacific would wipe out most signs of habitation.

During the beginning of the 1900s, the coast of Oregon became an attractive tourist destination, and travelers flocked to the area by the thousands. Particularly appealing to the visitors were the tranquil sandy beaches near the picturesque rocky headlands. Picnicking and swimming in the surf were the principal attractions.

One Lincoln County businessman, E. G. Caulkins, owned a popular stretch of beach. One section of the area was known as Three Rocks Beach. Caulkins enjoyed fishing in the bay with nets. One afternoon, as he was hauling in his nets, he brought up what he thought were the remains of a wooden vessel that had apparently sunk many years earlier. Caulkins claimed one could see the outline of the ship lying on the bottom sands. To Caulkins, it appeared to have once been a sailing vessel, and it was almost 150 feet long.

Caulkins, ever the developer and opportunist, decided he could make a lot of money by providing camping sites and facilities to tourists. He made arrangements to have a portion of the grassy field above the beach leveled. Using a large scraper pulled by a team of mules, Caulkins and his workers broke up several of the low humps and hillocks and smoothed out a selected area. From time to time, the scraper would break into one of the old shell mounds and expose some artifacts. Caulkins, long fascinated by American Indian culture, would always pause to examine them and often collected interesting pieces. From these middens* and the nearby ancient village, the businessman retrieved arrowheads, broken pottery, an occasional axe head, and other remnants of a bygone culture. During the course of leveling the beach, he accumulated four metal buckets of such things.

During the spring of 1931, Caulkins was overseeing a leveling of a section of the field that had become overgrown with sea grass when the scraper exposed some bones. The man operating the scraper examined the skeleton and determined it to be human. Calling Caulkins over, the men excavated deeper and found the remains of another human being.

One of the skeletons deeply impressed Caulkins. The thick bones belonged to a man who stood at least seven feet tall. Most of the bones of this skeleton had been broken, and the skull was crushed. More digging in the area over the next two weeks yielded over a dozen other skeletons.

Curious about his discovery, Caulkins contacted two acquaintances. Dr. John Horner was a well-known scholar who specialized in Oregon history. Dr. F. M. Carter was a physician who had a deep interest in West Coast American Indians. According to Carter, most of the skeletons uncovered by Caulkins were likely interred in a burial ground. After reconstructing the largest skeleton and examining it closely, Carter determined that it had once belonged to a large African American man. The nature of the broken bones and the crushed skull suggested that the man might have been tortured or beaten just prior to death.

Several weeks passed, and the discovery of the giant skeleton was eventually reported in newspapers. More time went by, and one morning, an elderly Indian appeared at the home of Caulkins, requesting an audience with the businessman. As Caulkins listened intently, the old man related an Indian legend about a strange ship arriving in the bay at Three Rocks Beach, the burial of a treasure chest, the killing of the giant guard, and his subsequent burial of his smaller companion above the pirate cache.

At the mention of the buried treasure, Caulkins grew interested and quizzed the Indian on various aspects of the past. When the old man left, Caulkins returned to the field with the intention of digging deeper into the ground where the huge skeleton had been found. When he arrived in the area, Caulkins realized he had done his job too well. The location had been completely leveled, and over an area of three acres in extent, everything was uniform. He was unable to pinpoint the location of the discovery. With the assistance of several of his workers,

Caulkins excavated a number of holes, but nothing was ever found.

Today, the pirate chest filled with gold and jewels still rests a few feet underground in the grassy meadow above Three Rocks Beach.

Selected References

Botting, Douglas. The Pirates. Boston, Massachusetts: Little Brown and Company. 1978.

Burl, Aubrey. Black Barty: Bartholomew Roberts and His Pirate Crew. Stroud, England: Sutton Publishing. 2006.

Conlin, Dan. Pirates of the Atlantic: Robbery, Murder, and Mayhem off the Canadian East Coast. Halifax, Nova Scotia: Formac Publishing. 2009.

Cordingly, David. Under the Black Flag: The Romance and the Reality of Life Among the Pirates. Fort Washington, Pennsylvania: Harvest Books. 1997.

Davis, William C. The Pirate Laffite: The Treacherous World of the Corsairs of the Gulf. New York: Houghton Mifflin Harcourt. 2006.

Ellms, Charles. The Pirates Own Book: Authentic Narratives of the Most Celebrated Sea Robbers. Salem, Massachusetts: Marine Research Society. 1924.

Gibbs, Joseph. Dead Men Tell No Tales: The Lives and Legends of the Pirate Charles Gibbs. Columbia: The University of South Carolina Press. 2007.

Gosse, Philip. The History of Piracy. New York: Tudor Publishing Company. 1934.

Howell, T. B. (ed.) "The Trial of Captain Kidd and Others, for Piracy and Robbery," A Complete Collection of State Trial and Proceedings for High Treason and Other Crimes and Misdemeanors. London: Longman, Hurst, Rees, Orme, and Brown. 1816.

Jameson, W. C. Florida's Lost and Buried Treasures. Clearwater, Florida: Garlic Press. 2012.

_____. Buried Treasures of the Mid-Atlantic States. Little Rock, Arkansas: August House Publishers, Inc. 2000.

_____. Buried Treasures of the Atlantic Coast. Little Rock, Arkansas: August House Publishers, Inc. 1998.

_____. Buried Treasures of the Pacific Northwest. Little Rock, Arkansas: August House Publishers, Inc. 1995.

_____. Buried Treasures of Texas. Little Rock, Arkansas: August House Publishers, Inc. 1991.

Johnson, Charles. A General History of the Pyrates. Courier Dover. 1742.

Konstam, Angus, and David, Rickman. Pirates: The Golden Age. Oxford, England: Osprey Publishing Company. 2011.

_____, and Kean, Roger Michael. Pirates: Predators of the Seas. New York: Skyhorse Publishing. 2007.

Landers, Jane. Atlantic Creoles in the Age of Revolutions. Cambridge, Massachusetts: Harvard University Press. 2010.

McCarthy, Kevin M. Twenty Florida Pirates. Sarasota, Florida: Pineapple Press. 1994.

Ramsay, Jack C. Jean Laffite: Prince of Pirates. Woodway, Texas: Eakin Press. 1996.

Rediker, Marcus. Villains of All Nations: Pirates in the Golden Age. Boston, Massachusetts: Beacon Press. 2004.

Ritchie, Robert C. Captain Kidd and the War Against the Pirates. Cambridge, Massachussetts: Harvard University Press. 1986.

Rogozinskie, Jan. Pirates, Brigands, Buccaneers, and Privateers in Fact, Fiction, and Legend. New York: Da Capo Press. 1996.

Sanders, Richard. If a Pirate I Must Be . . . The True Story of Black Bart, King of the Caribbean Pirates. London, England: Aurum Press, Ltd. 2007.

Snow, Edward Rowe. Ghosts, Gales, and Gold. New York: Dodd, Mead, and Company. 1972.

_____. True Tales of Buried Treasure. New York: Dodd, Mead, and Company. 1951.

_____. Pirates and Buccaneers of the Atlantic Coast. Boston, Massachussetts: Yankee Publishing Company. 1944.

Williams, Jeffrey. Pirate Spirit: The Adventures of Anne Bonney. New York: Guild Press. 2007.

Woodard, Colin. "The Last Days of Blackbeard," Smithsonian, February, 2014. Pp. 32–41.

_____. The Republic of Pirates. San Diego, California: Harcourt, Inc. 2007.

Zacks, Richard. The Pirate Hunter: The True Story of Captain Kidd. New York: Hyperion Books. 2002.

Glossary

Armament–Military weapons
Bandolier–Belt slung over the shoulder to carry ammunition
Bastion–Angular structure projecting outward from the wall of a fort
Booty–Stolen goods taken in war
Bowsprit–Spar projecting from the bow or front of a sailing ship
Brigand–An outlaw who carries out robberies and surprise attacks
Brigantine–Two-masted ship with square-rigged sails that were easy to maneuver
Cellar–Underground room, typically used for storage
Convoy–Group of ships sailing together for protection and support
Cutlass–Short sword, frequently used by pirates in combat, as well as for cutting ropes
Dhow–Traditional Arab ship with a triangular sail, typically used for fishing or trade
Emissary–Diplomatic representative from another country
Fencing–Illegally buying and reselling stolen goods or property
Flagship–Lead ship carrying the commanding officer
Fleet–Large group of warships
Flotilla–Small group of warships
Forge–Fireplace used to heat metal so it can be shaped into tools
Freebooter–Pirate, plunderer, or outlaw
Frigates–Armored warship designed and built for speed
Galleon–Large European sailing ships typically used for war
Gangplank–Removal ramp used to get on and off a ship
Garret–Small room or attic, typically with a slopping ceiling since it was constructed on the top floor
Garrison–Fort where military troops were stationed
Gibbet–Long pole used for hanging criminals for public execution and display
Gibbeted–Hanging the corpse of a convicted criminal in public display to deter crime
Grapeshot–Shot consisting of a cluster of small iron balls, typically used in short-range combat

Guerilla–Irregular warfare using surprise and secrecy against a well-organized army
Gunwales–Upper edge at the side of a ship or reinforced ridge to support guns
Halyard–Rope used to raise and lower sails (haul yard)
Magazine–Place to store munitions
Man of War–Heavily armed war ship
Marque–Legal authorization to seize a ship or property in another country's territory
Middens–Old trash or waste
Midshipman–Junior officer
Moored–Anchored or secured
Pauper–Someone who is very poor
Pieces of Eight–Spanish silver coins, often minted in Mexico
Purser's–Officer responsible for handling money on a ship
Quadrant–Instrument used to measure altitude for navigation
Quarry–Prey that is hunted or targeted
Quartermaster–Officer responsible for supplies
Rigger–Person assigned to work on the sails of a ship
Schooner–Fast sailing ships with at least two masts that could sail in shallow coastal waters
Scimitar–Sword with a curved blade believed to have originated in the Middle East
Scuttled–Deliberately sinking a ship
Shilling–British coin used in the United Kingdom
Skiff–Small flat-bottom, open boat
Sloop–Small single-mast sailing ship
Tender–Legal payment or financial obligation
Tiller–Handle attached to the rudder, used to steer a ship
Tories–Conservative political party in Great Britain that supported monarchy
Trove–Hidden or buried treasure
Weighed Anchor–To raise and secure the anchor
Whigs–Liberal political party in Great Britain and associated with constitutional monarchy

About the Author

W. C. Jameson is the award-winning author of over 100 books. As a professional treasure hunter, he has led more than 200 expeditions and has served as a consultant for film and television. He lives in Texas.

Other Titles by W.C. Jameson and August House

- Buried Treasure of New England
- Buried Treasure of the Appalachians
- Buried Treasure of the Ozarks
- Buried Treasure of the Mid-Atlantic States
- Buried Treasure of the Great Plains
- Buried Treasure of the Atlantic Coast
- Buried Treasure of California
- Buried Treasure of the American Southwest
- Buried Treasure of the Pacific Northwest
- Buried Treasure of the South
- Buried Treasure of Texas
- Buried Treasure of the Rocky Mountain West
- Finding Treasure: A Field Guide